UNCONTROLLED SPIN

The Power and Danger of Spin

Book One
Revised

Jerry Summers

Copyright @ 2016 Jerry Summers
ISBN: 1944577025
ISBN: Softcover: 9781944577025
e-Book: 9781944577032
Library of Congress Control Number: 2016936307
GeLaSy, Inc. Caldwell, ID
Revised Date: April 1, 2016

Special thanks to Sydney M. Radcliffe, for her patience in editing and revising, and constant alterations. Without your hard work and efforts, this book would have been much more labor intensive for ME. You Rock!

CONTENTS

CHAPTER 1
SPIN DOCTOR

S ean Green, CEO of Sean Green Marketing (SGM), sits behind
his elegant cherry wood desk, staring out the window of his One
Embarcadero Center corner office overlooking the San Francisco
Bay. The view is magnificent, and he feels smug in his accomplishments. *Not bad for a middle-class kid from the avenues of San Francisco who
dreamed of being an international corporate attorney,* he thinks. As a prominent marketing executive, he has become the spin doctor for some
of the world's largest corporations, generating revenues beyond his
clients' most vivid imaginations, and his bank accounts serve as silent
witnesses to his business acumen. Suddenly, his self-admiration is interrupted by a soft knock on his door.

"Come in," He hears the door close, and when he turns around,
he sees a stunning, jaw-dropping, gorgeous long-legged redhead.
Her athletic frame is accentuated, yet only modestly revealed, by
her simple black dress and high heels. She is adorned classically
with fine but understated gold jewelry; her earrings are half-carat
diamond posts. Sean rises to greet her as she extends her hand to
shake his.

"Jessica, Jessica Silva," she says, "and it's a pleasure to meet you, Mr. Green."

"Oh, please, call me Sean," he replies, "and may I call you Jessica?"

"No, it's Ms. Silva, and I prefer to address you as Mr. Green," Jessica says firmly.

"Very well. As you wish." He fixes his inquisitive gaze on her face and is not only captivated but also unsettled by the piercing green eyes that lock just as intently onto his gaze. "What can I do for you, Ms. Silva?" he asks as he gestures for her to have a seat. She settles into the plush office chair and gives a little wiggle, which he finds amusing. He senses that behind the confident exterior, she is a little nervous, and he wonders what could be next.

She clears her throat. "Mr. Green, I was given your name by Mark Stevens, of Global Metal Refining, who prearranged our meeting with Evelyn, your assistant, to ensure you would see me today," Jessica starts.

"I see," "and what is the purpose of our meeting?"

Jessica can tell by the tone of his voice and the look on his face that Mr. Green is not pleased about the prearranged meeting.

She hesitates slightly and then says, "Well, I am the CEO of Beauty Boutique Clothing, and I am in need of a dynamic innovative marketing firm to take the company brands to the next level. Mark and his wife suggested that you were the person to talk to."

Sean raises his eyebrows. "First of all, to clarify that I'm following you correctly, you mean Mark's new wife, Bonnie, correct?"

Jessica nods. "Yes, that's correct. Bonnie and I have been friends most of our lives."

"I understand, but I don't think SGM can be of any help to you. The apparel and fashion industries simply aren't an arena this firm is interested in pursuing. Perhaps I could find someone more appropriate for you to discuss this matter with?" he suggests, feeling slightly regretful that her proposal isn't as interesting as her eyes.

"Mr. Green, Mark and Bonnie both said you would probably react this way, but I must insist that your firm is the agency I'm interested in retaining."

Sean leans back in his chair, chuckles, then asks, "Jessica, what is your company's—ah, the Beauty something's—gross sales revenue?"

Jessica narrows her eyes. "Mr. Green, it's Ms. Silva. Beauty Boutique Clothing's sales are just under two million per annum."

Sean laughs, leans forward in his chair, and says, "Well, most of my clients' marketing budgets well exceed those figures on an annualized basis. Thank you, but I'm not interested in being retained by an apparel company with an adolescent name that can't afford this firm's expertise or fees." Rising from his desk, Sean extends his hand to shake hers once again and says, "Good day, Jessica. Thank you for considering our firm, but I don't believe your company is an appropriate fit for our client profile."

Jessica glances at his hand but doesn't extend her own. She turns and walks toward the door, grasps the handle, and, turning back to look at Sean, says, "*Mr. Green*, I believe you are wrong in your assessment of the Beauty Boutique. I must say I'm disgusted by your cold, callous, and rude dismissal of me here today."

Sean intensely locks onto her irritated glare. "*Ms. Silva*," he says, emphasizing the formality, "you are the one who sought my advice today, and I make no apology for clearly providing the advice you sought. Please give my best to Mark and Bonnie." He returns to his seat.

⋙┼ ┼⋘

Jessica closes the office door behind her and thanks Evelyn for scheduling the appointment. Evelyn notices Jessica's irritation and says, "I suspect things didn't go as you had hoped?"

Jessica admits as much and can't help asking, "Is he always abrupt and rude to clients he isn't interested in representing?"

Evelyn's kind facial expression assures Jessica she understands. She smiles. "Please don't take his bluntness as uncaring or cruel. It's just that he makes his living delivering messages succinctly and unemotionally to clients who often need to hear the content of the message, rather than the emotion associated with it. Mr. Green is very good at what he does. Emotion is placed into his marketing messaging, but not his negotiations."

Jessica nods and starts to walk away, but suddenly stops, turns, and asks Evelyn, "What does Mr. Green drink, and what are his favorite snacks?"

A surprised look flits across Evelyn's face as she says, "Well, he loves pistachios and dark chocolate. He enjoys merlot, and only drinks very expensive scotch. Why?"

Jessica replies, "I was just wondering what I could do to thank him for his time. I think he may have felt a bit ambushed by this meeting, since he had no say in arranging it." And she exits the office.

Jessica turns the key in her fire-engine red Miata. As she begins driving, she becomes angry for allowing herself to be dismissed like a college freshman from the professor's office. Noticing a Cost Plus World Market, she makes an abrupt lane change, squealing her tires as she whips into the parking lot.

She grabs a nice wicker basket, two pounds of pistachios, a Ghirardelli dark chocolate assortment, and two bottles of reasonably priced merlot. Next, Jess chooses a blank card and writes, "Mr. Green, Even though you're clueless, I appreciate you taking the time to meet with me. Enjoy the snacks." She then signs the card, "Ms. Silva, CEO of the 'adolescently named apparel company'." Her next stop is at a package delivery company to insist the package be delivered that day. She then heads to her office, desperately wanting to talk to Nate, her personal assistant, to get his read on today's events and Mr. Green's reaction to her visit.

When she enters the office, Nate immediately says, "Oh, honey, I can see it didn't go well. I'll be in your office with a double espresso and a twist of lemon in a jiffy. We can talk then." He scurries off to take care of her as only he can.

Jess plops into her desk chair, pushes all her working designs to one side, and silently wonders why all the considerate, compassionate, sensitive, and good-looking men are gay. Nate appears in the doorway holding a pewter tray with two double espressos, a twist of lemon, and biscotti. As he enters the room, Jessica is struck by his sense of style. She muses at his Armani, charcoal-colored tailored slacks and light purple Ralph Lauren shirt, heavily starched to reveal creases drill instructors would be envious of. His Cole Hann shoes are immaculately shined, just like his gold Rolex watch.

Nate serves her first, massages her neck and shoulders, releasing the tension, and then sits and locks onto her gaze. He doesn't say a word at first, but quickly loses his patience and quips, "Really, Jess? You're going to make me drag it out of you after I've made such exquisite espressos?"

Jessica smiles. "Of course not, and thank you. Why can't all men be like you?"

"Well, dear, if they were, you and many other women would be sexually frustrated and I wouldn't be as special as I am." He taps his foot. "I'm waiting."

"Oh, very well. It was horrible. Mr. Green was a pretentious, inconsiderate ass who said my company has an 'adolescent name' and can't afford SGM. Then he dismissed me, and like a college freshman, I let him. He mocked our annual revenues, and then finished the insult by telling me to give his best to Mark and Bonnie. Can you believe his audacity?" Jessica huffs.

Nate considers for a moment. "Well, he sounds to me to be the type of guy you're usually attracted to. Self-assured and controlling. Was he attractive?"

Jessica's look is deadpan. "His physical appearance was fine, but he's an asshole, and as soon as he opened his mouth, he became an even bigger prick. What does his appearance have to do with his actions?"

"It has nothing to do with his actions, but everything to do with yours," Nate says, averting his eyes and adjusting the espresso on the tray.

She narrows her eyes. "What is that supposed to mean?"

Nate clears his throat. "Well, let me see if I've got my assumed scenario correct. Your girl, Bonnie, told you Mr. Green was brilliant, attractive, wealthy, and maybe even your type. I bet he's even single, isn't he?"

"That's what Bonnie said, but I don't care about all of that, and it doesn't matter. He's a jerk," she asserts.

"Maybe so, but is he someone you think you need?"

"I don't just think it. He is," Jess protests.

"And what do you know about his business, clients, marketing industry preferences, and personal dislikes?" Nate asks.

"Nothing. Why are you being so difficult about this today?" Jess counters.

"I'm not. I'm simply pointing out to you why you were dismissed like a schoolgirl."

"Why's that, Nate? Do tell!" she snaps.

"Don't get testy with me when I'm trying to help you fix your mistake. Geez, it's my job. Besides, I love you."

She sighs and rubs her temples. "You're right. I'm sorry. Go on?"

Nate nods. "From my perspective, you completely underestimated Mr. Green. You walked into his office completely unprepared, and he ate you up and spit you out like an amateur business owner and not the professional CEO of a vibrant emerging fashion design company you have become. You were fascinated by Bonnie's characterization of Mr. Green, so much so you failed to prepare for your meeting. He clearly saw your weakness and exploited it without mercy. If you truly consider what he said to you, unemotionally, is there some validity from his perspective? Sean Green is known for being shrewd, even cutthroat. He takes no prisoners, and his agency is in very high demand with the nation's prominent business movers and shakers. Why on earth would you walk into a major business meeting and potentially serious negotiations unprepared? Jess, you got what you deserved."

"Damn it. I hate it when you present your thoughts without empathy for the other person's feelings." She frowns. "Especially mine."

Nate takes her hand. "Honey, I adore working for you and love you even more, but I have never lied to you. Quite frankly, you needed to hear where you screwed up. The only question now is what are we going to do to fix this dilemma? Assuming you still want to work with SGM…"

She sighs. "I don't know… Mr. Green really is a prick. I do think he felt we set him up though, by prearranging the meeting. That's why I stopped and had a 'thank you' gift sent over, in spite of his rudeness."

"That's good, Jess." Nate pats her hand. "You need to swallow your pride for once and recognize that if you are going to take the Beauty Boutique to the level you want to take it, you need Sean Green's help. Don't be afraid to quit thinking you have all the answers and listen carefully to what he tells you. Honey, he knows what he's talking about, even if he is a world class jerk. Tell me about the gift?"

Jess explains how she questioned Evelyn, about her stops at Cost Plus and the courier's office, the basket of goodies, and her note to Mr. Green. Nate listens closely but remains quiet as he ponders all the possible ramifications. When he finally speaks, it's with a touch of apprehension.

"Okay, the gift basket was a nice touch, but the note seems a bit pouty and immature. Here is what I suggest: don't call or contact Mr. Green until he attempts to contact you, either directly or through Mark or Bonnie. When he does call, don't take it. Force him to leave a message. That way, when you call back, you are in control. Let Bonnie know you were disappointed in how you were received, but don't elaborate on any of your discussion, because it would be inappropriate if she took it back to Mr. Green. Next, do your research on Sean and SGM. Get your design portfolio organized with your anticipated new lines and a put a presentation together for your next meeting with him," he pauses.

"Wait, why would I have another meeting with Mr. Green? He clearly isn't interested in representing Beauty Boutique Clothing," Jessica interrupts.

"Jess, let me tell you something about men like Sean Green. He is arrogant, maybe even a bit narcissistic, but he isn't stupid. If he thinks there is money to be made, and especially if it is copious amounts, he will be all in, ready to rock and roll—"

Jessica once again interrupts. "The dollars I'm looking at probably aren't large enough to get Mr. Green's attention."

Nate shakes his head. "Sister, you underestimate the Beauty Boutique's potential, and your personal charm. The easiest person to sell in the world is a salesman, and Mr. Green is nothing more than an extremely overpaid salesman." Nate finishes his espresso and lemon, gets up from the table, kisses Jess on top of the head, and says, "Get back to work on these designs. I'll do the research you need on SGM and Mr. Green."

Jessica smiles. "Nate, you are a lifesaver."

"You know it. Remember that when salary considerations come up again." He winks.

"I always do, love."

Nate giggles. "Sure you do. Now get back to work, dear."

CHAPTER 2
LESSONS IN ATTRACTION

The courier walks into the executive offices of SGM, and Evelyn chuckles to herself as he approaches her desk. "I have a delivery for Mr. Green. I was told he must receive it immediately," the courier says upon reaching her.

"I bet you were," Evelyn replies. "I'll personally make sure Mr. Green gets this package, thank you." Evelyn signs for the delivery and surveys the basket's contents. *Shrewd and classy with a touch of eloquence,* she thinks. She grabs the basket and heads into Sean's office. "I have a delivery for you," she announces, smiling, and places it on his desk with a flourish.

Sean looks at the contents and says, "Someone knows what I like. Who is it from?"

She shakes her head. "Well, I'm not sure, but I would suspect it's from Ms. Silva. You know, the woman you went out of your way to irritate and offend this morning?"

"Is that what she told you? I only explained reality to her in simplistic terms, so she could grasp the certainty of my decisions. But I'll give her more credit this afternoon than I did this morning. She obviously spoke to someone who knows me quite well to determine the contents of this gift." Sean smiles slyly. "Who could that have been?"

Evelyn shrugs on her way out of his office. "I have no idea. Maybe Mark or Bonnie?"

Sean chuckles. "Yeah, I'm sure that's it."

He grabs a handful of pistachios and settles behind his desk to open the enclosed card. It is blank, but made of expensive paper. He opens it and reads the enclosed message, then bursts out in laughter, apparently loud enough to draw attention, since Evelyn appears in his doorway, confused.

"I'm glad offending others is amusing to you, Mr. Green," she murmurs.

"Oh, come on! Read this drivel from Jessica Silva. It's full of childish drama. If she can't handle criticism, perhaps she should get married, have a couple of kids, and hire someone to run her fledgling apparel company with the god-awful name. What was it? Beauty Factory or some bullshit like that." He tosses the card onto his desk.

"It's Beauty Boutique Clothing, Sean," Evelyn says disapprovingly.

"Whatever, it's still a bad name!" Sean exclaims, not understanding what the big deal is.

"Then perhaps you should take on a fledgling company with a bad name to see if you're really as good at this business as you've convinced yourself you are," Evelyn says with a challenge in her eyes.

Sean raises his eyebrows. "Wow, you must really like Jessica. Or you're becoming more charitable in your advancing years."

She rolls her eyes. "You're an asshole. It's not just that I like Ms. Silva, which, by the way, I do. I really like her designs. She has found a niche market between retail outlet and designer stores; though I don't think she knows it yet. By the way, most of the clothes I wear that you like are Ms. Silva's designs, purchased at the Beauty Boutique's stores. So why don't you get over yourself and your success and help someone else for a change?"

He snorts. "Because I don't run a nonprofit organization. I do what I do because I make money, and lots of it." He pauses, considering those dazzling green eyes, then says, "But I tell you what. I'll make a deal with you. Please send Ms. Silva a bouquet of Asiatic blackout lilies with this note attached: 'Jessica, Thank you for the delightful snacks. They are appreciated very much. Please also accept my sincerest apologies since I apparently offended your delicate sensibilities. Sean.' Our deal is you cannot give Jessica any more advice or insight into me. If she contacts you, go ahead and schedule another meeting, and book this one for an hour. If she comes into this meeting prepared, I'll consider working out a benevolent contract with her to launch her organization and career. But the flip side is if Ms. Silva comes into the meeting unprepared, again, you will never bug me about her and her piss ant company again. Deal?"

"Boy, have you got yourself a deal. I'm going to have fun watching you represent Beauty Boutique Clothing."

Sean laughs. "We will see, won't we?"

Evelyn turns to go but stops partway through the door and says, "By the way, Mr. Green, I do believe you find Ms. Silva attractive."

"This is between you and me and has nothing to do with Ms. Silva's physical attributes," Sean says firmly.

Evelyn quirks an eyebrow. "Really? I have never been able to bait you into doing anything you didn't want to do, and appealing to your sense of benevolence never works. So why this time?"

Sean leans back in his chair, considering. "Well, you believe in Ms. Silva's product, and I have always respected your opinion. Therefore, I'll give her one more chance to prove me wrong."

Evelyn rolls her eyes. "That is such bullshit, and you know it!"

"Evelyn, just send her the lilies, and let's see how this chapter plays out, okay?" Sean says, frowning.

"Very well," Evelyn replies, exasperated.

Evelyn picks up the phone at her desk and dials the florist. She orders the lilies as instructed, reciting the note for the florist. She then instructs the florist to deliver the flowers first thing in the morning, to give Ms. Silva ample time to reflect upon the implied message and how to handle it appropriately.

Meanwhile, Sean sits at his desk and starts to analyze the fashion and apparel industries' annual sales. He quickly learns that the United States fashion sales are around $250 billion per annum. Additional inquiry demonstrates that the retail fashion industry is segmented into several niche markets, ranging from loungewear to high fashion. Further potential markets include children's wear, accessories, and fragrances. Sean also discovers that the typical retail fashion store averages $1.5 million annually, and that approximately 65 percent of the apparel industry is dominated by fifty of the largest companies, totaling approximately $97 billion annually. Sean's analysis reveals that the fashion industry has been in a steady but slight decline since 2005, which he quickly calculates as being due to the worldwide economic downturn. He writes a few notes to remind him to ask about the types of metrics Jessica uses to quantify her stores' performance against her competition, puts his new file on her away, and returns to more pressing client matters.

In reviewing his daily calendar, he sees he has a dinner meeting with Mark Stevens in an hour to discuss a marketing dilemma due to the questionable mining practices of one of Mark's vendors in Brazil. Sean reviews several options he wants to discuss with Mark, then wonders if he is going to get the full-court-press on Ms. Silva and her company. Sean picks up the phone and calls Mark.

"Want to do sushi tonight instead of French cuisine?" Sean asks when Mark picks up his phone.

Mark hesitates. "Bonnie is joining us tonight, and she has her heart set on French. Can we do sushi next time? You know how she dislikes sushi…"

Sean rolls his eyes, thinking, *What a pain in the ass Bonnie has become, constantly interfering with business decisions she knows absolutely nothing about while simultaneously imposing her social and environmental agendas on Mark and Global Metal Refining.* "No worries, of course we can. Anything for you two. Meet you at the usual place for French?"

Mark sighs in relief. "Yeah, thanks. I appreciate your flexibility. I know how you feel about constantly eating French food."

"Don't worry about it. I'll just have a little more really good French Bordeaux and a lot less of the cream sauces. See you and Bonnie at seven," Sean replies smoothly.

"Great," Mark says. "Oh, and let's keep our business discussion light and casual tonight. No storyboards or ad copy, okay?"

"Fine, but I don't think Bonnie is going to like some of my suggestions about this vendor. Should I fill you in now?"

"Yes, go ahead."

"My professional advice is that you publically separate Global Metal Refining from Diablo Mining, Inc., while privately supporting their contracts. Then I can work with Diablo Mining to improve their reputation not only in Brazil, but also in the United States. In essence, we can buy enough time so that they complete their contract with you, and after that we can let the negative publicity take its toll on Diablo. When the outrage starts to spill over, we will claim you were unaware of their environmentally unsafe procedures and Global Metal Refining won't do business with them again until they correct those deficiencies. You'll get the gold you contracted for, and this will position Global Metal Refining as a conscious, environmentally friendly, pragmatic, and stewardship-sensitive organization. I don't think Bonnie needs to be in on this, given her political views on the environment, but I needed you to know the back story. This way, my proposals will make much more sense to you, my friend."

"I understand. It sounds like a good plan, as always. Thanks for the heads up.". "See you at seven."

⊷⊹ ⊹⊶

Sean arrives at the restaurant promptly at 6:45 p.m., pulling his black BMW 633 CSi up to the valet. The valet opens his door, saying, "Good evening, Mr. Green. Will anyone be joining you tonight?"

"Good evening, Jim. I'm meeting Mr. and Mrs. Stevens this evening."

The valet passes on this information to the hostess, who ushers Sean to the Stevens' regular table, seats him, and says, "I'm sure the Stevens will be here shortly, but I'll have your waiter bring your drink. What is your pleasure tonight?"

"I'll wait for the Stevens to arrive, but I suspect it will be Bordeaux," he replies.

"As you wish, Mr. Green," she says, briskly departing the table.

Mark and Bonnie arrive shortly after, and Sean watches Bonnie stroll across the dining room as gracefully as ever. Her turquoise evening dress clings to her hips and is cut low enough to tastefully reveal her abundant cleavage. The gown is slit up the front to just above the knee. Sean muses; *Mark has always had great taste in women… especially blondes.* Sean stands up, hugs Bonnie, and then shakes Mark's hand before returning to his seat.

"Sean, you really need to get into designer suits. Those off-the-rack models are so unbecoming. God knows you can afford more than eight hundred dollars a suit." Bonnie shakes her head in disgust.

Instantly, Sean's mood sours. "Really, Bonnie? Are we going to go through this again? I don't need to pay for designer suits. I like my off-the-rack specials. I'll leave the designer clothing for you, my dear. I'm too cheap to spend that much money on clothing. Although I will admit you look stunning this evening."

14

Bonnie eyes him carefully. "If you weren't so charming, I would suspect you just insulted me."

Sean smiles. "I would never insult you. I just can't carry off designer clothing like you can."

She snorts. "Thank you, but I don't believe you one bit. And this time, my designer is Jessica Silva."

Sean raises an eyebrow, motions for the water, and, because of Bonnie's irritating presence, orders a Macallan triple, cask matured, twenty-five year old Speyside, single malt scotch. Then he looks at Mark and says, "What can I get for you and Bonnie?"

Bonnie orders a dirty martini and Mark orders Tanqueray gin with tonic and a wedge of lime.

While the waiter scurries to procure their drinks, Bonnie says to Sean, "I understand you met my friend, Jessica."

"Jessica?" Sean questions.

Bonnie resists the urge to roll her eyes. "You know, Jessica Silva? She owns Beauty Boutique Clothing."

"Oh, yes. I met Jessica."

"Sean, she really needs your help. I thought you would be the perfect person to—" Bonnie begins, but Sean interrupts.

"You did, did you?"

"Well, actually both Bonnie and I felt you'd be perfect," Mark interjects.

"Well, thank you both for you confidence in me, but I told Jessica I would help her find someone else. I'm not interested in delving into the fashion industry."

Bonnie gasps and touches Mark's arm. "Please, baby, get him to come to his senses! Jessica is terrific. Like I said, this dress is one of her designs. Sean, you simply must reconsider."

Sean sighs. "Thank you once again, but Jessica will do fine without my help. If she is as good as you say she is."

Bonnie lifts her chin. "Oh, she is."

Sean eyes Bonnie warily, "Anyway, Mark, I wanted to share some thoughts I have about your situation in Brazil—"

Bonnie interrupts, "Can't we eat dinner before you boys start talking shop? Afterwards I can excuse myself so you two can discuss any business you desire." Mark nods in acquiescence to Bonnie's desire, and Sean agrees as well, but only if the subject of Jessica Silva is also off the discussion table. Bonnie reluctantly agrees. The discussion remains light over dinner, and Mark orders a Grand Marnier soufflé dessert for everyone to sample. After dessert, Bonnie says, "Alright, I'll give you guys some time to talk. I'll head to the bar lounge and call Jessica while you two discuss your business." Mark and Sean stand as she does, and she nods to them as she leaves the table.

Once seated in the lounge, she telephones Jessica and asks how her meeting with Sean went.

Jessica tells Bonnie it was awful. "Sean is a pompous ass. He was callous and insulting. But I won't say any more, so don't ask, please."

Bonnie is shocked to hear this about Sean, because she has always found him to be gracious, even if he has always been a bit arrogant.

"Maybe he is so charming with you because your husband is his number one client," Jessica suggests.

Bonnie snorts. "Well then, I'll ask Mark to apply pressure in the right spots to make Sean reconsider representing you."

Jessica replies, horrified, "Girl, I love you for supporting me, but promise me you will do no such thing! If SGM is going to represent Beauty Boutique Clothing, it's going to be because I earned his respect and he sees the value in doing so. Not because he was pressured by my influential friends." Bonnie's silence on the issue announces her reluctance to agree. "Promise me, Bonnie!" Jess pushes.

"Okay, okay, I promise you I won't interfere in your business," Bonnie finally concedes. "I was just trying to help. And I still believe

Sean is amazing when it comes to marketing. His help would boost your business tremendously."

"I understand. I'm just not sure I can work with an ass like Sean Green," Jess replies.

Bonnie sighs. "All really successful men like Sean and Mark are assholes at some point. The secret you need to learn is the sexual power we women have over them. For them it's about the conquest, and for us it's about the victory. If you handle yourself correctly, by the time you give in to any man, you have achieved victory way before they have enjoyed their conquest."

"That's horrible! I would never screw a man simply to gain power over him."

Bonnie chuckles. "You are so naïve. Sexual attraction is a powerful weapon, and you have it at your disposal. You can use it for good or evil, but you are stupid if you think it isn't real or you haven't used it in the past. I'm not suggesting you seduce every man for everything you might want. That would make you a whore. What I'm suggesting is that all women use their sexual attraction to imply a man may have a chance in order to get the results they wish to achieve for themselves once in a while. If you're attracted to the man, there is nothing wrong with a quick romp in the sheets to cement the deal and release tension."

"You are unbelievable sometimes," Jess says.

"Don't you dare attempt to tell me you've never done such a thing, because I know better, and you know I do."

Jess finally relents. "Alright. I get your drift, but I'm not going to use my 'charm' on Sean Green. He's a major prick! I'm not even attracted to him."

Bonnie rolls her eyes. "He's a prick who knows his shit, and you'd do well to remember that. I just want you to get the best marketing firm around, and SGM is it. Good luck, and if you need some advice on using your feminine charms, just let me know."

"I think I can handle that area of my life on my own, but thanks for cheering me up," Jess replies, shaking her head and grinning.

Bonnie smiles. "No problem. Let me know if I can do anything to help outside of the feminine charm."

As Bonnie hangs up, Mark and Sean enter the lounge and ask if she is ready to go. Bonnie says, "It's about time you boys were done talking shop. I was getting lonely."

Sean cringes internally and says his goodbyes quickly. He heads to the valet to retrieve his car, and goes home.

Bonnie licks her lips seductively and suggests Mark needs to get her home soon. Mark grasps the significance of Bonnie's gesture and calls for his Mercedes to be brought around front as fast as humanly possible. As soon as it arrives, he tips the valet and helps Bonnie into the passenger seat. Bonnie shifts her dress as she slides into the car, exposing her leg to mid-thigh. She smiles shyly at Mark and says, "I think this night is only going to get better than it has already been. Thank you for a delightful dinner, baby."

"You're welcome, my lover," Mark replies, and hurries to get into the driver's seat.

CHAPTER 3
GETTING LUCKY

Mark and Bonnie turn into the driveway of their ten acre Marin County estate overlooking the well-manicured grounds, private pool, and cabana. It's a warm summer evening, and the illuminated home is truly palatial, yet still welcoming, basking in the warm glow of interior lighting. Walking into the vast entrance, Bonnie glances over her shoulder and tells Mark with a playful smile, "I'll make you a gin and tonic if you send the staff home for the evening."

Mark smiles in return and says, "Consider it done." Turning, Mark heads to the staff's quarters and gives the help the night off, then returns to the kitchen.

Bonnie hands him his gin and tonic with a wedge of lime and says, "Just the way you like it." She is holding her own drink, a dirty martini, as well. Mark smiles, and Bonnie puts her drink down to place her arms around his shoulders. She gives him a slow, sensual, lingering kiss. Mark puts his drink on the counter and places his hands on Bonnie's hips, then slowly brings them up her back. Bonnie spins in his arms, placing her rear against his front, and grabs Mark's salt-and-pepper hair. She pulls his head a little bit over her shoulder and kisses him passionately, tracing his lips with her tongue, then slipping it into his mouth more aggressively. Mark's hands come up from around her waist, cupping her breasts.

Bonnie continues to hold his head in place and tease him with her delicious tongue. She now intensifies her assault on his senses by pushing back into him and rotating her hips in a slight circular motion. She hears the pleasure in his breathing and feels it quickening along the side of her face. Mark gives a quick nibble on her ear, and Bonnie responds instinctively by arching her back, pushing her ass against Mark's crotch. Bonnie is rewarded by sensing his growing desire for her. She lets go of his hair and leans forward, placing both hands on the kitchen counter while simultaneously arching her back and grinding against Mark. He responds immediately by leaning forward and trapping both of her nipples between his thumbs and index fingers. Giving a slight pinch, he rolls both of her nipples through the cloth of her dress. Bonnie lets out a slight moan, then breaks away from his delicious torture, leaving him panting.

"Let's finish our drinks out by the pool, shall we?" she asks, slightly breathless, and snags their drinks off the counter on her way to the door. Mark sighs out of frustration and realizes Bonnie has every intention of driving him crazy tonight.

Then, he smiles his customary sly smile and says, "Sure, why not? After all, the staff is gone and we have all night, right?" She slinks out the door, and he follows her eagerly.

Bonnie sits at the table by the pool, allowing her dress to hike up as she does. She crosses her legs in front of Mark, exposing her thigh three-quarters of the way up. Bonnie lets Mark marvel at her thigh for a moment, and when his eyes meet hers, she locks onto his stare, takes a sip of her dirty martini, and says, "Oh, baby, you have no idea how long this evening is going to be for you."

She sees Mark shift in his chair in a slightly apprehensive manner as he says, "I can't wait."

"Oh, but you will, won't you?"

"Absolutely."

Bonnie takes another sip of her dirty martini and retrieves the olive with her tongue. She holds the olive between her teeth and playfully flicks it with her tongue. Mark watches intently, thinking, *how did I get so lucky?* Bonnie bites the olive and deliberately chews it while mesmerized with Mark's reactions to her not-so-subtle seduction routine. She gets up and takes the chair directly across from Mark's. as she settles into it, she purposefully allows her legs to open just enough to give Mark a quick peek at her lack of underwear before crossing her legs again, exposing even more of her thigh.

As they discuss the evening's events, she summarizes her conversation with Jess, and Jess's reaction to Sean. Mark tries to appear interested in the conversation but is extremely distracted by Bonnie's bouncing leg across from him. Bonnie recognizes Mark's faint attempt at listening and leans forward, allowing him a much more explicit view of her cleavage. Mark can no longer restrain his appreciation of her body and comments on the fact that she isn't wearing a bra. She smiles, knowing her seduction is having the effect she intends it to.

She gets up from her seat and takes a step over to Mark. Straddling his legs, she leans forward and kisses him passionately, then pulls his face into her bosom. She feels his hand slide up along her thigh until it reaches the junction between her legs. She moans as his hand brushes her, and she kisses him harder. She feels his finger slide along her and his middle finger penetrates her moist body, slowly and deliberately. Pulling away, she stands up, looking down into Mark's yearning eyes, and says, "See how much you excite me?"

She steps away from him. Looking down, she can see his sexual frustration and thinks of the power she now possesses over this man. She tells Mark to finish his drink. He gives her an inquisitive look as she pulls her dress over her head, exposing her naked body, and lingers as she watches Mark give her an approving once-over.

"I want to skinny dip. Interested?" she questions seductively. In no time at all, Mark is up and stripped, leaving his attraction open to her full view. She giggles. "Oh my, Mark. What are you hoping for besides swimming in the nude?"

Bonnie jumps into the warm pool and swims away from Mark, knowing he is staring at her backside. He quickly follows and swims up behind her. She turns around, places both arms around his neck, and kisses him, pressing her body against his. Then she whispers in his ear, "I love you so much, and you really, really turn me on." She gives him another kiss and swims away. He lingers for a moment, then follows her to the side of the pool. Drifting up behind her, Mark places his arms on either side of her, effectively pinning her in place. She once again looks over her shoulder at him and says innocently, "Sir, what are your intentions tonight?" She slides along the side of the pool, forcing Mark to move with her until they reach the shallow portion.

Mark still has his arms braced around her, so she pushes her ass up against him once again. Knowing this time he isn't going to relent, she reaches between her legs and firmly grips his cock, guiding it to her entrance and inserting the tip. Mark can no longer stand her teasing and slams his entire length into her. She cries out loudly, reaching back over her shoulder, and brings his mouth to hers. Her back arches, and she meets his thrusts, stroke for stroke, until they both cry out in mutual ecstasy. They linger along the side of the pool long enough to catch their breath, and then they allow themselves to drift for a while, basking in the glow of release. Bonnie gets out first and walks to the cabana to retrieve a couple of towels. As Mark gets out of the pool, she wraps him in a towel and says, "Let me get us another drink."

Returning from the kitchen with the drinks, she finds Mark lying totally exposed in the warm night air. She puts each of their drinks on the table, leans down, and gives him a quick kiss. She orders him to close his eyes and begins kissing down his body. Lingering at his nipples, she takes one in her mouth, flicking it rapidly with her tongue as she holds it between her teeth. Mark opens his eyes without permission, so Bonnie grabs her towel, which had fallen onto the pavement, and covers his face. She gives his nipple a firm bite, then tells him, "Behave. And don't move the towel." He twists from the combination of pleasure and pain, and complies with Bonnie's demands.

Leaving his nipple, Bonnie continues her soft kissing down his body to his belly button, where her kisses become more aggressive. Mark twists in anticipation, and she tells him to be still or she will quit. Mark once again complies with her order. Continuing lower, she finds his flaccid penis and begins subtle kisses along the underside to its base. She feels his approving reaction, then takes her tongue and drags it the entire length of his shaft. Mark opens his legs, allowing her better access, and moans, "Please, don't stop."

"I won't, as long as you follow my instructions." She kisses softly back down his shaft and moves back up with her tongue once again. With Mark's body fully responding to her enticements, she pauses to circle the head of his erect penis with her tongue, then slides the entire length of him into her mouth.

Mark cries out, "Oh, God!" and attempts to raise his hips. Bonnie holds him in place, releasing his shaft.

"Stay still or I'll stop what I'm doing. Acknowledge that you understand, verbally," she commands.

"Yes, Bonnie."

Bonnie slides up his body using her breasts to stimulate his senses, which is fully aware of her every little move. She places her labia over his shaft and slides down, then back up. As she continues moving up and down his shaft, she removes the towel from his face and tells him to look at her. She leans forward and places her breasts in Mark's face, ordering him to kiss them. Mark complies then takes her nipple into his mouth. Bonnie pulls back, lifting herself away from him, "I didn't tell you to do that. Now apologize!"

Immediately Mark replies, "I'm sorry." Bonnie places her hands on Mark's chest while moving her hips back onto his shaft and feeling herself slide down his entire length.

Mark moans in pure ecstasy. Holding his chest firmly down with her hands, Bonnie instructs Mark not to come before her. She increases her tempo, rocking forward and back on him. He can hear her breathing becoming shallower and instinctively knows she is getting close to her release. As her movements become frantic, he wonders if he can hold out. Then, suddenly, she comes hard, falls forward, and demands that he fuck her hard. Mark rolls her over onto her back, grabs her legs, lifting them above her hips, and drives hard into her over and over, causing her orgasm to extend and her to cry out his name, until he explodes deep inside her. He collapses on tops of her, and they pant until their breathing slowly calms. He pulls out of her body, suggesting they go for another swim. She follows him into the pool and thanks him for giving the help a night off.

He grins at her. "The pleasure was all mine, and I'll be happy to do it again anytime." They finish their drinks by the pool, then head inside for a quick shower and their comfortable bed.

CHAPTER 4

LILIES AND SCOTCH

J essica Silva arrives at her office at 9:00 a.m. sharp. As she walks in the front door, she is greeted by Nate, in his usual flawless apparel, with a cup of black coffee. He walks with Jess through the production area and says, "Jess, you must have been a really good girl last night!"

Jess pauses and turns to Nate, confused. "What on earth are you talking about? I went home, got into my sweats, and went for a short run. Then I felt sorry for myself and ate almost an entire pint of mint chip ice cream and a few Nilla wafers. Other than a brief conversation with Bonnie, nothing significant happened." Nate simply grins at her, and her eyes narrow. "Why?"

His grin broadens into a smile, "You'll see."

Jessica opens the door of her office and is overwhelmed with the intense smell of lilies. Across the room, she sees a stunning bouquet of some type of lily sitting on top of her desk. Taking a closer look, Jessica is intrigued by the combination of red and black in the flower and spies a card hidden in their midst. As she begins opening the card, Nate hovers in anxious anticipation to learn the source of the beautiful display. Jess, sensing Nate's anticipation, stops opening the card and says tauntingly, "Who could have sent such an amazing assortment to little old me?"

Nate cocks his hips, places both hands on them, and says, "Girlfriend, if you don't hurry and open up that card, I'm going to bitch-slap you. Who are they from? I'm dying here!"

She grins at him and opens the card with a flourish. Her mouth drops open, telling Nate everything he needs to know.

"They're from the illustrious Mr. Green, aren't they?" he asks, knowingly.

"Yes, yes they are. Oh God, they're beautiful," she says, fingering one of the stems as she reads the note.

"Sweetie, they are amazing in their beauty. Very exotic, even erotic, maybe?" Nate wiggles his eyebrows.

"Stop it, right there. I know where you're intending to go, and we are *not* going there, ever. Besides, they're lilies, which symbolize death, and Mr. Green's card is as demeaning as ever. He apologized for 'offending my delicate sensibilities.' What a royal asshole." She tosses her hair over her shoulder.

"Jess, why do you always have to assume the worst in everyone?"

"Not everyone! Just Mr. Green. He is such a pompous ass!"

Jessica hands Nate the card to read, and when he finishes, he stops to smell the flowers. Finally, he smiles and asks, "Didn't you ever stop to think this may be a sincere apology and there is no hidden agenda here? Perhaps he finds you attractive and can't express himself in his usual articulate manner?"

She rolls her eyes. "I told you not to go there, and I meant it. The only relationship I want with Mr. Green is a professional one!"

Nate wiggles a finger at her. "Tsk, tsk. I do believe thou doth protest too much. After all, I know you find him attractive."

Jess makes a face. "Bite me. Yes, his physical appearance I find attractive, but as soon as he opens his mouth, all is lost."

"Sister, this is me you're talking to. He is exactly the type of guy you have a weakness for. He's successful, confident, articulate, creative, and doesn't take your crap. What really pissed you off with Mr. Green is that he saw right through you and didn't let your beauty faze him in his business assessment of you. He caught you off your game and tossed you out like excess laundry, and you're not used to being treated like that."

Jess gapes at him and finally manages, "Damn right, I'm not."

Nate rolls his eyes. "Jess, let it go! It's in the past, and we need to concentrate on the future. Besides, any man this erotically creative has got to be good in bed. If Phillip and I weren't together, I'd ponder doing Mr. Green myself."

Jessica snorts. "Well, perhaps you should talk to Phillip about your man-crush. He might be willing to accommodate you in a ménage a trois!"

Nate sighs. "Now you're just being a mean spirited bitch."

She is quiet for a moment. "You're right. I went too far, I'm sorry."

Nate nods. "Besides, what Phillip and I have is so special. I would never share his magnificent body with anyone else."

"I said I'm sorry, and I meant it!" Jess exclaims, getting a wink from him in return.

"Yes, love, I know. I just wanted to use guilt to make you feel worse, simply because you're not the only bitch in this room."

She glares at him and then sighs. "What do you think I should do?"

Nate ponders in silence for what seems like hours, contemplating the right answer to her question. Suddenly, the light comes on, and he remembers Sean Green is a scotch snob. During his research, he found the only scotch Sean likes is obscenely expensive and ridiculously hard to find, but it seems like the best possible response to the display of lilies. He nods and says, "I think you should send him a bottle of scotch thanking him for the lilies, along with a suggestion to meet again in an attempt to get off on a better foot. If he responds positively, make your pitch with passion, determination, and professionalism. And if he still doesn't waver, we will find another marketing firm to move forward with your plans."

Jessica is surprised and responds, "Okay, but I don't know anything about scotch…"

Nate says, "I'll go get it right now and bring back the invoice from the liquor store in half an hour."

Jessica smiles and gives in. "Okay, make it happen. I want him to receive it today."

Already on his way out, Nate says, "No worries, I'll take care of everything."

Jessica sits at her desk and begins going through her e-mails. She's in the middle of responding to one of her clients when she is disturbed by Nate walking into her office with the invoice. Jessica just glances at it at first, then stares in disbelief. "Jesus Christ, Nate! *Really?* Sean drinks scotch that costs nearly eight hundred dollars a bottle? Shit, that's more than reasonable people pay for child support. I better get some mileage with this gift, or I'll dock it from your annual salary!"

Nate smiles at her idle threats and replies, "And if he agrees to represent Beauty Boutique Clothing, you'll double my annual bonus right?"

⇥ ⇤

Sean receives the delivery with Jessica's note. After opening the package, he yells for Evelyn to come into his office immediately. As she walks through the door, he says accusingly, "I thought we made a deal?"

Evelyn gives him a blank look. "What are you talking about?"

"Don't play coy with me. Look at what Jessica Silva just had delivered," he says, showing her the bottle of scotch.

Evelyn laughs. "Are you suggesting I told her about your scotch preference?"

He smirks. "How else would she have known?"

"Well, I don't know, but I promise I never spoke to her about the type of scotch you like. When she left after your meeting, she asked about your snack and drink preferences. I told her about the gifts you received, and I mentioned you only drink very expensive scotch, but I never mentioned the specific kind."

"Why would you tell her all of that?" Sean demands.

"Because she indicated she just wanted to thank you for your time. I have not spoken to her since our bet. Sean, maybe she is smarter than you've given her credit for, or maybe she got the information from Bonnie. Either way, I didn't say a word to her except what I've already told you."

Sean considers for a moment, "Then will you please call Ms. Silva and see if you can arrange a meeting between us, say, three weeks from today if she is available? If not, just schedule a meeting whenever we are both available."

Evelyn smiles. "She outclassed you this time."

He glares at her and points to the door. "Out! And don't forget to arrange the meeting!"

Evelyn shrugs and heads to the doorway. She is halfway out when Sean sighs and says, "Yes, okay, she outclassed me on this one. Perhaps I have misjudged her."

Evelyn represses a smile, nods once, and makes the telephone call to Beauty Boutique Clothing. She is transferred to Nate and tells him she would like to schedule an appointment for Mr. Green with Ms. Silva three weeks from today at 10:00 a.m.

Nate reviews Jessica's calendar and says, "She isn't available that day. Tentatively, a week later would work. I could put the appointment on her calendar, but Ms. Silva would have to confirm her availability with either you or Mr. Green next week."

Evelyn smiles and says, "That would be fine, but from Mr. Green's perspective, it's a firm appointment unless he hears otherwise."

"Thank you. Can I be of any further assistance to you, Evelyn?"

"No, but please tell Jessica for me that the scotch was an exquisite move on her part."

She hears Nate chuckle over the line. "Thank you for your time," he replies, then hangs up.

Nate casually strides to Jessica's office and lingers at the doorway until she looks up at him. He grins and says, "I made an appointment for you next month with Mr. Green, if you care to keep it."

Her mouth drops open. "Of course I want to keep it!"

"Well then, later next week you need to call Mr. Green and let him know you would like to confirm the appointment with him for next month. I think you should also thank him for the flowers and apologize for taking so long to get back to him. Maybe imply that your schedule has just been so darn hectic lately?"

Jess nods regretful approval. "Okay, but you know how I hate playing these types of games."

"I know, Jess, just trust me on this one please. You can stop once you meet with him."

Jess nods in agreement, then returns to her designs and begins scheduling the first production of the new line of products. She knows that afterward come the endless alterations and improvements, prior to finalizing the design. She works diligently for the next several days on color schemes, accessories, and final drawings for the design team.

Late Friday, she calls a meeting of her senior staff—consisting of the tailors, factory managers, Nate, seamstresses, and the in-house photographer for brochure advertising and posters. Jessica rolls out the new designs and gives her customary instructions for everyone to study them over the weekend and be prepared to reveal all their concerns or improvements during the follow-up meeting Monday morning.

"Is there anything else we need to discuss tonight?" she asks the group. No one voices any concerns, so she says, "Excellent. Thank you all and have a great weekend."

⚔ ⚔

Sean has Evelyn contact his pilot to let the pilot know he is heading to the airport for the scheduled flight to Brazil to meet with the president of Diablo Mining. The meeting is in order to outline the intended positioning of Mark Stevens and Global Metal Refining, Inc. in the United States and Brazil. He places the storyboard and the ad copy in his briefcase, then turns around and removes the $100,000 that Mark had given him to compensate Diablo Mining's president for the increased problem the marketing campaigns may create for them in Brazil. He places the money in the false-bottom portion of his briefcase, confident he will be passed through Brazilian customs without incident.

Sean tells Evelyn he will only be gone over the weekend and shall be back to work on Tuesday. He heads to his Sacramento Street penthouse apartment to pack for the weekend. As he enters his penthouse, Sean pauses momentarily in the living room to enjoy the view. The lights of downtown and the east bay are beginning to provide a subtle and comforting glow on the water. The spacious living area looks out over San Francisco Bay and Alcatraz, and he turns to his right and scans the skyline of downtown, briefly appreciating what all his hard work has gotten him. He grabs the necessities for Brazil and the weekend, then heads to meet the corporate chartered jet pilot. He boards the jet, and the stewardess, Rachel, hands him a scotch on the rocks. She gives him a smile and says, "We will be pushing away shortly. How have you been, Mr. Green?"

Sean takes a sip of his scotch, tips the glass toward her, and says, "Much better now."

She nods toward the drink. "I hope we got it right this time?"

"Absolutely you did. Thank you for remembering," Sean replies.

"Will you be dining with us tonight, or would you like to just sleep during this flight, sir?" Rachel asks.

He considers for a moment. "Actually, did you also remember the brie and smoked salmon?"

"Of course, Mr. Green. From Nova Scotia, correct?"

He nods. "Excellent. I think I would like the brie and salmon with red onion and capers, please. It'll go nicely with my scotch. Then I'll work for about an hour and retire for the evening."

"Of course, sir. I'll get it for you as soon as we hit our cruising altitude. About the time you'll be ready for your customary second glass of scotch, I believe?"

Sean smiles and says, "That will be perfect." He enjoys the snack and second scotch, works diligently for a little over an hour, and then heads to the fully equipped master bedroom in the rear of the plane.

He is woken by Rachel, who hands him a fresh cheese danish and a cup of French press coffee. "We'll be landing in about forty-five minutes. How did you sleep?"

Taking the cup from her, Sean says, "Very well, thank you."

She smiles. "The limousine will be waiting to take you to Mr. Stevens' villa for the weekend." Sean thanks her again and sips from his coffee cup. The jet lands and taxies to the terminal. Customs agents step onto the jet, greet Sean, sign off on all the necessary paperwork, and then wish him a great stay in Brazil.

CHAPTER 5

BRAZILIAN HOSPITALITY

S ean deplanes and gets into his awaiting limo. The driver Fernando says, "Good to see you again, Mr. Green. Is there anything special you need for this trip?"

Sean shakes his head. "Not this time Fernando, thank you." Upon arriving thirty minutes later at Mark's villa, the butler, Eduardo, tells him they have already arranged for an early dinner meeting on the veranda with Hugo Montes, president of Diablo Mining.

Sean thanks him and says with a smile, "I love it when you coordinate everything with Mark so I don't have to be concerned with any details other than what I'm going to present."

As Eduardo leads Sean through the house, he replies, "Well, Mr. Stevens told us he wanted you to be able to enjoy Brazil Sunday and Monday before your return flight to San Francisco. We have planned a five-course meal for you and Mr. Montes and hope you won't worry about anything in the time you're here." He pauses in the grand living room. "I hope lobster as a main course suits you tonight?"

"Sounds terrific to me."

Eduardo smiles and leaves the room. One of the maids directs Sean to his suite.

Sean is considering a swim when Eduardo knocks on his door with a mimosa. Sean says, "Thank you. Can I have that by the pool?"

Eduardo nods. "It will be waiting for you." Sean spends the rest of the day lounging by the pool, soaking up the sun's rays, before taking a cool shower and dressing for dinner with Mr. Montes.

Mr. Hugo Montes arrives and warmly welcomes Sean back to Brazil, saying, "It's always good to see you, my friend."

Sean responds, "You too, my friend. Have a seat, please. I'm not really sure what's for dinner tonight other than the main course. I hope lobster is acceptable for you?"

Hugo nods. "Sounds wonderful actually. And I'm sure Mr. Stevens' chef will prepare it to perfection. He always does."

"I suspect you are correct. What can I get you to drink?" Sean motions for the butler.

"Tequila with lime, please."

Eduardo nods. "It will be here momentarily."

Hugo thanks him, and Sean begins their discussion with an overview of the problem from Mr. Stevens' perspective, both in Brazil and the United States. He further elaborates about Mrs. Stevens' personal and political sensitivity on environmental issues and how important it is for her to see Global Metal Refining as an eco-friendly organization throughout this process.

Hugo nods in understanding. "But Mr. Green, Diablo Mining's practices are not unlawful in Brazil, even though environmental zealots seem to think otherwise. They are creating turmoil locally."

Sean counters, "Well, these same zealot groups have contacted their counterparts in the United States and are attacking the association between Diablo Mining and Global Metal Refining as co-conspirators in raping the precious rain forest of Brazil. Mr. Stevens has come under as much scrutiny in the U.S. as both of you have in Brazil, resulting in his company's stock prices falling thirteen percent as of yesterday. However, I have a solution." Sean shows Hugo the strategy adopted by Global Metal Refining while attempting to convince him of the importance of his participation in this plan with Mr. Stevens.

"But this effectively makes Diablo Mining look like the villain in this saga," Hugo protests.

Sean nods apologetically, "Mr. Stevens has also recognized this dilemma and how regrettable it is. He sent me with this consideration to soften the effect this will have on your personally." Sean stands and hands Hugo the duffel bag of U.S. dollars.

Hugo briskly opens it and raises his eyebrows. "It looks like about seventy-five thousand dollars?"

Sean corrects him. "It's actually one-hundred thousand U.S. dollars. Non-reportable, of course, so no worries about personal income tax. This is simply to offset the negative press Diablo Mining will soon have to endure." Sean clears his throat, then goes on to say, "Mr. Stevens has personally hired me to help with the negative press you're going to receive locally. But for now, let's enjoy dinner before concluding this discussion, shall we?"

Hugo places the duffel bag on the floor next to him, looking slightly dismayed, but agrees.

The dinner discussion becomes light and enjoyable, at least momentarily. After dinner and the appropriate compliments to the staff and the chef for a spectacular meal, they move their dealings into the formal living room of the villa. Sean lays out the storyboard and the ad copy for Hugo's consideration.

Hugo looks over everything, very obviously uncomfortable with the situation he has found himself in, and then makes it abundantly clear that he really isn't thrilled by the proposal. He runs a hand over his clean shaven face. "I suppose the extra money makes the deal acceptable. But I would like to make a few minor adjustments to the verbiage and plans."

He presents them, and they are eventually agreed upon by both men. They continue the evening over Courvoisier and cigars and once again the discussions center around much more pleasant subject matter.

During one of these lighter conversations, Sean seizes the opportunity to pick Hugo's brain about the fashion and apparel industries in Brazil and Latin America. Surprisingly to Sean, Hugo is very well versed on the subject, as well as the socioeconomic factors and the micro economy of Brazil. During the discussion, Sean learns that the Brazilian consumer market has been touted as a market with progressive policies targeted at foreign organizations for investment opportunities by the *Brazil Business Environment Report*. The two men discuss the sources and empirical studies that have referenced rising salaries and disposable incomes, and the discrepancies as to the actual amounts involved.

"For instance," Hugo explains, "one study claims that seventy percent of Brazil's population is made up of low-income classes, while *Business Monitor International* claims more than one-third of Brazil's population lives at or below the poverty level. The consumer behaviors reflected in Brazil's middle and upper classes continue to mirror their counterparts in developed countries, with consumer purchasing power continuing to rise. Yet the base of the pyramid consumers in Brazil continually strive for middle class identification, while the country's elite insist upon separation from the middle class." Hugo pauses to take a sip of his drink, and Sean does the same as he considers what Hugo has just said. Then Hugo continues, "As a result, all three segments of Brazilian culture and consumer markets engage in hedonic consumption as a means of gaining social identification and status. However, with all the positive economic reports on Brazil, the income separation and inequality remains a concern for many foreign investors. Research shows, contrary to this income and social inequality, base of the pyramid Brazilian consumers are willing to make specific economic sacrifices in order to purchase things they want, therefore satisfying their socioeconomic need for inclusion into the middle class or, at the minimum, projecting the appearance of not being excessively poor. The consumer consumption pattern has become well known with marketers in Brazil, like me, who use this type of purchasing pattern to increase brand loyalty by knowing that consumers cannot afford to purchase another product if they make the incorrect decision initially regarding the purchase of any item." Hugo spreads his hands and leans back in his chair.

"Additionally," he continues after a moment of letting Sean process this marketing strategy, "Brazil's labor market and job creation have lagged behind the growth in its labor force. Unemployment rates are high, and evidence clearly supports the notion that racial inequality, prejudice, and discrimination are a social reality. In the past, Brazil enjoyed the image of racial equality, but that has recently been revealed to be incorrect. While the majority of Brazilians don't even attain completion of high school or college, white men and women that complete at least twelve years of education are five times higher than Afro-Brazilian women. The average age for leaving school in Latin America is fourteen years old and seems to follow along socioeconomic lines. It has also been pointed out that the majority of Brazil's impoverished population may be the result of geographic polarization between the significantly more rural northeast compared to the more industrialized southeast. Government authorities within Brazil have been highly criticized for their failure to invest in education. This failure and the country's racial inequality become abundantly clear when one looks at the overcrowding in the schools of the industrialized southeast. It is apparent that, as an emerging marketplace, Brazil presents significant opportunities for business expansion as well as some real challenges." Hugo takes another sip of his drink.

Sean nods and says, "Nevertheless, the abundance of research and academic inquiry clearly delineates a pattern of social injustice based upon prejudices and socioeconomic stratification, correct?"

"Ah, yes," Hugo answers, "the majority of the individuals falling within Brazil's low-income category appear to include women, many of whom are single parents due to Brazil's high divorce rates, and the uneducated, many of whom are living in the agricultural northeast and racially are either Afro-Brazilian or members of Brazil's indigenous tribes. Individuals living in the southeast seems to fare better socioeconomically due to the greater access to education facilities and higher-paying employment opportunities. Clearly, the ethnographic tendency in Brazil's government is to either ignore or condone racial or social prejudice, based on geographical, economic, and employment stratifications." Hugo polishes off his drink as Sean considers all he has presented. Sean realizes there are tremendous opportunities for the right American company looking to make a difference, not only in Brazil, but also in the company's growth potential strategies.

"Very interesting," Sean tells Hugo. "You have been very helpful and have given me a lot to consider. Anyway, as I said before, Mr. Stevens has hired me to devise not only the current strategy for our environmental issues, but also a recovery strategy for Diablo Mining in Brazil and also worldwide."

Sean elaborates further by clarifying for Hugo that fees for his services will be handled entirely by Mr. Stevens. Hugo admits he is surprised and appreciates that Mr. Stevens is concerned enough about his ongoing relationship with Diablo Mining that he is willing to fix the problems they are about to create. Sean lays out for Hugo a two-pronged approach, starting in Brazil, which will be based upon the law-abiding practices of Diablo Mining.

"However," Sean says, "since many of the company's opponents have presented some valid points on this type of strip mining, we intend for you to be positioned as the driving force in correcting these practices. You will sponsor legislation in Brazil on new environmentally friendlier industry standards. Globally, you will become the face for environmentally sensitive mining and restoration after operational completion. You will design economically feasible solutions, and I will provide the marketing expertise to convince the concerned global citizens that these practices will allow the mining industry to coexist with the environment for the benefit of all concerned. If necessary, Mr. Stevens will provide up to two million U.S. dollars to Diablo Mining for industry lobbying and political contributions where necessary."

Hugo appears satisfied with the deal after the offer of this additional support, and the two once again return to more pleasant after dinner conversation.

After a few polite inquiries into Sean's business life, Hugo finally breaks down and asks what he's been wondering since Sean brought it up. "Why the sudden interest in the fashion industry and Brazil's marketing areas?"

Sean chuckles, "I had the CEO of a fledgling fashion apparel company come into my office with the desire that SGM represent her. I told her I wasn't interested in becoming involved in the fashion industry and dismissed her."

Hugo gives Sean an all-knowing smile, his teeth very white against his tanned skin. "She must be extremely attractive, eh? For you to be reconsidering…"

Sean looks slightly puzzled. "Why does everyone immediately jump to that conclusion?" Hugo gives him a deadpan look, and finally Sean nods, then recovers with, "But that isn't the reason I'm considering accepting her as a client. She recovered very nicely with a gift basket and good scotch, and so I did some research. The fashion industry is a two-hundred and fifty-billion-dollar industry in the United States alone, so I could see some tremendous income potential for the right designer. Furthermore, this woman's company is performing slightly better than the statistical norm."

Hugo sighs. "Ah, what we fools will do for a beautiful woman."

Sean chuckles but protests, "Not at all. My inquiry has been strictly for business purposes."

Hugo replies, "Well, if you are truly conducting business research, then you would probably be interested in knowing that my cousin owns an apparel factory that Nike has just abandoned. I believe my cousin would be willing to cut a very favorable lease deal for the right manufacturer. Since it's already set up for apparel, very little modification would need to be made for production to be up and running. It would take maybe six months? Would you be interested in seeing it tomorrow?"

Sean considers for a moment, then says slowly, "For research purposes only, of course. Why did Nike leave the factory?"

"They built one of their own. They were tired of leasing, I suppose."

The two men agree that Hugo will pick Sean up the next morning at 9:00 to tour the vacant factory, which is approximately a forty-five minute drive from the villa. They bid each other a good evening, and Sean retires to his suite.

⟨⟩

The next morning, Sean meets Hugo in the cobblestone driveway, and they travel forty-five minutes south of the villa. Upon arrival, they meet Hugo's cousin, Ricardo Montes. Sean is amazed by the condition of the well-manicured facility. After a tour, he is convinced it is state-of-the-art. It is air-conditioned, with a fully functional ventilation system and well-equipped work stations. Ricardo asks the typical questions associated with initial tenant evaluation, but he is also concerned about the integrity of the potential future business considering renting the facility.

Ricardo explains, "Most of the displaced workers who couldn't move with Nike are still in the area and would be available immediately to resume production with very little training necessary.

Are you sure that this business you are considering representing would be an appropriate fit? I do not want to get screwed over again, like I was with Nike."

Sean reassures Ricardo while attempting to process that these possibilities exist. A fully trained staff, a modern facility, and a landlord willing to bargain to fill an otherwise difficult facility to lease seemed too good to be true.

"I will be meeting with my potential client in a couple of weeks, and I will get back to you with some feedback early next month. Other than that, I can't really reassure you about much else."

Ricardo asks Hugo in Portuguese if Sean is seriously interested, and Hugo confirms that Sean is, in fact, a real bona fide prospect with the capability to have his clients deliver what he promises.

Ricardo turns back to Sean. "I have been delighted to meet you. I will e-mail a preliminary proposal to you, for your possible client's consideration."

"Thank you," Sean replies. "Are you willing to negotiate the terms?"

Ricardo nods hesitantly. "I'm willing to negotiate a fairly favorable contract for the right U.S. company willing to commit to at least a ten-year lease arrangement."

"And what about a right of first refusal to purchase and an option to buy?"

Ricardo says, "Absolutely, these provisions can be worked through and included in any arrangement."

Satisfied, Sean shakes Ricardo's hand. All three men go to a local cantina, enjoy more pleasant conversation and local cuisine, and then Hugo and Sean depart back to the villa.

When they arrive, Sean invites Hugo for drinks by the pool, and Hugo accepts and peppers Sean with many questions regarding his opinion of the factory.

Sean plays it very cool, being as vague as possible without being rude. "I have to discuss matters with my client, as I'm sure you understand. At the moment, I am unable to commit on her behalf."

Hugo frowns and Sean realizes he needs to throw some type of bone to maintain the opportunity. He sighs. "However, I'm delighted by the facility, and I can see several benefits for my prospective client, should she choose to utilize it in a global growth strategy, especially in the emerging Latin American markets we discussed last night. I will absolutely suggest this is the best move for her, but I will also need to explore her financial tolerance for this type of rapid expansion, as well as the appropriate timing for it within the fashion industry."

Hugo's informational needs are satisfied for the moment, and he stands and shakes Sean's hand before leaving the villa. "Thank you for your time, Mr. Green," he says, and Sean returns the pleasantry.

After Hugo has gone, Sean calls Mark Stevens to let him know the deal is completed with Diablo Mining and to thank him for the use of the villa over the weekend. Next, Sean begins the intense process of market research and preliminary outlines for his discussion with Jessica Silva, appreciating how delightful doing research is when it's done poolside.

CHAPTER 6
INITIAL ANALYSIS

As Sean considers the possibilities for Jessica's company, he is struck by the fact that for the first time in a long time, he will need to consider his client's financial ability to implement the strategy he develops. The relocation or opening of an additional facility is an aggressive transition into a new global strategy, which will most likely be beyond Jessica's ability to accomplish. He makes a note for himself to determine the strength of "Beauty Something's" brand within its niche market.

God, I need to get the name of this company into my brain correctly, then evaluate it solely upon its public recognition and credibility within the fashion industry. But to him, the name still seems trite, juvenile, and insignificant. *But hell, what do I know about women's fashion?* He decides to have Evelyn assign one of his best researchers to answer these questions prior to his next visit with Jessica.

Perhaps the most difficult issue to wrap his head around is the level of political corruption a U.S. company will be forced to deal with in Brazil's political environment. Mark, Hugo, and Ricardo will be able to shed some light on this issue and what will be expected in order to make things happen quickly. Next, Sean develops a preliminary benefits list for potential employees, health care coverage, marriage counseling, and family planning education, as well as literary and basic budgeting for the undereducated employees. Sean also makes sure the benefits include scholarship opportunities for the employees' children and educational programs so the workers will be able to complete high school and strive for college completion as well, in order to qualify for management positions within the organization. Considering the setup of the factory, Sean realizes there is also plenty of space to provide on-site day care for working moms, the costs of which the employees could reimburse, in full or just partially. Perhaps the biggest bonus the "Beauty Whatever" could offer is discounted clothing and bonuses paid in clothing to appease workers' need for social status along with their appetite for middle-class identification.

Most of the programs can be provided by the organization at limited or no expense for the facility employees, and can even be offered to the general public for a small fee to offset the organizations expenses, Sean thinks, nodding to himself. With the general concepts done, Sean starts to focus on the financial ramifications of this type of programming and expansion. Since he knows absolutely nothing about fashion costing per item, markup, or shipping expenses, he decides to speak with Mark, specifically about the ease or difficulty of getting the products out of the country and into the United States. He decides against doing it over the weekend, and then spends the majority of his time at the villa drawing out a variety of figures for the fashion industry, in preparation for checking costs.

⊶⊷

While on the corporate jet back to San Francisco, Sean calls Mark, then Evelyn. He discovers from Mark that shipping, via air service, to the United States will add approximately five percent to the overall production costs, regardless of the product, as long as none of the products are considered hazardous material. During his following conversation with Evelyn, Sean instructs her to have one of his researchers conduct preliminary market cost analysis on the fashion industry in the United States and Latin America, specifically focusing on production, shipping, and quality control issues in the niche market industry and on Beauty Boutique's market placement.

Evelyn quips, "Well, Mr. Green, seems to me like you have given considerable thought to the Beauty Boutique's representation."

Sean sighs into the phone. "I didn't say I was going to get involved. I'm simply trying to decide if the margins are large enough for SGM to engage in a realistic discussion with Ms. Silva."

"Mmh. I see," replies Evelyn knowingly.

"Just tell someone to have the damn preliminary research done by Thursday morning when I get into the office," Sean growls.

"Yes, Mr. Green. By the way, you have a meeting scheduled for 11:00 a.m. with Ms. Silva three weeks from today. It's only for an hour. Should I block out a longer time for you?"

"Yes. Block out two hours on my calendar, just in case we need a little longer depending on the research results. Also, please arrange for lunch to be catered by Basta Pasta, have my merlot available, and get a few cannolis from Stella's Pastry for dessert. I don't want us to go hungry if things go well, and if they don't I'll have a great lunch for myself."

"Is that it?" Evelyn asks, dripping sweetness.

He frowns at the phone. "For now, thank you. Oh, wait! Can you also schedule a dinner appointment with Mark Stevens this week? Tell him it's for sushi and it needs to be just between him and me. If he hesitates, tell him he owes me, and it will be all about business this time. We'll go to the usual spot."

"You got it," she answers, fake sweetness gone.

"Thanks, Evelyn," Sean says, then ends the call.

The jet touches down in the early evening in San Francisco. After a short ride from the airport, Sean pours himself a scotch and settles down on the couch with Sinatra playing softly in the background. He awakens early Tuesday morning slightly bemused about having spent the night on the couch. He packs up some clothes for work, dresses in sweats for the gym, and heads out for his normal workout.

He arrives at his office around 8:30 a.m. to a mound of messages, e-mails, and demands from Evelyn. When he finally allows an interruption to his work, it is Evelyn reminding him that it is nearly 5:30 p.m., and he is supposed to meet Mark for sushi at 6:00.

"Oh, shit. Thanks," he murmurs. He closes what he was working on, grabs his notes, and dashes out the door. Mark is already seated when Sean arrives in a whirlwind.

"I took the liberty of ordering us both a beer and the first round of sushi," Mark says with his generic smirk in place.

Sean huffs out a breath and runs his hand through his salt-and-pepper hair. "Great. Sorry I'm late. It's been one hell of a day." They exchange the normal pleasantries, with Sean asking about Bonnie and Mark asking about Brazil. A serious tone comes over Sean and catches Mark momentarily off guard.

Mark studies Sean's face as only he can. Sean finally breaks the silence and asks, "How well do you know Jessica Silva?"

Mark smiles and answers Sean's question with a question. "Are you asking me for a personal or business reference?"

Sean hesitates for a moment, slumps in his chair a little, then confesses to his friend, "Both I guess."

Mark chuckles and replies, "Well, she is an intelligent, beautiful woman, with enormous talent in the fashion design field. She has worked her ass off to get where she is and hasn't asked anyone for help. That is, until she asked you. Bonnie absolutely loves her, and from what I've seen of her, I don't think you could find a more honest, straight-shooting person. Why do you ask?"

Sean sighs. "Well, that helps I guess. As for why, you know she came to my office and was completely unprepared for any type of business discussion. I wasn't exactly accommodating." Mark nods, acknowledging Sean's statement. "However," Sean continues, "she recovered very well. And I responded with a snarky note and some flowers, to which she recovered well yet again, with an equally sarcastic note and a bottle of my expensive scotch. I've been doing a little research, and it looks like SGM might be able to help her, but in order to do so, she would need to expand rapidly, globally, and with a whole new line of products. I don't think her company has the capability to do so on its own, and I'm looking at possible options to help."

Mark gives Sean a curious look, wondering why Sean's talking to him about this in such detail. "Like what?"

"Well, my numbers are very preliminary at this point, but I expect she will need between $1.5 to 2 million, cash, to accomplish what I see as a possibility for her company. It's also the only way SGM could make a profit while assisting her."

"And what is this extremely expensive possibility?" Mark asks.

"Well, when I was in Brazil, I toured a fairly new apparel factory that had recently been abandoned by Nike Clothing. Hugo's cousin owns the property and is willing to negotiate a lucrative ten-year contract for the right renter. I think Jessica's company just might fit the profile. I don't believe many modifications would be needed to the factory, but you and I both know I don't know shit about fashion apparel production. I'd like for Jessica to tour the facility before anything else is decided. However, if the funds needed aren't available, I don't want her to get excited about the possibilities only to realize she is undercapitalized."

Mark analyzes Sean's words for a moment, then says, "You know, Sean, I wouldn't necessarily count Jessica out. My experience with her, as limited as it has been, has told me that she is a very capable and resourceful businesswoman. If she needs capital,

I suspect she would be able to raise whatever is necessary to accomplish her goals."

Sean nods, pleased with Mark's appraisal of Ms. Silva. "So do you think Beauty Boutique Clothing is a good risk?"

Mark raises his eyebrows. "Sean, quit beating around the bush. What exactly are you driving at today?"

"I'm not sure yet, and, as I've said, my numbers are only preliminary."

Mark rolls his eyes. "I have never known your numbers to be off more than ten percent, at the most. Out with it, my man. Now!"

Sean shifts in his chair and says, "I think I'm crazy for bringing this to you, but based on my initial analysis, I think Jessica has found a very viable niche market with enormous profit potential."

Mark sighs; realizing Sean is going to takes his time with whatever this proposal is aiming at. "Yeah, so?"

"I see the possibility that any investment into the Beauty Boutique could be doubled or tripled within the first full year of operation," Sean clarifies. "If you invest big…"

Mark leans back in his chair, puts his hands behind his head, and studies Sean's face. When he finally breaks his stare and silence, he says, "I only have one question for you at this point. Is your interest in Beauty Boutique Clothing and Jessica Silva personal or professional?"

"Professional," Sean says immediately. "I'm much more interested in making money than I am in chasing pussy. Hell, finding some split-tail to spend time with me in bed has never been an issue for me. You know that."

"True," Mark concedes, "but I'm sensing a different type of interest in Jessica Silva from you, and I just want to caution you. If you're analyzing this company as a possible investment vehicle, you need to view Jessica as a CEO and client only, not a possible conquest. Decide which it is before we continue with this discussion."

Without hesitation, Sean replies, "Mark, you have my word. I am more interested in the company's possibilities than I am in any possibilities with Jessica Silva."

Mark eyes Sean carefully before giving in. "Very well. What else?"

Sean shakes his head. "Nothing at this point, but I'd like you to consider investing one million dollars. I would do the same in order for this expansion to work for Ms. Silva, if she can't come up with the funds on her own."

Mark grins knowingly. "Well, here we are then. The actual purpose of this dinner meeting, eh? I'll tell you what; I'll consider this a preliminary proposal with results subject to your final analysis. But I would have one major condition."

"What's that?" Sean asks, smiling at Mark's directness.

"If I'm going to invest that much money in a fledgling clothing company, even if you're going to do the same, I want both of us to be seated on a board of directors. Good luck getting Jessica to agree to me sitting on the board, given her friendship with Bonnie. She'd see it as a conflict of interest."

"All right, fair enough. I'll take the challenge. And you'll consider it?"

Mark nods. "If you tell me it's a good investment and your analysis demonstrates it to be correct, I'll consider joining you in it. However, if you back away from putting your own funds into the company, I won't go forward either. Fair enough?"

"Fair enough," Sean answers, appreciating the deal-making banter. "Now, what else do you want to eat? I'm starving."

CHAPTER 7
WOULD YOU?

Thursday morning, Sean meets with Evelyn and Bradley Jenkins, a classically dressed, geeky young man in his early thirties. Bradley is a well-educated market researcher and statistician. He works for SGM, and Sean personally considers him to be the best on board, but Bradley doesn't know it. Bradley starts off the meeting explaining mode, medium, deviations, and variations.

Sean fakes a snore then interrupts Bradley. "I never was interested in the mechanics of statistical analysis in graduate school and I'm not interested in it now. That's why I hired you. I understand the significance and interconnection of certain variations, and that's all I really need to know. Tell me, Bradley, if you were going to invest two million dollars in Beauty Boutique Clothing, given their position in their niche market, and you wanted to double or triple the return on that investment in, say, one to two years, knowing SGM would be doing the marketing, would you invest?"

Bradley begins with a disclaimer and qualifications and is again interrupted.

"It's simply a yes or no question," Sean says, "Would you risk two million dollars developing this company? Does the research warrant such an investment? Yes or no?"

Bradley squirms in his seat. Sean focuses on him with a piercing stare, then asks again, "Yes, or no?"

Bradley looks at his feet, wrings his hands, glances at Evelyn, who purses her lips, then finally looks up at Sean's laser gaze and says, "The market research warrants such an investment."

Sean nods, relaxing slightly. "Okay. But would you, personally, risk two million of your own hard-earned dollars with such an investment?"

Sean notices Bradley seems a little annoyed at his persistence when he straightens up and his face goes stiff. "Well, that's not really a fair question, is it, since I don't have two million dollars to invest!" He snaps. "Sir, I told you, the research indicates the parameters established in your question are possible to achieve. But there are still many variables that can change your dynamic dramatically, which haven't yet been fully explored."

Sean sits back fully, trying not to chuckle, and lets him off the hook. "Okay, fair enough. Now that you know my parameters, explore some of the other concerns that could change the dynamic and get back to me in two days. Oh, one more thing. Look at the possibility of moving production into Brazil and factor that into your equation. Don't worry about the cost of building a production facility. One has already been identified on a very favorable long-term lease arrangement. I'm only concerned with the market and industry conditions at this point. That will be all for now."

Bradley seems to shake himself out of his defensive stance as he stands. "Yes, Mr. Green," he says on his way out.

Evelyn shoots a disgusted look at Sean and says, "Do you always have to mess with people's minds? You had him so unsettled by the time you dismissed him, it was actually unpleasant to watch."

Sean scoffs. "Oh, come on, some of this has got to be for me. Besides, if Bradley is a little unsettled, he'll do better research and his analysis will be more detailed because he doesn't want to be caught off guard again.

Evelyn gives Sean a cockeyed, quizzical look from under her dark pixie-cut hair and asks, "So, where are we going with all this research?"

Sean smirks back at Evelyn, saying, "I don't know yet. SGM is still in the analysis phase of client selection. Ms. Silva appears to have established a nice niche for her company. However, she is right in her contention that without some significant marketing help, her company's profits will level off at best, and stagnate at worst, neither of which will suit her desires. On the other hand, Beauty Boutique Clothing isn't significant enough in its revenue stream to threaten major designers or industry movers and shakers. What I'm struggling with is entering into the realm of fashion marketing, especially for a company as small as Beauty Boutique. You said many of your outfits were Jessica Silva designs, correct? Why do you like them enough to purchase them?"

Evelyn looks slightly taken aback. "Well, Jessica Silva designs clothing that is flattering to women who aren't anorexic like some fashion models. Her clothes are classy, sexy, and an excellent economical choice for professional women. In other words, she designs clothing for people like herself. She is athletic but not anorexic, and she has curves like most women. Her prices are above off-the-rack department store clothing, but so is the quality. She really has targeted the professional women's market in comfort, fit, and pricing. If you're an entry-level businesswoman, her clothing might be too expensive, but if you fit into the upwardly mobile or professional level of employment, the quality, costs, and designs are a perfect fit. She chose her perfect market. Let me put it into perspective for you. Why don't you wear designer suits? You can obviously afford them."

He chuckles and answers immediately, "Because I am too damn cheap to spend that kind of money when an eight-hundred-dollar suit works just as well for me as a two thousand dollar one would."

Evelyn nods. "Exactly. If Jessica Silva were designing men's suits, her prices would range between eight hundred and fifty dollars and one thousand two hundred dollars. Rival designer suits in style and quality are currently selling for over two thousand dollars. If you could find less expensive suits that have the same quality as the more expensive ones, would you buy them rather than what you can get off the rack?"

Sean nods, beginning to understand. "Yes, of course I would."

"There you have it. That's what Jessica has accomplished with her designs. So, how are we going to market Beauty Boutique Clothing?"

Sean laughs and insists, "I haven't agreed to do so yet!"

She rolls her eyes. "I've been with you too long to accept your bullshit. Admit it. You're intrigued by the possibilities and challenges of taking on something so foreign to you that it actually excites you, doesn't it?"

Sean smiles, "Yes, it does. I'm just not sure Ms. Silva can afford SGM, and I'm not very benevolent when it comes to our fees for services. We are good at what we do, and this type of expertise comes with a hefty price."

"Understood, but if she can, can you help her take her company to the next level?"

He nods slowly. "Yes, I could help her, but the next level for her is to establish a global market and international recognition. With that comes the threat of hostile takeovers and buyouts. Is Ms. Silva ready to play in that arena? I'm not sure she is. Nothing from our last meeting was convincing."

"Well, you were an asshole during your last meeting, and you know it," Evelyn chides.

"I agree, but many people are going to be assholes to her if she goes international. I have my doubts about her, Evelyn, and only she can change that."

⊨⊣ ⊢⊨

Tuesday morning, Evelyn and Bradley are back in Sean's office. Evelyn is amazed by how calm Bradley looks and recognizes why as soon as Sean opens the conversation with, "So, Bradley, what did you discover?"

Bradley sits up straighter. "Well, Mr. Green, the fashion market exceeds two hundred and fifty million dollars in the United States alone and is dominated by roughly fifty large international designers. Accessories expand the market by another one hundred million dollars. On top of that, you have fragrances, shoes, and men's clothing. In other words, there is plenty of growth potential for Beauty Boutique Clothing. Production in emerging growth countries like Brazil is definitely viable with production costs being cut by forty percent, with a fifty percent reduction not being out of the realm of possibilities. Two major hurdles any American company will face in relocating into Latin America are political corruption or payoffs and a relatively unskilled labor force. Shipping costs to the United States will add approximately five to eight percent of the overall production costs. Brazil is a little better off in both of these arenas because the country is encouraging United States company investments, so the political payoffs will be more reasonable than other Latin American countries. Apparel industry labor is a little stronger because of Nike apparel and others that have production facilities already established in Latin America. There is a strong national identification with the Brazilian soccer team association, and any support shown for them will increase name recognition and branding dramatically, as demonstrated recently by Nike's marketing strategy in Brazil. The fashion industry is an emerging market in Brazil. A designer or quasi-designer label will garner a premium sales price due to status bias or identification needs of the local population. Purchasing power is on the rise in Latin America. Locals are hard working, and women especially are becoming a much more predominant force in the labor market than ever before, due to the very high divorce rate and single-parent family dynamic. There is tremendous potential for a small designer and manufacturer to thrive, because the market isn't large enough yet to attract large designers. It will be much easier to establish a market presence in Latin America at this point. Therefore, the potential to capture significant market penetration in the fashion apparel industry is virtually unhindered by any significant competition. There is, however, significant risk in being industry leader in emerging untested markets. If the producer has an established market elsewhere, the ability to produce product at a significantly reduced cost without inducing child labor will increase profitability in the already established distribution channels and ultimately will enhance vertical integration and increased sales. Capitalization will be a major concern for smaller manufacturers, and turnaround times will be slower until employees are fully trained." Bradley finished with a proud look on his face and waits for Sean's response.

Finally, Sean asks, "What about quality control issues?"

Bradley immediately answers, "That will depend on the organizations training programs and procedures. I believe it would be a short-term issue with proper training for the relatively uneducated labor pool. But once the staff is fully trained, I don't see it being any more significant than at any other facility worldwide. Finally, initial calculations indicate an increased profit margin of at least twenty-five percent in existing markets if production is done in Latin America, perhaps higher once the labor pool is properly trained and production is at or near capacity. In short, the scenario you laid out to me last week is, in my estimation, totally viable given no dramatic shift in political or economic times, globally."

Sean nods his approval. "Thank you. You've done an excellent job on your research, and I appreciate the speed at which you accomplished everything. Well done!"

CHAPTER 8

FINDING YOUR NICHE

Monday morning is a sweltering day in San Francisco, with temperatures in the mid-nineties. It's the type of day single professional men love in the business district—the type of day when women remove their business jackets and wear silk tops. The gentle breezes off the bay often cause the blouses to lie tight against the women's bodies, leaving the male imagination reeling. Sean, however, is completely oblivious to these facts.

He arrives at his office early and is finishing his final calculations and inserting them into his presentation when Evelyn gently knocks on his door, peeks in, and says, "Ms. Silva is here for your eleven o'clock."

"Thank you. Please show her in to the conference room. I'll be in shortly," Sean replies, barely glancing up from his work.

Evelyn nods and obliges. After Jessica is seated at the conference table, Evelyn gets her fresh fruit and coffee, and tells her Sean will be in momentarily. Jessica thanks her and looks out the conference room windows.

What an absolutely stunning view of San Francisco Bay, she thinks. She becomes mesmerized by the brilliant colors on the sails of the many sailboats and wonders how many employees skipped work to enjoy such a gorgeous day. Her thoughts are interrupted when Sean enters the room and apologizes for running behind schedule. He gets a small plate of fruit and a cup of coffee before sitting with her at the table.

After a moment, he opens the conversation. "Jessica, thank you for the gift basket and scotch. They were very much appreciated."

She raises a fine-haired eyebrow and corrects him, "First, it's Ms. Silva, and second, you're very welcome. Thank you for the lilies."

Sean leans back in his chair with his usual smirk and says, "Okay, then. *Ms.* Silva, we need to get something straight before we begin today. I loathe formalities. I work on a first-name basis with all of my potential and existing clientele. My calling you by your first name isn't a sign of disrespect, and I apologize if it has been regarded as such in the past. What we do here at SGM requires us to develop a deep trusting relationship with our clients, and I find that trust can be hindered by such formalities as titles and gender designations. That being said, can we please talk on a first-name basis as we move forward?"

Jessica looks surprised, considers for a moment, and then gives him a small, dainty smile and nods affirmatively.

"Very well then. Thank you, Jessica. I also need to extend to you an additional apology, as I have been told I was quite rude to you during our last meeting. In fact, Evelyn told me I was an asshole."

Jessica laughs aloud, nods again, and says, "Yes, you were actually very annoying. But I will never be dismissed like that again as long as I live, so I guess I owe you a thank you for giving me that wake-up call."

Sean smiles belatedly. "I understand, and again, I am sorry. I felt set-up and blindsided. Bonnie has that effect sometimes, I'm sure you know. Since then, I have been doing a lot of research and have asked my staff to do the same. We compared notes based upon our independent findings and have come to virtually the same conclusion. But before we get into the particulars of our findings, I want to hear from you what you are hoping SGM could do to help you take Beauty Boutique Clothing to the next level. What are your hopes, visions, and strategic plans to accomplish the goals you have?"

Jessica is momentarily stunned. *What the hell happened with this guy? I was expecting a rude, pompous ass, yet today he seems genuinely interested in understanding and perhaps even helping me...*

"Well, this may take a little while. I don't want to interfere with your schedule. Shall we set up another meeting and just cover the basics today?" she asks.

Sean waves a hand, his watch flashing in the sunlight let in by the large windows. "Don't concern yourself. I'm sorry I neglected to tell you, but I have allotted two hours today and have arranged for lunch to be catered. I can also free my afternoon, if we are making progress today. That is, of course, if you have the time in your schedule?"

She considers for a moment, then says, "Let me make a few phone calls to rearrange a few minor appointments. I'm delighted you are at least willing to consider a proposal from the Beauty Boutique."

Sean nods. "Absolutely. Let me know when you are ready."

Both Jess and Sean clear their schedules for the rest of the day, and Jessica begins to lay out her dreams for her company in the coming years. She tells Sean she believes her company has hit a point where sales and profits will level off if there isn't some expansion into foreign markets.

"I understand there will be a need to capitalize such a business expansion, but I'm not sure where and how it should be undertaken. I know my niche market very well. I'm between off-the-rack department store clothing and designer labels, and I want to stay there." She looks up from her notes, directly into Sean's eyes, captivating him yet again. "I want to dominate the professional women's clothing market."

Sean asks, "What about lines other than clothing? Say, shoes or handbags or fragrances?"

Jessica slightly shakes her head. "I'm a clothing designer. I'm good at it. I don't know a thing about fragrances or handbags. In my estimation, the footwear market has too many significant players who design incredible products for me to compete with. A new company could be undercut in pricing from the start and forced out of the market before any real success is experienced. Beauty Boutique Clothing has a unique niche, and I've had tremendous success filling a need that high fashion designers aren't interested in, and the department store clothing lacks in quality. I have established lower prices and extreme quality as the norm. I don't think I could keep that promise in other categories. I also don't believe I have the financial capability to expand into France, Italy, or Germany, so I have been looking at the former Soviet Union markets. I know there is a major pent-up demand, but I'm not sure about the consumer purchasing power quite yet."

Sean nods, satisfied with her answers, then says, "You also have to deal with a significant political environment that is unstable at best and completely corrupt at worst, without any real indication which force will prevail. Where do you see your sales in two years without any expansion? Where do you see them with expansion? What are your projections for any type of expansion you may consider? How do you see Beauty Boutique Clothing implementing your expansion strategy? Finally, what are your capitalization or financing needs and plans for this considered expansion?"

Jessica pauses to think for a moment, and Sean can almost hear the wheels turning in her brain. He's finding that he enjoys discussing business with her. "Well, let's see if I can handle those questions in order. In two years, without expansion, I see the Beauty Boutique's revenues leveling out right around two million dollars per annum and remaining stable with minor rises and declines in the ten percent range. With a proper expansion and choosing the right market, I see us doubling or tripling our sales revenue with perhaps a decline of profitability initially of five-to-ten percent due to higher distribution costs. Once our distribution systems, both vertically and horizontally, get the bugs worked out, profitability should increase by ten-to-fifteen perfect per unit sold. My projections are based primarily upon increased distribution costs, with manufacturing remaining in the United States and finding appropriate commercial space to showcase and sell our designs via our own outlets in whatever market or markets we choose to pursue. Our expansion strategy would be to continue what we are currently doing and marketing through our own stores. In this manner, I can maintain control of customer service and the high quality of the shopping experience we have successfully developed thus far—"

Sean interrupts, "So, just to clarify, you intend to manufacture in the United States, increase production, and market through individually owned storefronts? Is that correct?"

Jessica nods. "Yes, exactly. In this manner, the major costs are finding and securing appropriate commercial spaces for retail sales in the new market or markets. Finally, I plan to fund this expansion through savings and increased sales."

"I see," Sean replies, considering her drive and strategies. There is a knock on the door, and Evelyn pokes her head in.

"Lunch has arrived," she tells them.

"Let's take a breather momentarily to enjoy our meal," Sean says, and Jessica nods agreement.

They enjoy their catered lunch with Sean's merlot and dessert cannoli, including small talk about the weather and their mutual friends, Mark and Bonnie. When Sean resumes the business discussion, he begins by telling Jessica he has a proposal he wants her to consider.

"Since our first meeting, I have done a fair amount of research and thinking about how SGM could help the Beauty Boutique. What I have discovered is that you have a very interesting niche market that has tremendous growth potential, as most designers have neglected it. Jessica Silva designs, as I've been told, are appreciated for their quality and pricing, but because of your limited exposure to various markets, you are virtually unknown except to the very few in your target market. One of the problems I see is, once your success becomes known and other designers see the market potential, competition could become quite intense, and you should have at least three or four years of designs ready to roll out on very short notice. I agree with you that the Beauty Boutique needs to develop deep market penetration and market share by the time this niche market potential is recognized by others. Much like the footwear industry, you need to be prepared to drive newcomers in your niche market out by way of pricing and tight profit margins. This brings us to the fact that your distribution channels are extremely shallow, even anorexic, since they are limited to your corporate-owned boutique. Research indicates you have resisted selling outside your properties, and unless you intend to open a vast number of outlets, your market penetration will remain insignificant compared to others in the industry. Your profit margin per piece is very good for an American-manufactured product, but you'll need to cut the price by at least thirty-five percent if you intend to dominate the niche market."

Jessica interrupts Sean and says, "That's impossible if I want to maintain the same quality. It's not realistic and you can't fake quality."

Sean smiles. "That's a good assessment, if you're manufacturing in the United States."

Jessica mildly shakes her head, processing, then says, "If you're outside the United States, you have labor force issues, distribution issues, and quality control concerns. Additionally, I am vehemently opposed to using child labor or sweatshops and will go bankrupt before I will consider either of those options."

Sean smiles again genially. "Have I suggested either of those options?"

She gives him a suspicious look. "Not yet, no."

"Nor do I ever intend to. You jumped to several conclusions that are way off the mark. First, let me point out you already have distribution issues much larger than you have anticipated. Quality control is always an issue in your chosen industry, and salaries make up your largest labor force issue in the United States. So these concerns aren't going away no matter what is eventually decided."

Jessica nods, her red hair falling softly over her shoulder. "Well, you have a point there."

Sean clears his throat and continues, "What I have envisioned for the Beauty Boutique is a four-pronged approach that will required a two million dollar minimum capitalization within the next ninety days. It will also require establishing a production facility outside the United States, and I have identified a possible site in Brazil. It will require some innovative benefits, and it will require allowing your designs to be sold outside of your privately owned boutiques at a slightly higher pricing premium than what can be expected in your facilities." Sean notices Jessica becoming uneasy as she fidgets with her pen, so he pauses for a moment, compelling her to make eye contact, then says, "This outside distribution will be limited in both time and scope. The intent is to get the deeper market penetration via a much broader distribution channel with the strategic focus of replacing this distribution method with corporate-owned facilities after a primary market is established. So let me get a pulse check before I continue. Do you currently have two million dollars in liquidity you can access within ninety days?"

Jessica replies, "Not personally, but I believe I can get it in that time frame."

Sean inclines his head, slightly surprised. "Very well then, let's continue."

Jessica interrupts. "Wait, why Brazil?"

"Well, there are several reasons. First, the government is actively soliciting U.S. companies to consider expanding into Brazil. It's an emerging market with a desire, even a hunger, for products manufactured locally. Second, the labor force is better skilled than other emerging countries, and politically, the corruption is minimal in comparison to other Latin America governments. And third, Nike recently abandoned what appears to me to be a fairly well-equipped clothing facility forty-five minutes south of Mark and Bonnie's villa. I would like to fly you to Brazil so you can tour the facility with me in two weeks at no cost to you. Mark has already offered us his villa while we are there. If the facility is a possible option, we can develop this strategy much further. If it isn't, we will have to put our heads together and develop another one. Jessica, this is in no way a commitment on either of our parts to continue beyond the initial investigative phase, but in order for my first draft proposal to work, this factory must be a fit for your company. Since I know nothing about clothing manufacturing, I would like you to educate me, at least a little bit."

Jessica says, "I'm not sure about the size of the expansion you're proposing. What about my employees? I can't relocate them."

"Understood. I am not proposing you relocate all your employees. I see the initial production being completed in Brazil, then shipped to your facility here for quality control and finishing touches before distribution. Once you have the staff and management trained in Brazil, then, and only then, can orders be shipped directly to the markets."

Jessica nods slowly, taking in Sean's ideas. "You mentioned earlier distribution being outside of my own outlets. What did you have in mind?"

"I would like to see you partner with a footwear manufacturer or designer only to share retail space, then cross-train employees, yours and theirs, to sell each other's line of products on a commission basis. In other words, you each pay your own employees as normal, but when one of your employees sell shoes with an outfit, they will receive a commission on the shoe sale and vice versa. It gives the employees of both designers incentive to cross-sell and match outfits under one roof. Then their customers can match outfits with shoe purchases, and your customers can purchase matching shoes for their clothing purchase," Sean answers, pleased with his idea.

Jessica raises a single eyebrow and says, "I see where this type of arrangement might work. I'm just not sure it is the way I want to market my designs."

"Well, we are just brainstorming right now, so please just keep an open mind. Don't feel the need to accept or reject any suggestion at this point, as there will be plenty of time to study the merits and pitfalls of everything we have discussed here today. There are significant pros and cons to everything that needs to be considered. On that note, are you able to clear your calendar for a weekend to fly to Brazil, say, two weeks from now?"

"Yes, I can, but it's a huge step to even consider this type of expansion…" Jess replies, sounding a little unsure and clicking her pen again.

"I know it is. But you told me you wanted to dominate the professional women's clothing market, and I'm a firm believer that any type of domination requires significant risk and vision. Are you and Beauty Boutique Clothing ready for this type of bold move and strategy?" He pauses and gives her a quizzical look, then holds up a hand. "Don't answer. Just ponder it, and if you decide it's not for you, call me in a day or two and we'll cancel our trip to Brazil. Otherwise, I'll pick you up two weeks from Thursday at 8:00 p.m., and we'll fly to Brazil. We will start work as soon as we land and clear customs. Fair enough?"

Jessica agrees, thanking Sean for his time and energy, and leaves his office. Her head is reeling from all the possibilities, and she decides she needs to talk to Nate, and then Bonnie.

CHAPTER 9

BUSINESS OR PLEASURE?

When Jessica arrives back at her office, everyone has left except Nate. He is waiting, not so patiently, for a blow-by-blow description of how Jessica's meeting with Sean went. He has just started tapping his foot when she breezes through the door. She looks determined and happy at the same time, and as they make eye contact she says, "We have so much to discuss, but right now, I need to pee, and you need to make us both some very strong coffee. Call Phillip. Let him know it's going to be a long evening for both of us. I'll make it up to him by giving you another holiday soon."

She turns in the direction of the restroom as Nate begins to smile, then says, "Honey, don't worry about Phillip. He's working late himself and totally understands what's going on in our world right now." She flashes him a grin over her shoulder, and he heads to the kitchen.

Jess is sitting at the conference room table with preliminary design improvements scattered all around in front of her when Nate comes in with the coffee and sits down daintily.

She looks up at him and reaches for her coffee. "All I can say is *wow*. Sean was a complete gentleman, he apologized for being an asshole, and he actually *thanked* me for the gifts I sent. He planned to take the time to have a proper meeting today, had lunch catered, and served the merlot I gave him, which I thought was a very classy touch, by the way. He asked seriously about what I expect for Beauty Boutique Clothing in the near future and we had a great discussion of where to go from here. He works at a pace that would send anyone's head spinning. I found myself wondering what he was up to today... He had personally done an enormous amount of research into my industry and the outcomes look pretty favorable. He doesn't like the idea of expanding into the Soviet Union, but he looked at a factory in Brazil that he wants me to go check out in two weeks to see if it would meet our needs. He's talking a big expansion, Nate. I'm going to need two million dollars of capitalization to fund it, within ninety days. I told him I can raise the funds in that time frame."

Jess pauses to take a breath, and Nate interrupts. "How in the hell do you plan to get that much money?"

She gives him a sly smile and says, "I haven't a fucking clue at this point."

Nate giggles. "Nice bluff. Did he believe you?"

She shrugs, tossing her hair over her shoulder and leaning back in her chair. "I don't think it mattered much to him at that moment."

"Well, are you going to Brazil? How much do we need to set aside for the trip?"

"Yes, I'm going, and nothing." Jessica smiles and shakes her head, still amazed. "Sean is flying us down on his corporate jet at no expense to me, and we will be staying at Mark and Bonnie's villa. Apparently, the factory is a forty-five minute drive from there."

"And what if the factory won't work for us? Then what?"

Jessica sighs. "Well, Sean said we would have to regroup and devise a different strategy for any possible expansion."

"So he has decided to take us on as a client then," he pauses, realizing a change, and gives Jessica a knowing look. "And I can't help but notice that it's *Sean* now, and not Mr. Green. What's up with that, sister?"

She waves her hand, brushing off the innuendo. "It's not like that at all. Sean explained that he loathes formalities and will only work with his clients on a first-name basis, that's all. He thinks it helps build trust and rapport."

"Oh. Well, then it has to be Sean. I see." He resists the urge to giggle again.

She rolls her eyes. "Wipe that cat-swallowed-the-canary look right off your face. This is strictly going to be a business relationship, nothing more! He wants me to have three or four seasons of designs ready by the time we undertake any type of expansion. Finally, we have an understanding that neither of us has made any type of commitment to solidify a working relationship. We're each just exploring options at this point in time." She pauses, gazing at a sketch and gracefully corrects a line, then looks up at Nate. "So what are your thoughts?"

"I believe you have a lot to think about and a lot of work to do just to keep Sean interested in pursuing expansion options with us. I also believe he has done his research and has concluded there is money to be made for both Beauty Boutique Clothing and SGM. If you pursue expansion plans with Sean, you will be stretched beyond anything you have ever experienced before and at an operational tempo you haven't even imagined. Sean could be a great mentor, or he could be a vicious colleague. He obviously has great expectations for you and believes you have the ability to perform at the level of his expectations, or he wouldn't invest his time or resources getting you to Brazil. Do you know what his expectations, especially financially, from the Beauty Boutique are? What are we going to end up paying for SGM representation during this expansion?"

"Well, that's what has me concerned. When I tried to cover that subject, he blew it off and told me there will be time later to discuss such mundane topics. First, he wants to see if the factory in Brazil will ever work. He said if it does, we will go into much greater detail about finances."

Nate cocks a dark eyebrow at her. "Well, darling, I suspect you should be prepared for a bill somewhere in the million dollar range for SGM's representation."

Jessica sighs. "Shit. You know we don't have that kind of money. For the expansion maybe, but not for both…"

Nate nods practically. "Then I suggest you tell Sean fairly soon and see if he is interested in working out some type of arrangement. Because at this point, I see an expansion costing in the neighborhood of three million dollars and our gross receipts are currently sitting at one million, eight hundred, thirty-one thousand dollars and twenty-two cents."

She cringes at the comparison of numbers, hugging her coffee mug closer. "I know, but couldn't we assume a significant increase in revenue will accompany this type of expansion?" she asks, fishing hopefully for a good answer.

He shrugs. "Probably. But in what time frame, and will it be enough to make up the difference?"

"I just don't know right now…" she says, plopping her cheek into one hand.

"Jess, I think it's wonderful that SGM has gone this far with us, and God knows we need this expansion desperately. But before we get caught up in the possibilities of what could be, let's bring our situation back down to earth and have a very frank discussion with Sean about our financial position. You have done a magnificent job with this company, but now that we are seriously talking about entering into the international realm of fashion design, we will be playing in the big leagues against the big names. I just want us to approach everything realistically, honestly, and cautiously so Beauty Boutique Clothing doesn't become another statistic of promising fashion companies that expanded too rapidly and are no longer in existence."

"So what are you suggesting?" she asks, looking slightly deflated.

"Well, what I'm saying is, let's proceed full steam ahead but with due caution and circumspection, that's all. This is an enormous step—the payoffs could be outrageous, and the pitfalls could be devastating. You're a very intelligent businesswoman, so let's continue to check and double-check the risks versus rewards ratio and make sure we can handle both appropriately for the sake of everyone involved in this expansion. You have a great team assembled. We all love you because you have always considered the impact that every decision you have made could have on everyone on the team. Let's never lose sight of that quality of leadership."

"Of course not. Without each of you, I wouldn't be where I am today. I want to make sure, if we do expand, that everyone feels and receives the benefit of our increased profitability."

"We all know you will do the right thing, and we all have confidence in you and the Beauty Boutique's future. Everyone here is rooting for you. So go to Brazil with Sean, check out his plan and the facility, and we can regroup after you have a better idea of everything involved with such a bold move. In the meantime, I just need you to start finalizing this season's fashions, then focus on finalizing the next three seasons, per Sean's suggestion. Even if you decide not to expand, having those designs finalized that far in advance could never be a bad thing."

Jessica smiles. "You're right, as usual. Tomorrow let's call a meeting with the design team and develop a scheduled time frame to make sure the new designs are accomplished in the next sixty days. We have a huge start in that direction already. I think sixty days is plenty of time to accomplish that goal without stressing everyone to the max. Do you agree?"

Nate nods. "Definitely. Now go home and get some rest. It sounds like the next couple of months are going to be brutal for us both."

⊨⊩ ⊪⊨

Jessica arrives home later than usual, thinks about going for a run, and decides against it. Instead, she plans to draw a hot bath, light some candles, and read a good murder mystery. As she is heading to the bathroom, her cellphone rings. She looks at the caller ID with every intention of ignoring it until she sees it is Bonnie. From much experience, she knows if she doesn't answer, Bonnie will keep calling her until she picks up. With a huge sigh, she answers the phone. "What's up, girl?"

Bonnie launches right in. "Did you meet with Sean today? Was he a dick to you like before?" Jess smiles to herself, "Yes, I did, and no, he wasn't."

She hears Bonnie gasp over the line. "Why did you leave a sister hanging all day long? I have been *dying* to hear all about it."

Jess's smile turns rueful as she watches her dreams of a bath dissipate. "I didn't leave you hanging. I was just walking in the door when you called me."

"Tell me all about it."

With a huff, Jess plops into her favorite armchair and kicks her feet over the side. "Okay. I was actually pleasantly surprised. Sean was a complete gentleman. He was thoughtful in his approach and even apologized for being an ass. He has done a lot of research and wants me to go to Brazil with him in a couple of weeks. He said we would be staying at your villa, is that okay?"

"Of course it is, sweetie, even if I didn't know anything about it." Bonnie chuckles. "Is this trip for business or pleasure, my dear?"

Jessica snorts, picturing Bonnie wiggling her eyebrows. "It's all business. He wants me to tour a factory south of your villa to see if it could be converted for the use of Beauty Boutique Clothing."

"Oh, do you mean the old Nike factory?"

"That's the one,"

"It's a fabulous facility. You'll love it. How did Sean find out about it?"

"Apparently when he was down there last month, he toured the factory with the Beauty Boutique in mind, and he has a preliminary strategy for our expansion if the facility works for us." Jess finds herself smiling again and makes a face.

"Honey, that's amazing. So SGM is going to represent you?"

Jessica sighs again. "Not so fast, girl. All of our discussions are preliminary right now. Besides, I'm not sure I can afford SGM."

"If Sean's gone to that extent for preliminary discussions, he has something in mind, and he sees real potential in you and Beauty Boutique Clothing. Otherwise, he would have never gone to that extreme. I would bet you a million bucks that Sean smells money, and a *lot* of it, or he wouldn't be going back with you, even on a preliminary basis. Unless, of course, he intends to fuck you at the villa."

Jessica gasps. "Bonnie!"

"Well, why not? You're a beautiful, sexy woman, and if I were male, I'd want my dick inside you."

Jess shakes her head, chuckling a little. "You're disgusting. Do you really think he would be plotting something like that?" she asks, a hint of concern tingeing her voice.

Bonnie chuckles. "You'd think you'd be used to me by now. And no, I have never known Sean to mix business and money with carnal pleasures. I'm just screwing around with you. The fact of the matter is that Sean probably sees an opportunity to make lots of cash, and that's why he has done so much work before getting you signed as a client. He is also probably fully aware of where you stand financially, so he has something in mind there too, that he hasn't revealed to anyone yet. But mark my words; he is interested in representing you. So when are you leaving for Brazil?"

"Two weeks from Thursday. Sean is picking me up at 8:00 p.m."

"Very nice. Just remember, it's a ten-and-a-half-hour flight in Sean's jet, and there's the time difference. Brazil is four hours ahead of us, so if you're in the air by 9:00 p.m., you'll arrive at 7:30 a.m. our time, and it will be almost noon in Brazil. You'll need to sleep on the plane, and keep your toothbrush with you so you won't have morning breath when you arrive."

"Thanks for the advice," Jess says gratefully. "Sean says he wants to hit the ground running."

Bonnie laughs, "Hang on to your panties, because when he makes statements like that, he has a lot of work planned immediately. Be sure to rest and get ready to work at a pace only obsessed people work at. Oh, who am I talking to? You'll be just fine; you're a work obsessed woman. One bit of advice though: take some time for yourself over the weekend. The villa is beautiful, the staff is fabulous, and Brazil is a kick in the ass, so make time for you to have a mini vacation, okay?"

"Okay, I promise I'll save some me time and enjoy Brazil, with or without Sean Green."

"Oh, yeah!" Bonnie exclaims, laughing. "When you meet the factory owner, Ricardo Montes, check out his ass. He is the cousin of Mark's business partner, Hugo. Single, rich, maybe a little creepy, but *very* sexy. Maybe you and he could—"

Jessica interrupts with a laugh and says, "Stop trying to get me laid! I'm good to go in that arena."

She can practically feel Bonnie rolling her eyes over the phone. "Stop trying to convince me of that. What's it been? Seven months for you?"

"Not that it's any of your business, but I have been very busy with work."

Bonnie snorts. "How long?"

Jess huffs out a breath, hesitating. "Well, if you really must know, it's been a year and a month, and it wasn't very good the last time, anyway."

"Holy shit, girl, you better pack some lube because you have probably already dried up down under, if you know what I mean."

"Oh my God, Bonnie, not everyone has to have as much sex as you do to be happy!" Jess exclaims.

"Bullshit!" Bonnie scolds in her crass manner, "You need to go get pounded, and soon, before you become an old spinster. Maybe you should consider one of those Internet fuck buddy sites." She pauses as if considering which would be best, and Jessica cuts in.

"Okay, you know I love you dearly, but I'm not taking sex advice from a woman who would drop her panties for someone new every day if she wasn't happily married. I'm not like you. You'd think you'd be used to *that* by now."

"Well, honestly, that's why I married Mark. He's a pervert, and I love that about him," Bonnie replies smugly.

"Oh, jeez," Jess says, feeling her face pale at the images that popped into her brain. "That's way more than I needed to know about Mark. Besides, it's late. I'm going to bed to get some much needed rest."

Bonnie grunts. "At least take care of yourself before you sleep."

Jess makes a sound of frustration and exclaims, "Goodnight, Bonnie!" She immediately hangs up the phone, glaring at it for a moment before she rises and heads to her bedroom.

On the other end, Bonnie laughs and shakes her head, thinking, *Jesus Christ. After over a year without sex, I'd be such a bitch. How does she even do that and remain sane?*

CHAPTER 10

TACTILE

Two weeks pass very quickly, and Jessica is finishing up her packing Thursday evening when she hears her doorbell ring. She looks at the clock beside her bed and smiles. *Right on time. He is prompt,* she muses. She makes her way to her front door and opens it to Sean, dressed in blue jeans and what appears to be a collared linen shirt.

"Hi, Sean. I'm a very tactile person. Is your shirt linen?" she asks, eyeing him.

He smiles at her abruptness. "No, it's actually pima cotton."

"May I touch it?"

"Um, sure. Why not?"

Jessica puts her hand on Sean's chest and is amazed at the feel of his shirt, then realizes he is an extremely fit man with very firm pecs. She removes her hand from his chest, flushing, and to distract herself asks, "Why pima cotton over linen?"

Sean immediately says, "I think it breathes better and it doesn't wrinkle like linen. I hate wearing wrinkled shirts, so pima is a better choice for me. Are you ready?"

Jessica nods. "Absolutely. I have two bags. Would you mind grabbing one for me?" Sean nods, and they grab her bags and leave her house.

Sean opens the trunk of his BMW, places Jessica's bags inside, then opens the passenger door for her.

She looks around the interior of his car, noting the extreme cleanliness, and asks, "Are you always this fastidious in everything?"

Sean laughs, "I had the car detailed this morning so you wouldn't be offended. Fastidious? No. Obsessive compulsive and a bit narcissistic?" He shrugs. "Probably."

Jess laughs, too. "Narcissistic, definitely. I'll let you know about the obsessive compulsive by the end of the weekend."

Sean smiles over at her and says sarcastically, "Well, that is really something to look forward to."

"Hey, you pointed out your flaws. I'll just let you know if I agree with them by the time we return to San Francisco."

"Well, funny, I don't recall inviting such an analysis," Sean chides good-naturedly.

"Too bad. It's actually a habit of mine when it comes to business partners," Jess responds, grinning.

They enjoy small talk during their drive to the airport, and Sean tells Jessica that she can have the sleeping berth on the jet. He will take the secondary sleep space for himself.

Jessica protests, "Oh, I couldn't I wouldn't want to put you out during the trip."

Sean insists, saying, "It's no imposition. Besides, this way you will have complete privacy so you can actually get some rest." He drives up to the Cessna Citation and opens his trunk so the suitcases can be loaded while they board the jet. Jessica stops at the entrance of the jet, and her mouth drops open. The interior is luxurious, with a leather sofa and chairs, end tables, and a complete bedroom in the back.

The stewardess, Rachel, nods to her and gestures for her to come all the way on board. "Welcome, Ms. Silva. What can I get you to drink before we push off? Mr. Green, your scotch will be ready in a moment."

Jessica settles into a plush chair. "How about some tequila with a few wedges of crushed orange and cinnamon sprinkled in it?"

Rachel gives Jess a funny look and says, "Very well. Is Patron okay with you, Ms. Silva?"

Jessica nods. "Yes, that will be fine. And please, call me Jessica."

"Okay, Jessica," Rachel says with a smile, "I'll have that ready for you momentarily." She turns and heads back toward the stewardess station.

Sean sits in a chair slightly diagonally from Jess and says, "I forgot to ask if you were allergic to any foods or what your food preferences were, I'm sorry. I have requested two light snacks to be served immediately. The first is a Capresé salad, which consists of mozzarella cheese, Roma tomatoes, and balsamic vinegar dressing. The second is French brie with cold smoked salmon from Nova Scotia. Will that be fine with you? Otherwise, I'm sure we can have something else prepared for you."

Jess is practically drooling. "That actually sounds delicious. There is no need to prepare anything else for me."

Rachel places Jess's drink on the side table next to Jessica. Sean nods to her and Rachel says, "It sounds like everything is in order. The food will be served as soon as we reach cruising altitude. About that time, Mr. Green always has a second scotch. Would you like another drink as well, Jessica?"

Jess nods gratefully. "Thank you, very much."

As Rachel departs, Sean says, "I haven't planned for an in-flight movie, so I don't know what is available right now, but—"

Jessica interrupts, "Perhaps we could just talk and get to know a little bit more about each other."

Sean considers and then replies, "That would actually be lovely and quite relaxing."

The doors close on the jet, and they begin to push off from the gate. Jessica says, "I really must admit, I have never travelled in such style and comfort."

Sean laughs, "Then you should enjoy this trip. It's one of the luxuries I allow myself these days. Besides, this is all deductible for me."

"Well, it may be deductible, but you still have to pay the bill every month," Jess counters, taking a sip of her drink.

He just smiles, raises his glass, and nods.

As they reach cruising altitude, the stewardess returns with the Caprésé salad and the brie and salmon with capers and red onion. She also brings their second round of cocktails. Jessica surveys the snacks placed before them.

"This looks absolutely wonderful," she comments, scooping some brie onto a baguette crisp. "So, tell me about yourself as a kid, what you truly enjoy in life, and what makes you tick." Sean starts to interrupt, but Jess holds up a hand. "Wait, the one condition I have with these questions is that you can't talk about your work. I want to know about the boy who grew into the man you have become." For the very first time since she met him, Jessica sees Sean Green squirm uncomfortably.

He looks down at his feet, then around the plane, and finally back at her. "It's not at all very interesting. How about you? Where did you grow up?"

She smiles at him. "Oh no, you don't. You first. Then I'll tell you about myself. I don't usually go away for a weekend with a man I know absolutely nothing about, so I need something to justify doing this."

Sean laughs out loud. "Well, I can assure you, I'm absolutely safe, but fair enough. Let's see, I was born in Ohio, and my parents moved to San Francisco when I was ten. We lived in an apartment on Fifteenth Avenue and Geary Boulevard until my parents moved to the family home on Forty-First Avenue and Fulton. I spent most of my evenings and weekends at Ocean Beach, drinking beer, smoking dope, and bodysurfing. I graduated from George Washington High School, received a full-ride academic and athletic scholarship to Stanford, and there I earned a bachelor's in business and an MBA in marketing. I started SGM in 1990—"

Jessica interrupts, "Uh-uh! I'm not interested in your career, remember?"

He clears his throat. "Sorry, I forgot. I was the middle child of three. I have an older sister, who is a nurse, and a younger brother, who is a certified public accountant for Pacific Gas and Electric. My father was in law enforcement, and my mother worked for an insurance company in San Francisco. My childhood was good for a middle-class kid. Dad died young from a heart attack, and Mom died seventeen years later. I enjoy photography, swimming, camping, hiking, fly-fishing, and traveling. I usually vacation in McCall, Idaho, every summer to get my outdoor fix for the year."

He pauses, and Jessica asks, "Where the hell is McCall, Idaho?"

"It's about one hundred miles north of Boise, in the mountains. It's a quaint little town nestled on lower Payette Lake. The local Native American Indian tribe, the Nez Perce, believe the area has an oppressive evil spirit surrounding the town, which makes perfect sense if you passively observe the petty political drama that occurs in the city. It really is a Peyton Place, where if there isn't any drama occurring, the city's residents or leaders create some. Anyway, it's a beautiful area if you don't consider the antigrowth tree huggers or the town's local leadership. I own a home on the lake off of Warren Wagon Road, where Mark, Bonnie, and I often spend time together. It's not as nice as the villa we're going to stay at this weekend, but it's comfortable."

He takes a sip of his scotch, and Jessica thinks, *if it's anything like this plane, I'm sure it's absolutely beautiful.*

"Enough about me, Jessica. Now it's your turn to share."

She takes a contemplative breath and asks, "What type of athletic scholarship?"

Sean eyes her for a moment, then replies, "Swimming. I was a competitive swimmer in high school and college. Your turn."

She nods. "Well, I grew up in Los Altos, attended private schools throughout high school and then Dartmouth in Boston.

I earned a business degree, then moved to London and received my graduate degree in fashion entrepreneurship and innovation from the London College of Fashion – University of Arts. Growing up, I ran track, and I still love running even now. Mom and Dad still live in Los Altos, and I visit them at least once a month for a weekend or so. Both of them were big corporate attorneys and still maintain a small practice for a select group of clients. Bonnie and I have been best friends since first grade, even though she is so different than me in her worldview and personal relationships. I know she can be aggravating with her ideology and very narrow in her views, but she means well. She has such a great heart and kind soul, and I love her to death. Mark spoils her completely, which has only cemented her beliefs into her psyche."

Sean chuckles, then asks, "Has Bonnie always been so flighty?"

Jess smiles, remembering. "Ever since we were fifteen years old. She discovered the manipulative power of her sex appeal and pretended helplessness on people, especially powerful men like Mark. But I do truly think she loves him."

"Well, sex sells in marketing, and in life. That's why it's used so effectively. Bonnie just markets her attributes well, and it's been very beneficial to her most of her life."

Jessica shakes her head. "That may be true, but her looks will eventually fade, and then where will she be? It worries me sometimes."

Sean smiles reassuringly. "Don't worry. She really is a kind woman, and Mark is batshit crazy over her, so things seem to have worked out well for the both of them."

"But what if Mark decides he wants a younger, firmer model one of these days?"

"I don't see that happening, but even if it did, Bonnie would be set for life," Sean answers.

"I suppose she would, but her sense of self-worth would be absolutely destroyed. That's why it's such a slippery slope to rely on one's physical beauty." Jess catches herself and stifles a yawn as best she can. Sean looks at his watch.

"Maybe we should try to get some sleep. Tomorrow's schedule is extremely full."

Jess nods. "You really should take the bedroom—"

Sean shakes his head. "No, really. You're my guest, and it's all set up for you anyway."

She finally relents, thanks him, and heads for the bedroom.

When she enters the sleeping berth, she just smiles. She walks over to the bed and picks up an Italian chocolate mint that, evidently, Sean had the stewardess place on the pillow. The covers are turned down, and a vase of roses sits on the headboard shelf. Jess thinks, *I know those roses weren't placed there for Sean's benefit. That was very thoughtful of him, and they made the entire sleeping quarter smell marvelous.*

It seems like she has just fallen asleep when Rachel places a tray containing a pot of French press coffee, a bowl of fresh fruit, and a large wine glass filled with organic granola and Greek yogurt next to the bed. Softly, she says, "Good morning, Jessica. We will be landing in about an hour. Please let me know if there is anything else I can get you."

Jess rubs the sleep from her eyes. "Thank you, this looks wonderful. I need to freshen up a bit, and then I'll be right out."

"No hurry. Mr. Green is working on some project deadline."

Jessica raises an eyebrow. "Does he ever slow down?"

Rachel smiles, "If he does, I've never seen that side of him. Enjoy your breakfast."

The sleeping berth door opens and Jess pads out softly, carrying her heels for the day instead of wearing them. Sean closes his computer, smiles at her, and asks, "How did you sleep?"

"I slept great. How about you?"

Sean, still smiling, replies, "Fine. I really don't sleep much at all. If I get four or five hours a night, I'm terrific."

Jess shakes her head, sitting in one of the plush leather chairs and placing her shoes on the floor next to her. "Wow, not me. I need at least six hours of sleep, or I turn into a raging bitch."

Sean chuckles. "I'm glad you let me know. I will certainly keep that in mind, for my own personal health. Have you ever been to Mark and Bonnie's villa?"

She shakes her head. "Not this new one, but I visited the previous one a few times."

"Well, you're going to be amazed. There is absolutely no comparison to the new one. Bonnie, of course, insisted that Mark buy this estate, and it is truly magnificent. She has a good eye. Now, here is our itinerary for today." He passes her a folder.

Jessica gives it a quick glance and thinks, *Holy shit, it's packed with meetings. How are we going to get to all of these?*

Sean studies Jessica's reaction, noting that her eyes widen slightly, and then offers, "I know it looks crazy, but it's really not that bad. With the exception of the factory tour, all of the meetings will be at the villa in a very relaxed setting."

She passes the folder back to him and says, "Well, that's good to know, because it looks totally crazy to me."

"We do have a lot to accomplish in a very short time frame. Both Mark and Bonnie insisted on me promising to give you Sunday off so you can sightsee and enjoy Brazil. It seems you are in need of some quality time off, to soak up rays, read, or do whatever you wish, even if it's only for one day. I promised, and I intend to keep my promise," he says, sliding the folder back into his briefcase and grinning at her.

Jess simply sits back and nods, slightly perturbed that her friends would make such a request on her behalf.

The jet lands smoothly and as soon as it has come to a complete stop on the tarmac, the door opens, and Brazilian customs agents board. They check the plane's paperwork; shake Sean's hand, and say, "Everything looks to be in order, as usual. Welcome back to Brazil, Mr. Green." Sean nods his thanks and introduces Jessica to the agents, who are charming and cordial to her.

They welcome them both once again and depart. Rachel appears to help them with their carry-on luggage and says to Sean, "Mr. Montes will be awaiting your arrival at the factory, and your limousine is already here for you." Everything is loaded into the limousine by the time they deplane, and the driver asks if they want something to drink before they begin their drive to the factory.

Jessica shakes her head and says, "Not for me, thanks. It's still morning."

Sean laughs and declines a drink as well. During the drive, he briefs Jessica on some of the local customs and Mr. Ricardo Montes. He advises her to be reserved in her reactions to the factory and to appear only mildly interested, even if it is perfect. She shoots him a look for questioning her ability to play it cool.

He shrugs and explains, "The culture in Brazil is different than America, and if Mr. Montes thinks you are excited about the possibilities, he'll raise the price and try to squeeze us both."

Again, Jessica shoots him a sardonic look. "How is that different from America?" she asks, and doesn't wait for an answer, "Who is Lidia Espinoza, on the schedule?" She points to the name on the itinerary.

"She is the appointed spokeswoman for the displaced Nike workers and has the best handle on the workers' knowledge, skills, and abilities. She will be sizing you up, as well as trying to sell you on the factory and workers. I believe her primary objective is to convince you to invest in Brazil, especially in the factory, so everything she says must be weighed carefully." Sean looks out the window and says, "We're almost there. Remember, Mr. Montes is charming. He fancies himself a ladies' man, so stay alert with him, because he's really good at reading people, especially women."

Jessica looks disgusted. "I got it the first time, Sean."

He nods once, still looking slightly worried. "Good, because we're here and the show is about to begin."

She turns and looks out the window. *Wow, this place looks really promising.* The limousine driver opens the door and helps her out, then immediately introduces Jessica to Mr. Montes. *Oh my,* Jess thinks, *Bonnie was right. He certainly is very sexy and charming.*

"Hello, Mr. Montes—" she starts as they begin to walk around the factory.

He interrupts smoothly. "Ricardo. Please, call me Ricardo."

She nods. "Very well. Ricardo, how many square feet of usable production space is within this facility?"

"Well, Ms. Silva—"

"Please, call me Jessica," she interrupts with a smile.

"Very well, Jessica. There is currently forty thousand square feet of production work space, with an additional thirty thousand feet of expandable space and another thirty thousand square feet of storage capacity in the main warehouse. Office space and showroom space add an additional seventeen thousand square feet in the administration building."

Jess gives Ricardo a blank, yet polite, stare and simply says, "Thank you." She turns and walks up the walkway to the door.

Surprised by her reaction, Ricardo follows her and asks, "Is that sufficient?"

She allows a small smile and says, "It will be fine, as long as the production space is adequate."

Sean watches this interaction and notes Ricardo becoming unnerved. *She'll do just fine in all of our meetings,* he thinks, breathing a sigh of relief.

Ricardo presses his lips together. "Well, let's go inside and see if this will work for you." As he unlocks the door and walks through, Jessica chances a glance at his ass and thinks, *Bonnie sure knows how to pick them. His ass is fantastic. She was spot on.*

They walk down a short hallway, and Ricardo flings the doors to the facility open with a grandiose flare, expecting a gasp, only to get Jessica glancing at Sean and saying, "Oh, Sean, I don't know."

Sean holds back a smile and cautions her to reserve judgment until the entire tour is completed.

"Very well," she replies with a sigh. Sean notices that now Ricardo looks a little nervous, and Sean likes the fact that Jessica can put him on guard so quickly. She then begins to point out positive features of the facility but lacks enthusiasm, causing both Sean and Ricardo to doubt her interest in the facility. They conclude the tour. Jessica thanks Ricardo for his time, then immediately gets into the limousine without further discussion.

Sean shakes Ricardo's hand. "I'll speak with her later tonight and someone will get back to you with some sort of indication as to Jessica's level of interest or lack thereof. Thank you." Sean turns and gets into the limo. As they head toward the villa, Sean asks the driver to close the window between the back and front compartments.

He turns to Jess and says, "I suspect you weren't that impressed."

She shakes her head vigorously. "Oh my gosh, on the contrary, the facility is fantastic. It will need about a quarter of a million in renovations to be just right to fit our needs, but it's a thousand times better than what we have right now."

Sean gapes at her, trying to figure out where he lost track of her real opinion. "Wow. You played that situation really well. You had both Ricardo and me convinced that you were totally unimpressed."

She raises her eyebrows. "I've been a businesswoman for quite some time, and I'm not as naïve as you may have surmised me to be."

He clears his throat, thoroughly embarrassed about his blatant doubt of her abilities. "Apparently I misjudged you."

She gives him a coy smile. "Is now a good time to say *duh*?"

Sean chuckles, and she requests the folder containing their schedule. She studies it a little closer, then suggests, "I think you should invite Ricardo to dinner with Lidia, so we can all meet jointly."

He shakes his head hesitantly. "I don't think it's a good idea for Lidia to know what types of negotiations are going on between Ricardo and the Beauty Boutique."

"Trust me," Jess says, completely confident, "we need to meet them together. Also, my staff knows exactly where we stand with regard to income and expenses on a monthly basis, and I believe this would be a uniquely new experience for Lidia. I also believe she'll probably have inside information on Ricardo's position and will keep him in check if she thinks I'll walk. I think I'll be able to negotiate better terms and conditions with her present. Can we have this arranged before dinner, please?"

Sean considers, realizing she might be right, and nods. "Very well."

As the limo enters the grounds of the villa, Jess looks at Sean and says, "You were right. This landscape is absolutely spectacular."

Sean smiles and says, "Wait until you see the actual estate."

The limo swings around the circular cobblestone drive and stops at the main entrance. The building is a terra cotta stucco with brightly arranged tiles on the stairs that lead to an ornate wooden door with an intricate carving of the sun setting halfway below the horizon. In the spacious foyer, a large fountain made out of Italian marble is the centerpiece. Surrounded by a wide variety of native plants, the foyer provides serenity and warmth reminiscent of a spiritual retreat. The formal living and dining rooms are decorated exquisitely with local artists' furniture, paintings, and crafts.

Jessica pauses for a moment, realizes that her mouth has been open in awe the entire time, and snaps it shut. "Well, you were right again. This place is nothing like the last. It's a showcase for interior design excellence, and yet it still feels like a home. I don't know how Bonnie does that."

Again, Sean smiles. "Yes, she does a magnificent job, doesn't she?" he says, breathing in the aroma of fresh tropical air.

The maid, a quiet, mousy little thing, shows Jessica to her room on the second-floor wing, and Eduardo Sean to his usual room, on the first floor. Both of their rooms have terraces that overlook the courtyard and pool. Jessica tells the maid she is going to shower and dress for their dinner guests. She pauses then asks, "What kind of attire is expected at dinner?"

The maid suggests she speak to Mr. Green, as there is no designated dress code, then bobs a curtsey and hurries from the room. Jess hears water splash around in the pool, opens her door, and steps onto her balcony. She watches Sean swim several laps with incredible flip turns before she yells down to him. He doesn't hear her the first time, so Eduardo gets his attention in the shallow end. Sean stops and stands up with his back to Jessica as he speaks to the butler. She is pleasantly surprised by what she sees.

He has broad, muscular shoulders, his back muscles are very defined, and as he turns to look at her, she is amazed at the chest and abs that defy his age. She feels a slight tingle at the junction between her legs, then shakes herself and says, "How are we dressing for our dinner meetings?"

Sean replies, "Cocktail informal. I'm going to wear a suit without a tie, so any evening gown or dress would work."

She thanks him and turns back into her room, reminding herself she is here on business, even if she didn't really realize just how fine Sean Green really is. She relaxes for a while in her room, settling in for the weekend, then showers and prepares for their dinner meetings. She is thankful she was able to get a full night's sleep on the plane. Perusing the clothes she brought, she decides to wear one of her new designs, just to see how it is received by

Sean, Ricardo, and Lidia. She tries not to think about the fact that Sean's opinion is the one she is most interested in.

She slides into a full-length, sleeveless purple evening gown with a v-neckline and a split in the front that ends two inches above the knee. She adds a hammered silver arm cuff about two inches wide and silver, Egyptian-style necklace, then completes the outfit with three-inch-heeled silver sandals. Shaking her hair out, she decides to leave the long, dark red locks down, and gives herself a quick once-over in the full-length mirror provided in the bathroom. She adjusts the gown, and a satisfied smile flits across her face. She likes what she sees. Leaving her room, she heads downstairs toward the veranda, where she finds a seat facing what is preparing to be a beautiful sunset.

Her enjoyment of the sunset is interrupted by the household waiter, who asks if she would like anything to drink.

"Yes, of course. Could I please have a fresh, blended mango margarita?"

He nods and disappears momentarily, then reappears with one of the most exquisite blended margaritas she has ever tasted in her life. As she is daydreaming, overlooking the incredible estate grounds, she hears Sean walk onto the veranda behind her.

When she turns to greet him, he stops dead in his tracks, then catches himself, clears his throat, and manages, "You look absolutely stunning this evening. Is that one of your designs?"

Jessica blushes a little, then feels a powerful sense of pride in knowing he really likes how she looks. "Yes, it's one of the new designs that we are still working on perfecting."

Sean, stammering a little, asks, "W-what needs to be perfected?"

She smiles at his stutter. "Well, for example, we will consider whether the slit should be in the front or on the side, and whether the neckline should be squared, rather than a v-neckline." She shrugs. "Those types of things."

As he moves to a seat across from her, Sean says, "Well, from a man's point of view, I much prefer front slits to side slits and v-necklines to squared ones."

Jessica nods as she thinks, *Of course you do.* "And why is that?" she asks, humoring him.

"Well, if you must know, the front slit always reveals more of the woman's legs, and the v-neckline, I believe, is more flattering to any woman regardless of her physical endowments." He grins at her. "In my humble, but accurate, opinion, if she is big busted, it makes her breasts less overpowering, and if she is small breasted, the fact isn't as noticeable."

Jessica chuckles. "Really? Men look at women's fashion like that?"

Sean shrugs and replies, "I don't believe it's the fashion we are concerned about as much as the woman wearing the clothing."

She nods, understanding, but says, "Okay, but not every man is attracted to every woman, so then what?"

"I can look at a woman I'm not attracted to and appreciate how she looks in clothing she is wearing without 'lust in my heart,' as President Jimmy Carter said. If she has taken the time to put herself together, I can appreciate her effort without wanting to bed her," Sean explains.

"I see," replies Jessica, suppressing a smile.

Just then, Ricardo Montes and Lidia Espinoza arrive. As the pair comes down the steps onto the veranda, Sean notices Lidia is wearing a dress with a side slit. He turns and looks at Jessica, seated on the veranda with her legs crossed, one exposed to just above the knee, and says, "I definitely prefer front-slits." Jessica is somewhat confused by his out-of-the-blue comment, but then she notices Ms. Espinoza's dress and wonders if it is the clothing or the person he finds more becoming, silently hoping it is the latter.

Sean and Jessica stand and greet Ricardo and Lidia. Lidia is an attractive, dark skinned woman in her early 40s. She is slightly shorter and more full-figured than Jessica, with captivating eyes and a calm demeanor. Jessica is pleased with the way she presents herself. After exchanging initial pleasantries, everyone moves into the formal living room for their more businesslike discussion about the factory and displaced Nike workers. Jessica begins the conversation with Lidia by asking about daily, weekly, and monthly production numbers from previous work. She is impressed with the reports she hears as to output and the low percentage of flawed pieces. She asks, "If I seriously entertain reopening the factory, what is most important to the workers?"

Lidia thinks for a moment and then replies, "Most of us are single women with children, so a livable wage, the ability to flex schedules, and shifts that start earlier in the morning or after the kids have gotten to day care or school are extremely important. Some type of career advancement training and recognition program, maybe including some type of bonus or merit pay incentives, would also be appreciated." Jessica nods and files the information away for future reference.

Lidia continues, "Your gown is absolutely beautiful. Very elegant. Is it one of your designs?"

Jessica smiles. "Thank you. Yes, it's a new design that is still being adjusted."

Lidia again says, "It's beautiful, and I don't think it would be difficult to produce in Brazil. I also believe the design would be very well received, here and in other parts of Latin America. Would you be expanding your company farther than Brazil, or would all the clothing be shipped back to the United States?"

Jessica considers for a moment. "I believe, initially, the work produced in Brazil will be shipped to me at my San Francisco factory to ensure quality control. However, once I am satisfied with the quality of the garments produced in Brazil, the end product will be shipped directly from the factory and we will start producing clothing to sell here as well," she answers.

Lidia gives her an encouraging smile. "You will be pleased with the quality of work and surprised at how fast my workers can have garments made and then shipped directly from the factory to retailers."

Jessica nods, "What do you think this dress would sell for in Brazil?" She is surprised and pleased to find that, if Lidia's numbers are correct, she could increase the margin she maintains in the United States by twenty-five percent in Latin America. With the reduced cost of manufacturing in Brazil, she also estimates a forty-five percent overall profit increase in the United States.

Ricardo interrupts and asks Lidia in Portuguese, Brazil's native tongue, if Jessica is the real deal and if she truly knows what she is doing in the fashion industry. Lidia answers, also in Portuguese, "I believe so. I did some checking on the Beauty Boutique before agreeing to this meeting, and Jessica has a great reputation as an up-and-coming designer. She is an astute businesswoman and has a reputation for taking care of her employees. You would be stupid not to work out a deal with her on favorable terms, because if you don't, this factory will remain vacant for a long time to come."

Unbeknownst to Lidia, Ricardo, and Sean, Jessica is fluent in Portuguese and allows herself a private smile at the compliments Lidia has paid her, and also at the fact that Ricardo is in a delicate position with the factory.

Just then, the butler, Eduardo, interrupts, "Ladies and gentlemen, dinner is served."

It is a four-course meal consisting of cold melon soup, artichokes, grilled sea bass, and flan. The conversation throughout the meal is light and pleasant, revolving around Jessica's new designs, trends in the fashion industry, the Beauty Boutique's market, thoughts on Latin American markets, fabric availability, shipping, costs, and pricing.

Ricardo touches Jessica's hand. "You do look very beautiful this evening. I hope we can establish a, how you say, long-term relationship with you." Sean has remained quiet thus far, and Ricardo wonders what strategy he is employing. He turns to Sean and says, "You have been awfully quiet, my friend."

Sean smiles and says, "I wanted the two of you and Ms. Silva to become better acquainted and comfortable with each other, and I thought my silence might allow for that. Shall we retire to the veranda? Brandy anyone?"

As they all settle on the veranda, after-dinner drinks are served all around. Ricardo asks Jessica point-blank, "What was your impression of the factory?"

She surprises him by saying, "It is a fabulous facility, and it would certainly meet the Beauty Boutique's needs."

Both Sean and Ricardo are stunned by Jessica's shortness, having expected her to list all the factory's shortcomings. Ricardo recovers first and says, "Wonderful! But I'm still sensing some hesitation from you."

She nods. "Of course you are, because there will always be some hesitation with a major decision such as this." Then she turns the tide on him and bluntly asks, "What are you expecting to get for this facility with a ten-year lease arrangement?"

Ricardo stutters a little, caught off guard by her deliberate negotiation style. Before he can respond, Jessica continues, "Let me clarify what I'm looking for. It is obvious you will have a problem leasing a property that can only be a single-user facility. Yes, you could modify or change that facility, but we both know your maximum return is to find a tenant, like Beauty Boutique Clothing, who can move in with little modification needed. I need to expand, internationally. But I am not restricted as to where I can open a new factory. I will admit having one basically already built to suit is a major plus. However, I'm not sure Brazil is where I need to expand, so sell it to me. Sell me on Brazil and its fashion industry, and tell me what you're going to do to make this facility the one for me." She leans back in her chair and takes a sip of her brandy.

Sean struggles to hide a smile as Ricardo turns to Lidia and says in Portuguese, "I'm not sure how to answer that question. Any suggestions?"

Lidia nods, steps in, and says in English, "Perhaps I should be the one to handle this question for you, since Ricardo doesn't have as much experience as I do in the Latin American fashion industry?"

Jessica nods to Lidia to go ahead. Lidia begins with the basic economic information Sean briefed Jessica on earlier. Lidia goes on to say, "There are a group of trained workers ready, willing, and able to hit the ground running with the reopening of the factory, and I believe the Beauty Boutique's designs would be readily accepted and welcomed in Latin America, if the design you are wearing tonight is a representative example of the rest."

Jessica smiles and asks Lidia, "How many of these workers will still be ready to work in six months? I'm sure many will move on to other jobs in the area after that amount of time."

Before Lidia considers the implications of her statement she blurts out, "What other jobs?"

Ricardo snaps at her in Portuguese. "Mind your place, woman! You've said too much!"

Jessica looks taken aback. "Thank you, Lidia," she says, then turns to Ricardo and asks, "How long would it take to get the necessary permits or permissions from the Brazilian government to be up and running, and how much would be needed in payoffs?"

Ricardo regains his composure and replies, after a final glare at Lidia, "A couple of months and probably one hundred thousand dollars, if you wanted to be up and running in less than six months."

Jessica says, "I understand. And what are you willing to do for me if I decide to lease this facility?"

Ricardo smiles and begins with bullshit. "Well, there are several businesses interested in this facility." Jessica watches Lidia's head snap toward Ricardo at the statement and knows for sure he's bluffing. She concludes she is currently the only viable candidate interested in the factory, but she listens to his speech anyway. Ricardo explains how this is a state-of-the-art building, in high demand, and he isn't in a rush to lease it to just any business. Instead, he wants to make sure he has the right business leasing his property.

Jessica is very patient with Ricardo, but after forty-five minutes of hearing him expound upon the facility's virtues and potential clients, she can't take any more. "Ricardo, do you want to discuss the deal parameters or not?" Ricardo nods yes, his thin-pressed lips giving away his annoyance at being interrupted.

"Very well. Allow me to outline what I suspect," Jessica continues. "You have a wonderful building, and I am interested in it. I haven't tried to bullshit you about that fact, but I'm also not naïve or stupid. I suspect I'm your only viable candidate right now, and the longer it sits empty, the less valuable it becomes, for several reasons. First, the longer those machines sit unused, the more they are likely to experience mechanical problems when they are fired up. Second, you have a ready-made workforce of factory workers who haven't re-located with Nike for a reason. Either they weren't welcome to move with Nike, in which case I probably don't want them either, or they couldn't for whatever personal reasons. In either case, they will need to get jobs to help support their families. If they do, the probability of having to remodel the facility only increases. Finally, this factory, as lovely as it is, is located quite a distance from the major fashion industry markets in Brazil, which increases shipping cost to the producer. You really only have forty thousand square feet of production space. The rest is storage, retail, and administrative. If you aren't ready to discuss possible parameters, that's fine, but let me tell you what I'm thinking. I would be interested in leasing the entire facility on a very long-term basis and investing the two hundred and fifty thousand dollars necessary to make the modifications. I would pay rent at thirty U.S. cents per square foot for the usable production space, fifteen cents per foot for the administrative space, and five cents for the storage and retail space, which in my mind is still only storage space. This equates to eleven thousand, five hundred and fifty dollars per month. I would be willing to entertain ten thousand dollars a month and agree to step up the rent to existing prices when the additional square footage becomes operational production space. I would also entertain a specific percentage rent increase beginning after the second year, but it must be a fixed percentage. I would also require a right of first refusal on any sale of the property." She pauses, giving Ricardo a chance to process the agreement she has laid out.

Ricardo smirks, then turns to Lidia and, in Portuguese, says, "This woman is out of her mind if she thinks I'm going to jump on this offer right away."

Lidia responds, "Ricardo, you know that's a reasonable offer and she would be paying just a little less than the previous tenant was paying for a brand-new facility. Furthermore, you know she's right that even if you sell the production equipment, you'll make more leasing it for the long term. Additionally, you must consider everyone here that really needs this employer in order to survive."

A slight snarl curls Ricardo's top lip. "Mind your own business. I'm not interested in your assessment of potential rent schedules or the needs of the local unemployed." Turning to Jessica, he nods, smiles, and says, "I don't think we have an agreement, but we have a starting point from which we can negotiate."

She gives him a tight smile in return and replies, "Well, Mr. Montes, I believe I have made a fair offer. Perhaps you could send whatever proposal you find agreeable to my office in San Francisco? However, I can assure you my offer is fairly firm, so any major deviation from those terms will be rejected outright." Catching Eduardo's eye, she motions for another brandy, wondering if she can deal with a man who speaks so negatively to another human being.

Ricardo responds, "I am not accustomed to acquiescing to straight-out demands."

Jessica smirks and takes a sip of her new drink. "And I am not accustomed to playing games. Mr. Montes, either my terms are acceptable, or at least close, or they aren't. Either way, it's okay with me. I'm not interested in spending much time in concluding if we can come to terms or not. I know, roughly, what works for me, and we are either in the ballpark or we're not. So, are these numbers in your ballpark, or should I begin looking elsewhere?"

Ricardo clenches and unclenches his fists, then grinds out between clenched teeth, "Ms. Silva, I'll need some time to consider your proposal, but I think it is something we can work with. However, this attitude of yours—"

At this point, Sean interrupts, "Well, I think this has been a very productive day. Shall we all relax and enjoy the beautiful evening."

Everyone agrees, but the tension diminishes slowly. The butler makes a point to replenish their drinks frequently as they begin to appreciate the warm evening air.

"I think I will take a look at that lovely garden at the end of the pool," Ricardo says, rising. Lidia takes her cue and follows with a sigh. As they peruse the garden, Jessica hears Lidia tell Ricardo in Portuguese, "You better not let this company get away. She offered you a more than fair deal, and you know it."

Ricardo replies, "I have no intention of letting this deal slip by me, but I don't want to appear anxious, and I don't like a woman giving me what amounts to an ultimatum. I want to try and get a little more money out of her. If she says no, I'll take the deal she offered, but on my terms."

Lidia sighs with relief and says, "Great, I'll let the factory women know it looks very promising." Jessica smiles slightly to herself, knowing she has a deal if she wants it. Now all she has to do is figure out how to pay for it all.

Once Ricardo and Lidia return to the veranda, conversation turns to more pleasant matters.

"How long will you be in Brazil?" Ricardo asks Sean. "Have you made any plans to show Jessica around?"

"We will leave early Monday morning. We have a few more meetings to deal with tomorrow, and I want to speak with Hugo and some local government officials—"

Jessica suddenly has a great idea, interrupts, and asks, "Lidia, could you arrange a meeting at the factory with as many of the displaced workers as possible? Perhaps in the late afternoon tomorrow?" Lidia nods yes.

Sean returns to his conversation with Ricardo. "I promised both Mark and Bonnie I would leave Sunday open so Jessica could see the sights if she wished."

Ricardo seizes the opportunity to put pressure on Jessica about the factory. "I could act as your tour guide and show you all Brazil has to offer," he suggests with a sleazy smile.

She manages a smile in return and replies, "Perhaps next time. This Sunday I just want to lie around this magnificent pool and do nothing. I'm not accustomed to working at the pace Mr. Green set for us this trip."

Ricardo laughs and says, "I seriously doubt that. During your next visit, it would be my pleasure to show you a good time."

"We'll see," Jess replies, hiding her expression in her glass.

Eduardo appears and asks if anyone would like coffee. All agree that coffee would be nice, and all compliment him on the dinner. He smiles and says he will have the chef help him serve the coffee so everyone can pay their compliments to him, personally. The chef is pleased to hear his meal was regarded highly and invites them all back again.

After coffee, they call it a night and bid each other good evening. As Ricardo and Lidia are leaving, Sean asks Jessica if he can have about an hour of her time to recap the day's events.

"Of course," she says. Sean asks that two creamy grasshoppers be brought to them in the colossal, yet comfortable living room.

"I'm glad you liked the factory, but I believe you should have reserved your negotiations for a later date. Ricardo will never accept an offer so demanding," Sean tells Jessica after they are seated with their drinks.

She laughs out loud. "Tell you what... I'll bet you dinner, winner's choice as to the restaurant, and drinks that Ricardo will take my deal."

Sean chuckles and replies, "You'd better be fairly sure, because I think you're going to owe me dinner, and I'm not cheap."

Jessica sips her grasshopper, eyes sparkling. "Call it woman's intuition. And neither am I."

His lips quirk into a grin, and he wonders for a moment if she is flirting with him, then disregards it. "So, tell me, are you committed to establishing a production facility here?"

She nods. "I needed to know whether or not the factory expenses were viable, and at what I quoted, everything looks really good on the production side, even if the factory workers weren't trained, and when talking with Lidia, I decided they are probably pretty close to what I would expect in trained production workers. If I'm correct, the deal I offered would be terrific for Beauty Boutique Clothing."

Sean considers. "That might be so, but Ricardo isn't going to take that deal because you challenged him in front of everyone. His ego won't allow him to be treated in such a manner. He is a macho, Latino male who always needs to be in control."

Jess raises an eyebrow and says, "He'll accept my deal because he knows it's fair, and he really doesn't have any other viable options in the works right now, no matter how much he bluffs that he does. What's on the agenda for tomorrow?"

Sean gives her a look. "We'll see. I suggest we have breakfast around 8:00 a.m. and start our meetings at 11:00 a.m. We have a lunch meeting here at noon with Hugo Montes and two of Brazil's government officials. Then we can meet your factory workers at

4:00 p.m. Dinner is at seven, and we'll recap all of our business meetings, and then Sunday is all yours. If you want to go somewhere, I can arrange that. If not, you can lie in the sun all day. Whatever your heart desires, my lady."

He gives her a playful mock bow, and she grins. "Well, thank you, sir."

They finish their dessert drinks, then head off to their rooms for the night. Jessica decides she will get up early and go for a run and swim before breakfast. Sean decides he will sleep in.

CHAPTER 11

SURPRISE

Sean awakens the next morning to a noise he isn't used to hearing at the villa. Walking out on the patio, he sees Jessica standing in a black one-piece bathing suit, her red hair falling just past her shoulders. The suit has horizontal slits up each side from her waits to just below her breast. A high French cut accentuates her long muscular legs. He watches her dive into the pool, and then he silently slips back into his room, thinking, *what a seriously gorgeous woman she is.* Then, catching himself, he reigns in his thoughts. Looking at the clock, he sees it is only seven in the morning and decides to take a long hot shower before he heads to breakfast.

Jessica finishes her swim, heads for the shower, and then dresses for breakfast as well. She decides to wear another new design, donning a white linen suit with a high waist and a sleeveless, burgundy button-down silk shirt, then completes it with a single string of pearls. When she walks into the dining room, Sean stands to greet her and exclaims, "Wow!"

She smiles and does a quick twirl. "It's another new design. I'm glad you like it."

"Like it? You look fantastic."

"But Sean," she teases, "it's linen, not pima cotton."

He returns her teasing with a mock glare. "I said I didn't want to look wrinkled, not that I didn't *like* linen."

She barely hides a grin by saying, "Well, you look very nice as well in your charcoal slacks and blue polo."

He inclines his head. "Thank you. Mimosa?"

"Not for me. I'm happy with plain orange juice and some fruit," taking the seat he offers her at the table.

"Well, it's a little late for that, I'm afraid. My understanding is that fresh banana crepes, coffee, and bran muffins are on the menu for today."

Jessica giggles a little. "Oh, good. I'm starving, but I didn't want to put anyone out."

Sean shakes his head at her, mystified that one of Mark and Bonnie's closest friends could be so simplistic in her demands. "Don't be ridiculous. The Stevens always make sure their guests are well taken care of, and you of all people should know that."

"Good point," she replies.

After their delicious breakfast is finished, Jessica and Sean discuss and agree upon a strategy for their first meeting. Jessica decides to remain quiet for most of the meeting and let Sean and Hugo carry the conversation. Occasionally, she can interject a question, but her role in the meeting is one of silent observation. Jessica reminds Sean she will need to know what kind of "fees" would have to be paid in order to have production running full bore in six months or less.

Sean smiles. "Of course. So, it looks like this will work for you?"

Jessica gives a big sigh, then says, "There are a lot of details to work out first. The lease and the factory improvements, even the hiring of employees, are minor issues. Honestly, the largest concern for me at this point is SGM's fees."

Sean laughs. "Don't concern yourself with those. We will make it work if you truly want to retain us."

Jessica smiles slightly. "You know I do, and you've known it since our first meeting when you dismissed me so rudely."

"Yes, I have known, but you weren't the first, nor will you be the last, CEO I'm blunt with," he replies with a sly smile.

"Oh, so now it's blunt instead of rude?" Jessica prods.

He chuckles. "I'm always blunt with clients, never rude."

Both laugh, then Jess asks, "So what will your contract look like? I suspect it will be in the million-dollar range?"

Sean suddenly grows serious, stares intently at Jessica, then says forebodingly, "Actually, you will owe me your soul by the time we have finished negotiating my contract."

She stares at him for a moment. "Well, that's too bad, because I already sold my soul for my fashion niche."

He laughs out loud, enjoying the banter. "Seriously, don't worry about my contract. We will make it all work if we both decide to work together. What else is bothering you?"

She considers. "Well, I suspect the type of undertaking we are looking at will require a two-million-dollar outlay in an eighteen-to-twenty-four-month period. I have plenty of designs for this expansion, and my staff is prepared. Even with previous preparations, the large amount of revenue outlay will require me to either raise capital through investor infusion or to obtain a substantial loan. I have always run my business on a cash basis with all my equipment, real estate holdings, and inventory free and clear of any encumbrances. The only other option I have, if I need funds in an emergency, is financing for a five-year period, in which case I will pay everything off in two years. Currently, Beauty Boutique Clothing is debt-free, but this expansion could be a game changer in that department."

Sean nods. "I have every confidence in your ability to become this type of change agent. Otherwise, I wouldn't have spent any time researching the fashion industry."

She inclines her head. "Thank you. I appreciate your confidence. I just need some time to consider. This is a huge decision and commitment for me."

"I understand."

Eduardo comes into the living room and announces, "Mr. Hugo Montes and Mr. Juan Zamora have arrived." Sean asks him to seat them outside under the cabana for lunch so everyone can feel comfortable speaking freely.

Eduardo nods. "Very good, Mr. Green."

They stand and Sean touches Jessica's arm. "We arrange it like this so the government official, Mr. Zamora, can have confidence he isn't being recorded."

Jessica makes a face. "Wow, I never would have thought about that."

Sean chuckles, steering her toward the door, and says, "Then it's a good thing I did, eh?"

Once outside, Sean introduces Jessica to Hugo and Juan. Both are enamored by her beauty and choice in clothing. Sean mentions the outfit she is wearing is a new design of hers that she hopes to manufacture and market in Brazil.

Juan nods intently. "My wife would love that outfit. How much are you selling it for?"

Jessica smiles and replies, "I haven't priced it yet, but if you get me her sizes, I'll be happy to ship her a complimentary outfit so she can help get my name known in the proper circles here."

Juan beams with delight. "I will have them by the end of this meeting."

Sean gives Jessica a quick nod of approval, and she returns a sneaky wink of acknowledgement. Their conversations are casual while the lunch of fajitas is prepared in front of them, then served with margaritas, tequila, and beer. After the plates are cleared and dessert is served with coffee, Juan turns to Jessica and says, "I understand you might be interested in retaining the old Nike facility for your organization."

She nods. "I'm interested in the facility, but I'm not sure we will be able to reach an agreement with Ricardo Montes."

Juan turns to Hugo and asks in Portuguese, "What is the problem?"

Hugo replies, "When I spoke to my cousin, he told me he believes they have a deal, but he would like to try and squeeze her a little harder."

Juan looks upset. "Come on, she is a lovely lady who designs beautiful clothing, and we all should do what we can to help her open the old factory!" He returns his attention to Jessica. "How can we help?" he asks, switching back to English.

Sean interjects, "Well, Jessica isn't familiar with the business requirements here. Hugo and I are helping to guide her through them, and any assistance you could provide with the appropriate authorities would be most beneficial."

Juan nods and asks, "What time frame are we looking at if a satisfactory agreement can be reached about the facility?"

Sean glances at Jessica and replies, "Correct me if I'm wrong, but it looks like four to six months after a property agreement can be reached."

Jess nods. "That is an excellent time frame as long as what has been represented to me about the displaced workers is correct and we can hit the ground running as hard and fast as anticipated. I'll have a better idea after I meet with the workers this afternoon."

Juan smiles encouragingly. "I'm sure you will find these workers as eager and able to perform as you hope and anticipate. This is a very tight time frame for officials here, and I'm sure you could anticipate extra fees in order to expedite such a request."

Jess nods and Sean says, "We anticipated that would be the case. We just need to know the range of fees we should expect."

"I'll have to check the expedited fee schedule at the office, but I would think somewhere in the fifty-to-one hundred thousand range," Juan replies. Then, turning to Jessica, he says, "I'll have those figures for you well before you sign an agreement—and probably even before you leave Brazil Monday morning. In fact, I'd like to bring my wife by to meet you. I think it would be easier for you to get the proper sizing for her that way, and she will have an opportunity to get to know you before she discusses your designs with her friends."

Jessica smiles. "Juan, I would be delighted to meet your wife and give her my personal attention. In fact, I might even be able to get the factory workers to produce a copy of this design for her on Sunday, if I can get some linen tomorrow. It would be a test run for everyone."

Juan is visibly excited by the possibility. "I believe my wife would be delighted if that could happen."

Jess nods her head. "I will do my utmost, but it will only be possible if the workers have the ability and we can get the linen."

Hugo interrupts and says, "The linen won't be a problem. However, how will the factory workers produce any garment without a design?"

"I have designs for every outfit I brought with me, so that as I wear them, I can make notes about what I like and don't like," Jess replies with a smile. "Juan, it looks like your wife and I are going to spend a couple of hours together tomorrow. By the way, what is her name?"

"It's Carmen."

"Well, please tell Carmen I am looking forward to meeting her and creating the first Beauty Boutique design ever manufactured in Brazil for her."

Juan turns to Hugo and, reverting to Portuguese, says, "This is terrific. Carmen will be amazed this could be arranged for her. Make sure Jessica has the fabric she needs, and have Lidia and Ricardo insist to the workers this is a test. The garment must be completed on time and of the quality deemed necessary."

Hugo replies, "Of course, Mr. Zamora. Anything for your Carmen."

Juan chuckles, "I'm sure if this truly happens, most of the governmental barriers can be removed for Ms. Silva's company to open—"

"Juan," Jessica interrupts quietly, still not acknowledging that she speaks Portuguese, and slightly tired of being so rudely cut out of conversations. "Perhaps it would be nice to find Carmen a necklace to go with her new outfit and give it to her at the same time? Let's make the next couple of days very special for her, and who knows? It might turn out to be a very special couple of nights for you as well." She smiles and gives him a seductive wink.

Juan grins. "I believe that is a fabulous idea."

Sean, Jessica, Hugo, Ricardo, Juan, and his wife, Carmen, arrive at the factory promptly at four o'clock and are greeted by Lidia and the displaced factory workers. After all the proper introductions are exchanged, Jessica takes control of the meeting. She finally reveals her secret—much to the surprise and discomfort of Hugo, Ricardo, Juan, and Lidia—and explains in fluent Portuguese the goals she wishes to accomplish. She instructs the workers that Lidia hand-chose to get Carmen Zamora properly measured and fitted for the first ever Beauty Boutique original design crafted outside the U.S. Jessica explains that this outfit is to be of the highest quality for Carmen, as it will serve as the showpiece for any future production in Brazil.

"I will pay you," Jessica says to the workers, "and also you, Lidia, as a production supervisor. Ricardo, I will also reimburse you for any expenses associated with this single production request."

After the initial shock at her fluency in his native tongue, Ricardo smiles wickedly and responds, "That won't be necessary, as you already know my position on your proposal based on what we thought were private conversations. I suspect we have reached a verbal agreement."

"Yes, we have an agreement." Jessica replies, then adds, "As long as you don't try to squeeze me any harder."

At that, a cheer resounds through the factory. Sean stands there, dumbfounded, not understanding what just happened, and turns to Jessica with a questioning look.

Hugo, laughing, tells Sean in English, "Let me explain this to you, my friend."

Jess winks at Sean as he says, "Please do."

Hugo explains quietly so as not to interrupt while Jessica speaks to the workers. "None of us knew Ms. Silva spoke fluent Portuguese, and it seems there were some unintentionally unguarded conversations revealing Ricardo's willingness to accept her proposal. Also revealed in those conversations were his plans to get more money out of her. However, even though it is clear now that he can't, they still have a deal. Jessica had a very big trump card, and Ricardo was forced to acquiesce to her or lose face in front of everyone present."

Jess moves to stand by Sean as everyone talks excitedly about the reopening of the factory. "You owe me dinner."

Sean shakes his head incredulously. "You tricked me into the bet. You knew you had a deal before we even talked about it, didn't you?" Jessica just nods and smiles. Sean continues, "Well, then I would be honored to buy you dinner. Well played."

"Thank you. I'm delighted to accept your dinner invitation," she says, then turns and explains that she will meet Carmen, Lidia, and the assigned workers at the factory Sunday morning at nine o'clock. Jessica excuses herself and Carmen so she can verify Carmen's measurements for tomorrow's production.

Juan interrupts before Jessica and Carmen can go to a private room and says, "I have a gift to give Carmen before everyone gets focused upon the work at hand." Carmen looks surprised as Juan presents her with a beautiful diamond necklace. He clears his throat. "On such a special occasion as this, I could not miss the opportunity to make it truly special for the love of my life. Do you like it?" Carmen, unable to respond, cries tears of joy and hugs and passionately kisses Juan.

After Carmen's fitting is complete, Jessica walks the staff through the design and production expectations. Everyone agrees to meet at nine o'clock the next day, and the meeting is concluded.

During the drive back to the villa, Sean and Jessica discuss their impressions of the day's events.

Sean asks, "Why didn't you tell me you spoke Portuguese?"

Jessica's answer is simple. "A girl has to have some secrets."

He makes a face. "Well, I guess so."

"Besides," she continues, "if you knew that, you wouldn't have accepted my bet, and I wouldn't be getting a free dinner. I told you my culinary desires aren't cheap and neither is my choice of wines, although I must admit, it won't rival your expensive taste in scotch."

Sean nods, chuckling. "Well, I guess I'm fairly safe then."

Jess smiles, "I'm not sure I'd go that far." Her face then becomes very serious, and she says, "Sean, apparently this expansion is looking like it's realistic and the details are coming together nicely, so we are going to have to make a decision on how your contract is going to fit into everything."

Sean, looking equally serious, replies, "SGM hasn't agreed to represent Beauty Boutique Clothing yet."

Jessica's mouth drops open as she gapes at him. Sean can't maintain his straight face and begins to laugh, to which Jessica makes a disgusted sound. "Oh, Jesus, Sean, you're such an asshole!"

Sean, still chuckling, replies, "Relax. I told you, we will structure my contract in a manner that will work for the Beauty Boutique's budget. What that looks like, I'm not prepared to go into right now."

Carmen tells Juan on their ride home how impressed she is with him, how beautiful the necklace is, and how gracious Jessica is to produce her first design in Brazil just for Carmen.

"Yes, it's wonderful of her to do this for both you and me, but it is also a way for her to test the factory workers."

"Nevertheless, if the design is as beautiful as I suspect it will be, promise me you will open all the necessary doors to ensure her time frames are met as cheaply as possible?"

Juan smiles. "Of course I will, my love, but only if you are thrilled with the finished product." As Juan is pulling into their estate, Carmen reaches over and strokes his inner thigh upward until she reaches his crotch.

She gives it a little squeeze and says, "I think I'll take a shower before dinner, if you don't mind. The factory was a little bit dusty after going unused so long."

"Of course I don't mind," Juan says as he walks into the living room to make himelf a drink. Carmen heads upstairs for her shower.

Juan enjoys his drink and settles into his favorite wing-backed arm chair to contemplate what this evening might have in store when his anticipation is abruptly interrupted by Carmen's screams. Juan jumps from his chair and rushes upstairs, suspecting Carmen has found another scorpion in their bedroom, as had been the case many times before. Juan rushes into the bedroom to find Carmen holding two drinks and wearing nothing by the diamond necklace and gold stilettos.

Juan pauses momentarily, taking in the view, and then asks with a tinge of humor, "Is something wrong?"

Carmen gives him a sultry smile. "No, nothing is wrong. I just figured that was the quickest way to get you upstairs. Would you like your drink here, or would you prefer to join me in the tub?"

Juan smiles and says, "I would love to join you in the tub."

Carmen walks seductively to him, hands him his drink, rubs his crotch long enough to sense his excitement, then says, "Good. I hoped that would be your choice." She turns and walks toward their colossal granite bathroom.

Juan stays behind, enjoying the way Carmen's hips sway, and when she looks over her shoulder and asks if he is coming, Juan says, "Yes. I was just taking a moment to admire the view." Carmen giggles and bends over to undo the straps of her stilettos, observing Juan's appreciation from between her long legs. Juan undresses and, upon entering the bathroom, finds the bubble bath has already been drawn. Carmen steps in and lounges comfortably, covered in bubbles and sipping on her drink.

He eases himself into the bathtub after her and offers a toast. "May my love and admiration for you grow each day, and may this evening hold pleasures beyond each of our wildest imaginations."

Carmen sits forward, purposefully exposing the sparkling necklace and her breasts, and says, "I can drink to that." She kisses him slowly and seductively, lingering long enough to feel his warm and increased breath upon her lips. The time passes quickly, spent teasing each other in the bath until the water becomes cold, and then they retire to the bed.

Juan's attention is focused only on Carmen's tanned body. He begins kissing her neck, and then moves to her shoulder, inching inward to seize her left breast in his mouth. His tongue finds her nipple and circles it rapidly. Carmen responds instinctively by arching her back and letting out a pleasure filled whimper that excites them both. Juan holds her nipple between his teeth and intensifies his approach by flicking the nipple with the tip of his tongue, making her squirm with pleasure. He reaches up with his right hand and cups her right breast. Pinching the nipple between his thumb and forefinger, he then begins gently twisting. Carmen's breathing quickens and deepens, signaling her intense excitement.

After a moment, Juan's right hand leaves her nipple and strokes the junction between her legs, causing Carmen to moan deeply when his index finger penetrates her moist, unhindered body. She begins moving her lower body in response to Juan's caresses. He gradually begins kissing his way down her torso to her abdomen and lingers at her belly button momentarily before moving even lower at a painstakingly slow rate. Finally, Carmen feels his breath against her labia. In an aggravating gesture, Juan suddenly turns and begins kissing her inner thigh.

She makes a frustrated sound, running her fingers through his hair to guide him back to where she wants him, but he switches to the other leg and moves down to the knee, then crosses back over, positioning his body between her legs. There he remains, motionless for what seems to Carmen like an eternity before she finally feels his tongue stroke up the entire length of her eager womanhood. She grabs his head, interlacing her fingers through his hair, and Juan gives her another stroke of his tongue.

Carmen cries out, "Oh God, don't stop!"

Juan places his hands over her hip bones and, using his thumbs, he spreads her labia and exposes her clitoris, which he attacks with his flickering tongue, causing a sweet torment that leads to a prolonged and intense orgasm.

After the waves subside a bit, Carmen pushes Juan onto his back, straddles his hips, and with one fluid motion drops down on the entire length of his shaft. Juan groans as Carmen places her palms on his chest, pushing his upper body into the mattress as she rocks back and forth on his shaft. Her desire builds quickly yet again, and her rocking becomes frantic as she explodes into another shattering orgasm. At this point, Juan can no longer be patient as his desire and need reach a fevered pitch. He throws Carmen onto her back and slams his entire manhood into her over and over again. Sensing she is close again, he continues his relentless pounding until their frenzied pants give way to audible cries, and Juan finds his release deep inside her.

He collapses on top of her and lies there as each of them catches their breath, feeling the tiny convulsions of sexual satisfaction from each other's bodies and basking in the fact that their love-making surpassed both of their expectations. They doze off and on for a bit, then order a light snack to be had in bed before sleeping blissfully until the alarm goes off in time for them to make the nine o'clock appointment at the factory.

═◄─ ─►═

Everyone is assembled at the factory by the time Carmen and Juan arrive. Carmen is showing her personal style wearing blue jeans, a maroon silk blouse, and her stilettos from last night, along with the diamond necklace Juan had given her. Hugo and Ricardo have supplied both white and black linen, and Jessica gives Carmen the choice between the two. Carmen chooses the black linen. As the work begins, Jessica constantly checks the stitching, the measurements, and the specifications. She realizes she is pleasantly surprised by the competency the workers are displaying.

Lidia catches a stitching flaw and runs it by Jessica, who is impressed that Lidia caught something she missed. The first fitting for Carmen is extremely close to perfection. When Jessica suggests a few minor alterations to have the garment tailored for Carmen's figure, the results are stunning. Carmen is ecstatic, Juan's jaw drops when he sees his wife wearing the design, and Sean, Hugo, and Ricardo just applaud. Lidia and the factory staff are pleased with their work, and Jessica feels their craftsmanship is phenomenal. Carmen and Juan can't thank Jessica enough, and Jessica can't give enough credit to Lidia and her crew; she even praises Lidia for catching the flawed work that she missed.

Everyone leaves satisfied with the way the day has gone. Juan and Carmen have a local photographer memorialize this creation and promise Jessica her Brazilian designs will be showcased in all the right social circle. Juan speaks to Sean later, via telephone, and has him pass on to Jessica the message that the expedited governmental approval fees will not exceed fifty thousand U.S. dollars, which Sean knows is well below normal standards, probably because of how well Carmen was treated. Sean congratulates Jessica on her extremely successful business maneuvers, and they share a toast in celebration of a job well done.

CHAPTER 12

GO BIG OR GO HOME

Tuesday morning, Jessica enters Beauty Boutique Clothing's offices in San Francisco at nine o'clock sharp to find Nate and her senior staff eagerly waiting to hear about her trip. She begins briefing everyone on how well the two new designs she took with her were received. She explains all about her negotiations with Ricardo, Lidia, Juan, and Sean, and gives a blow-by-blow of testing the factory workers with the production of Carmen's outfit and receiving rave reviews. She explains to her senior production staff the quality of the factory, its equipment, and the potential of available, well-trained local workers. Several production and quality control department heads appear concerned, and they question Jessica about their need to relocate to Brazil. She recognizes their concern and unspoken questions, which cause her to explain in further detail.

"First, let me assure all of you that no one will be required to relocate to Brazil, and that each of you is secure in your job here, in San Francisco. For some, it may be necessary to spend time, perhaps two or three months, at the new factory to ensure production is set up and moving along correctly. However, based on my observations of the displaced Nike factory workers' production skills, my expectation is that all the difficulties can be resolved in less than a year, with our international operation being on its own within that time frame, should the Beauty Boutique choose to undertake this expansion."

She fields multiple questions regarding quality control, distribution, political factors, and time commitment. Then, she surprises everyone in the room, including Nate, when she says, "The decision to expand our operations into Brazil and to open international markets at this time will not be undertaken unless the majority in this room votes to do so. I am fully aware I would not be where I am today had it not been for each of you, your dedication, and your hard work on behalf of the Beauty Boutique. In the next few weeks, Nate and I will be examining all the possible options for financing this type of expansion. I will negotiate the marketing contract with Sean Green Marketing, then bring back to this room the costs and benefits analysis so that everyone knows what we're getting into. We're either in agreement going forward, or we will not expand at this time. The success of this organization has always been because of the unity within the leadership team, and this company will never risk disunity, because when this team fractures, so does the organization. We either succeed or fail together." Jessica finishes her speech to an appreciative round of applause. She briefly waits for anyone to comment while making a point to make eye contact with everyone present, and then finishes, "Thank you all for you time today. See you for our meeting next week." She walks out of the board room.

Nate follows closely behind and into her office. "Darling, I don't want to be a killjoy, and that was a marvelous speech, but how in the hell do you plan on pulling this type of expansion off?"

"What do you mean?" asks Jessica, distracted by the design modification lists on her desk.

"Really, you have to ask?" he sighs, "This is a two-million-dollar capitalization project, at least. Where are the funds coming from?"

She shrugs and says, "Between the equity I have in my home and savings, I believe I can raise one million, and my parents should be good for five hundred thousand. We can use half of our line of credit for the other five hundred thousand, which gets us to two million."

Nate nods slowly. "Yes, it does, and it also straps us in completely with regard to carrying costs, production breakdowns, and any type of industry-wide slowdown or strike. If I was thinking of risking all of my personal assets, I'd examine investor or bank financing options first."

Jess shakes her head. "You know I hate anything that interferes with our management decision-making processes in any way. Both of those options would come with management oversight and limitations, putting the Beauty Boutique's ability to respond quickly to industry shifts at risk. Our flexibility and ability to react quickly have kept us at the forefront of our niche market. I simply don't want to lose that type of competitive advantage, especially in the circumstances you just described."

Nate huffs out a breath. "Okay, part of that is understandable, but Jess, you're talking about risking everything you have worked so hard to achieve."

"Well, perhaps it's time to go big or go home."

"Not when the other option is to go broke, even if we think we're ready to go big," Nate retorts.

Jessica rubs her temples. "Look, I understand that everything you say could be true. The worst could happen. But the fact remains that we have a competitive advantage that is going to require us to expand or risk a challenge from some unknown competitor. If we continue to strengthen our position within this niche market, we can become the dominating fish in a relatively small pond. I think we should take that opportunity."

"That's true, but by expanding our pond size, don't we also reveal our niche and open ourselves up to the unknown competitive threat?"

"Perhaps, but let me pose a question. Why has no one recently entered the fashion shoe market?"

"Well," Nate says, considering, "because any newcomer entering that field would be driven out by those who dominate the market by undercutting the competitors pricing..." He trails off, realization dawning on his face.

"Exactly. Beauty Boutique Clothing needs to be the company that dominates the career women's fashion market. Currently we do, and by taking this expansion, I aim to keep it that way."

Nate sighs and gives in. "Very well. Then let's get to work and figure out how to make this feat happen."

Just then, Jessica is paged through the office phone. "Bonnie Stevens is on line three, Ms. Silva," says the secretary through the intercom.

Jess sighs and tells Nate, "Please contact Evelyn at Mr. Green's office and see when the Beauty Boutique can expect a draft proposal from SGM." Nate nods and leaves Jessica to her phone call.

She picks up the line and says, "Hi sweetie, I've been expecting a call from you for a while."

"Well, why didn't you call me last night then?" Bonnie replies tartly.

"Sean and I have had a pretty busy schedule. I was exhausted when we got in, so I went straight to bed," Jess replies, soothing Bonnie's distress.

"Alone?" Bonnie asks, and Jessica snorts.

"Yes, of course alone. Who was I supposed to go to bed with this time?" Jess asks sarcastically.

"Well, Sean. Duh."

"No! I told you, our relationship is completely professional."

Bonnie giggles. "Oh, you slut. I didn't realize you would make him pay for it. How do you do that?"

Jess represses a groan with a surge of willpower. "Ack, do you ever stop?"

"Okay, okay," Bonnie says, giving in. "Seriously though, how was Brazil?"

"Well, the villa is outrageous, and your chef is phenomenal."

"I know!" Bonnie exclaims. "That's why I insisted Mark hire him."

"Oh, and you are absolutely right about Ricardo's ass. Wow, what a fine piece," Jess says.

"I know! Since Sean is out of the question for you, did you at least take a ride on Ricardo?"

"Bonnie…" Jess says warningly.

"Fine. Did he at least show you what Brazil has to offer?"

"No. His ass may be nice, but he definitely isn't. Besides, I worked on Sunday, kissing up to Juan Zamora's wife by getting her outfitted in a free, brand new Beauty Boutique outfit."

"Goddamn it! Sean was supposed to leave Sunday open for you so you could have some fun before you came back to the states to work again."

"Oh, don't blame Sean. He did leave the day open. I was the one who decided to give Carmen that gift. I believe the Beauty Boutique will get more mileage in the right circles out of that simple gesture than any other type of advertising."

Bonnie sighs. "Probably, but let me see if I've got this straight. You worked, didn't get laid, didn't sightsee, and didn't party."

Jess nods ruefully, thinking that it sounds pretty bad when put in that light. "Pretty much."

"God, you and I have to go out drinking sometime so I can remind you how to have a good time. You need to lighten up, and you definitely need to get laid soon."

"I'm a little busy right now and somewhat stressed about this expansion, raising capital, and the new designs Sean demanded I have available."

"Okay, but if you don't start enjoying your life soon, you're going to turn around one day and most of your life will have passed you by, my dear. Hey, I've got an idea. You and I should go to the villa for a weekend, just by ourselves. Sean is going to McCall shortly. Mark and I usually join him for the week, but we can let the two of them go be boys, and we can head to the villa for girl time! I won't take no for an answer. You need some time to let your hair down and relax a bit."

Jessica doesn't bother trying to say no, knowing Bonnie will pester her until she gives in anyway. "That sounds great. When is all this happening?"

Bonnie replies, "It will be early next month. I'll get the dates from Mark, and then we can figure out what we will need to take."

Jessica considers for a moment. "Okay, but if we really do go, I don't want any pressure to do anything. Just lying by the pool and catching up with you sounds perfect to me. Don't even try to set me up with anyone, or I swear I'm not going. Promise?"

Bonnie sighs, then says dramatically, "Very well, as you wish. I'll leave your deceased love life to you. But I've got to say it's pathetic, and you need a seriously freaky guy to reignite some passion in your life."

"Ugh. Whatever."

"So we have a deal? When Sean goes to Idaho, I'll send Mark with him, and you and I will head to Brazil?"

"Only on the conditions I specified," Jess clarifies.

"Of course, sweetheart. Your dusty vagina is your issue, not mine."

"Ugh!" Jess exclaims. "You're disgusting. But I'll look forward to our vacation. Get me the dates so I can schedule them into my calendar as soon as possible?"

"Absolutely, dear. I'll call you in a couple of days with them," Bonnie says, and then they end the call.

∗ ∗ ∗

Sean begins his morning in much the same manner as Jessica. He arrives at his office at the usual time of eight o'clock, briefs Evelyn on the results in Brazil, and asks her to get the standard proposal for services ready for presentation to the Beauty Boutique, but to leave payment rates and schedules open for his adjustments.

Evelyn smirks at Sean, then says, sarcastically, "I thought this wasn't a charity organization and you weren't a very benevolent person?"

He sighs. "Well, I'll inform you, just to protect my reputation, that I am not benevolent and I will make copious amounts of money off of the Beauty Boutique's contract. It will just be structured very differently because of the special needs of this particular client, that's all."

Evelyn resists the urge to snort. "Of course, Mr. Green."

Sean raises his eyebrows and asks, "What else needs addressing immediately?"

Evelyn picks up her notes, but she is interrupted by Sean's private line ringing. "Just a minute," Sean says, and picks up the phone. Mark is on the other line and sounds unsettled, something Sean hasn't heard him sound like in years. Sean asks Mark to hang on for just a minute and then tells Evelyn he will be a little bit with the call and he will get back to her. Evelyn excuses herself from his office, and Sean returns to his conversation with Mark.

"I'm sorry for the interruption. Evelyn was in my office, and I wanted to excuse her before I returned to this conversation. What's going on? You didn't sound well a minute ago."

Mark's voice is tight when he speaks. "I just got off the phone with Hugo Montes. He is very angry because someone claiming to be associated with the environmentalist watchdog group in the United States just shot holes in five of his diesel pumps, to the tune of one hundred thousand dollars. He said he's pissed for two reasons. First, Diablo Mining, Inc. is taking most of the political and environmental heat in Brazil, and second, now the money we gave him has to be used to replace his pumps."

Sean rubs his eyes with one hand. "Well, we knew this was a possibility, and so did he."

"Yes, but he is now demanding we get him another two hundred thousand dollars, off the books, for his grief. I told him no, our deal was set, and that's when he threatened to go to Bonnie and show her our deal. Sean, you know how Bonnie will react. I don't need any drama in our relationship. Things are going really well for us. On the other hand, if I pay his demands, then when will it end?"

"What if we agree to reimburse him for his loss in the amount of five hundred thousand dollars but tell him it has to come off of the two million in advertising you were paying me to represent Diablo Mining, Inc.? Then we won't pay him any more in cash. All we need is another month and his contract with Global Metal Refining is concluded and you'll be in the clear. If he talks to Bonnie after that, we can deny that's what we meant with the contract and we were still willing to help him, but now that he is being personally and professionally immature, we have cut all ties with him and his eco-insensitive practices. I also think it is time we begin to get proactive here in the United States. Let's release our first statement today explaining you understand there have been some concerns raised because of one of your suppliers' practices in Brazil. Let's say it's your understanding that Diablo mining has and is complying with all national and environmental regulatory laws in Brazil, and Global Metal Refining is currently evaluating its associations. I had hoped to get another month before this hit, but we both knew this was coming."

"I know. I just don't want Bonnie involved in this, or things will get ugly at home. Right now, I like how everything is going at home. Go ahead and make the deal with Hugo, *quickly*. I'll release the statement after your meeting is set," Mark replies, sounding a little bit more at ease.

"Okay, let me make some arrangements, and I'll get back to you later."

After they hang up, Sean calls Hugo and explains the deal to him. Hugo agrees to meet Sean back in Brazil at the villa in two days. Sean calls Mark and tells him he needs the five hundred thousand tomorrow, because he will be heading to Brazil as soon as he gets the cash.

"Okay. I'll stop by your office first thing in the morning."

Sean tells Evelyn to schedule the jet for his trip, due to problems with Global Metal Refining's vendors. He emphasizes the need to keep this trip confidential and then returns to his office to finish his work for the day.

⚒ ⚒

The next morning, Mark arrives at Sean's office early. He delivers the cash and leaves, virtually unseen. Sean boards the jet to Brazil with preset meetings he personally arranged. Upon his arrival, he passes through customs without incident, as usual, and arrives at the villa in time for a drink and a light snack, then heads to bed. He meets Hugo by the pool fairly early the next morning and confirms Mark's offer, which delights Hugo.

Sean holds out the bag of cash, allowing Hugo to grasp one of the handles before saying, "Your threat to Mark's home life and marriage was not appreciated. It will not be tolerated in the future. If you would like to continue these profitable business arrangements with us, please make sure it doesn't happen again."

Hugo, still holding onto his handle, asks Sean for clarification as to the specific issue.

Sean maintains a pleasant tone, but also infuses authority. "Mark takes the position that his business life and personal life are always separate, and should a vendor of his violate that provision, such as involving his wife in a deal, Mark wouldn't be inclined to do business with them again. Ever."

Hugo eyes Sean for a moment, then says, "Of course. Please extend my apologies to Mark. I assure you this will not be a problem again, given that the situation has been handled fairly and honorably."

Sean nods and releases the bag to Hugo's possession. "Care to join me for breakfast?" Sean asks, and Hugo accepts. They enjoy breakfast, then each heads their separate directions. Sean briefly telephones Mark to assure him everything is once again under control and extends Hugo's apologies with a touch of irony.

Mark laughs, saying, "If that bastard threatens me again, I will destroy his business and his life."

Sean nods, expecting an answer like that. "I gave him the message loud and clear. I suspect he won't be a problem again."

After their conversation, Sean boards his jet once again and heads back to San Francisco, feeling content that another potential crisis has been avoided.

Hugo sees Mark's press release the day after meeting with Sean and is furious. He calls SGM, demanding to speak with him immediately. Evelyn interrupts Sean's meeting with Jessica, just after he had begun to ask her for suggestions about how to best structure his proposal for services so as not to interfere with any potential cash flow issues he isn't aware of in the fashion industry.

"Evelyn, I'm in a meeting. It will have to wait," Sean says, attempting to get back to Jessica.

Evelyn clears her throat. "I'm sorry, Mr. Green, but it's regarding your meeting yesterday, and it seems very important."

"I see." Sean sighs and turns to Jessica. "Do you mind if I take this call in the conference room? This is a critical situation that is currently in the developmental stages."

Jessica glances up from his proposal and says, "Not at all."

He excuses himself and moves to the conference room to handle the telephone call. He picks up the phone, and even thousands of miles away the tension is palpable.

"I am very disappointed by the most recent press release of Global Metal Refining, and I must say, I feel I have been somewhat misled," Hugo begins.

Sean reminds him of their very first deal. "The statement yesterday was just a simple statement to strengthen Global Metal Refining's corporate reputation in the United States. It in no way placed any blame on Diablo Mining. Did it not please you that Mark clearly indicated Diablo Mining was following all appropriate environmental laws in Brazil?"

Hugo explains, "Yes, that was fine. But the Brazilian environmental zealots are beginning to make my life miserable, and several of my business partners and clients are beginning to distance themselves from myself and my business."

Sean rubs a hand over his face. "Once again, this was all to be expected. We need to stick to my marketing plan. This is why you were treated so honorably, over and above your demands. All of this will blow over in a few months if you just keep your dignity about you, as you always do. In the end, you will be positioned as your country's environmental leader for the mining industry and recognized for your work internationally."

Hugo sighs over the line and thanks Sean. "I will stay the course of your plan and call you if I have any further concerns."

"Thank you, please do stay in touch," Sean replies and hangs up the phone.

Returning to his meeting with Jessica, Sean apologizes for the rude interruption, assuring her that he usually doesn't let anything interrupt his meetings, but the situation was critical.

Jessica nods. "I understand. Shall we?" He nods in return and takes his seat.

She lays out most of her concerns, including several industry timing issues.

"Perhaps we should structure SGM's fee payments to coincide with the cash flow received for international operations, if you decide to undertake them? The fees can be a percentage that is proportional to the funds received, with the stop gap being my normal monthly rate. This way, the maximum payment would be my standard monthly fee and a proportional percentage of the receipts can be paid to SGM instead, so we can avoid undue burden on the Beauty Boutique," Sean suggests, and Jessica nods, so he continues, "The full amount would still be owed, of course, but the contract for these services could then be extended until payment in full is reached." He passes her a contract that states the annual fee will be four hundred and eighty thousand dollars.

Jessica sits speechless for a moment, staring at the document, then says incredulously, "Sean, this isn't even half your usual annual fee. Why?"

Sean laughs and replies, "You, and Evelyn, have convinced me this is a good opportunity for SGM. I really don't know much about the fashion industry, so you'll have some teaching to do. That's where the difference is, because I cut my inexperience in the fashion industry out of my fees. Also, if this is as successful as I hope it will be, I'll make up for it in subsequent years. Fair enough?"

Jessica shakes her head disbelievingly. "This is amazing," she says, "but you know, several things need to be put into place before I sign this agreement."

Sean replies, "Absolutely, and I understand. I just didn't want to be the reason you didn't take the opportunity."

She starts to stand. "Thank you, so much."

He stands as well, to shake her hand, but Jessica steps in and hugs him.

Sean clears his throat. "Uh, welcome to SGM as our newest and smallest client." Jessica's head is spinning as to why she is hugging him, and then she realizes just how marvelous he feels and smells. For the first time in over a year, she finds herself wanting to see any man, but especially *this* man, naked. She snaps herself out of it and breaks away from his embrace.

"Um, sorry about that," she murmurs, gathering up her things.

"No need to apologize. I enjoyed it. I mean—" He clears his throat again. "I enjoy the fact we are beginning to build trust within our professional relationship."

Jessica nods, finishes packing up her stuff, and leaves Sean's office, thinking, *what in the hell did I do that for?*

Sean sits behind his desk, dazed, thinking, *Shit, why did I clarify the professional relationship?*

Evelyn stands in the doorway watching Sean for a moment, then asks, "Well, what has you so deep in contemplation, Mr. Green?"

Sean is startled back to reality and looks up at Evelyn, saying, "I just proposed a very benevolent contract to the Beauty Boutique and was questioning whether or not it was the right thing to do."

Evelyn picks the copy of the contract up off Sean's desk and looks at the fee payment schedule. Stunned, she says with a coy smile, "Is there anything else I need to know about this new client?"

"Yes," Sean retorts, "they are our smallest client. And it's your fault that I was so generous."

"Oh, I hope so," Evelyn replies, then snorts. "Anything else?"

Sean glares at her. "Like what? Oh, yes, actually. Please make a note in the file that I am to be notified if they miss any payment to us so I can immediately cancel this pathetic deal."

Evelyn sighs, rolls her eyes, and turns to leave his office. "Consider it done. You know, for a moment there, I thought you actually had a heart."

CHAPTER 13

NO PUN INTENDED

Jessica leaves Sean's office with her thoughts reeling about what had happened, on both a personal and professional level. Her personal feelings about Sean Green changed somewhere along the line, and she has no idea when or how it happened. She closes the door of her Vallejo Street home behind her and drops all of her stuff in the entry. She immediately walks into the kitchen, pours herself a large glass of wine, and telephones Bonnie. When Bonnie hears the deal Sean cut for Jessica, she is excited. Bonnie tells Jessica it is a wonderful contract and SGM will take the Beauty Boutique to a much higher level than it is already on.

Bonnie senses Jessica is troubled by something, even among the excitement of the day, and she starts to probe. Initially, Jessica resists and tries to play off her distraction as fatigue, but Bonnie isn't buying any of it.

"Girl, please, we have been friends all of our lives. I know when something is bugging you, so out with it!"

There is a pause while Jess considers simply hanging up. Then she sighs, takes a big gulp of her wine, and says, "If you insist, but this could take a while."

"Well, I'm listening, and I've got all night," replies Bonnie.

"Okay, here it goes..." Jessica begins to divulge her concerns, fears, and confusion. She explains she is excited to have SGM agree to represent Beauty Boutique Clothing, especially given the rocky start, but she is also understandably concerned about risking everything she has worked for thus far, not to mention all of her financial resources and her staff's future.

"Honey, there are investors constantly looking for good opportunities, and I am sure the Beauty Boutique could attract many of them," Bonnie reminds her.

Jessica acknowledges that this is probably true. "But I was hoping to keep control of my company, rather than allowing a lender's board to take over. Right now, I could probably risk my assets and still swing the deal," she replies. Bonnie listens patiently as Jessica brings up one pitfall after another. "SGM's contract is a terrific deal, but it would impact company cash flow and potentially profits," Jess continues. "The travel time necessary to ensure the factory in Brazil would be up and running to my standards as quickly as possible is a huge chunk of time I don't usually have, and there's also the increased cost of flying back and forth..."

As Jessica trails off, Bonnie suddenly figures out what is really bugging her and blurts out, "Oh my God! Jessica, you think Sean is hot and he scares you to death!"

Jess groans. "Damn it, I hate it when I'm transparent!"

Bonnie laughs and says, "You're not. I just know you better than most, and you would *not* be this scared if it was just money you were risking. Omigod!" Bonnie's voice jumps an octave. "Did you guys do it in Brazil? How could you hold out on me?"

"No!" Jessica exclaims. "But I saw him swimming, and he has really taken care of himself. He was a complete gentleman, charming, thoughtful, witty, and even patient with me..."

"So, what's the problem then?"

Jess considers. "Well, I don't have time to get involved in any significant type of relationship, especially with a business associate like Sean."

Bonnie thinks for a minute and then clarifies what she has perceived from the conversation. "Let me see if I've got this straight. You seriously like Sean, and you're thinking he could be much more than a casual fling, aren't you?"

Jessica stutters, "W-well, m-maybe, but I'm at a point in my life where one night stands and casual romances aren't worth the trouble. I am happy with who I am and my success. The only way I would consider becoming involved with anyone is in an exclusive and committed structure."

"So? What's the problem?"

"I don't think Sean would be of the same mindset, and we will be working very closely together. We need to maintain a professional relationship, or things could get really awkward, really fast."

"Why do you think he wouldn't have the same mindset?" Bonnie asks.

"Well, just because I think we're in a different place. And platonic is the way our relationship should be," Jess replies, unable to come up with a more specific reason.

"You're scared, aren't you? How do you know Sean isn't feeling the same way you are?"

Jess shakes her head. "I don't. It's just not appropriate, given the circumstances."

"Oh, I see. So two successful people can't fall in love and work together, is that it?" Bonnie asks sarcastically.

"Yes, precisely!"

"Bullshit! You're just scared to let anyone close to you after that last douche bag. I think you should just take it one day at a time and leave yourself open to anything that may pop up." She chuckles. "No pun intended, but that too. Anyway, Mark and

Sean are heading to Sean's place in McCall in two weeks. Are we still going to the villa?"

Jessica sighs with relief that the interrogation has ended. "Yes, we should still go."

"Okay. Mark told me they're going for an 'off-site strategy meeting' regarding Diablo Mining and the environmental disasters they are dealing with. Personally, I think it's going to be a weekend away so they can get drunk and sit around in their boxers scratching their balls without a woman telling them they are being disgusting cavemen. Mark is going up Friday night before Sean arrives Saturday afternoon, and they will both be back Monday morning. Can you get that whole weekend off, or will you be at your parents that weekend?"

Jess considers and then replies, "I'll see my parents this weekend so I can spend the whole weekend alone with my best friend. It has been a really long time since we did that."

"Great. I'll tell Mark we will take his jet and they can arrange to get to Idaho in Sean's jet. This will be fun, and I can't wait to spend some quality time with you. We can discuss anything and everything!"

"Yeah, it'll be nice," replies Jessica. "So, what's going on with Mark and Diablo Mining?"

"Ugh. It's a travesty. Ricardo's cousin, Hugo, the one you met at the factory, owns Diablo Mining. Mark is finishing up a gold contract with him shortly, but Mother Earth Cooperative discovered Hugo's company is raping the forest in Brazil to get the gold that's part of their contract. After checking environmental laws in Brazil, it appears Diablo is within the letter of the law, but their practices are way out of line environmentally. Mother Earth Cooperative has targeted Global Metal Refining here in the United States as the financer of the unethical environmental practices and has started a media campaign aimed at exposing both organizations in hopes of creating boycotts in the U.S. Mark has assured me that he had no knowledge of these practices and as soon as the contract is completed he will never work with Diablo Mining again without drastic changes on their part. Mark is concerned because Global Metal Refining stock has suddenly become very volatile, and it affects liquidity and investor morale. Sean and Mark are devising a marketing campaign to combat all the negative press Mark is starting to get. I understand Hugo isn't happy about how Diablo Mining is being portrayed, especially internationally. It's just a really ugly situation for everyone involved. I'm sure Sean will work his spin magic and Global Metal Refining will emerge stronger than ever because they are such an eco-friendly organization."

"Wow, I had no idea you and Mark were going through such an ordeal. I'm so sorry. I have been so wrapped up in all my issues that I haven't been a very good friend," Jess says.

"Don't be silly, we understand. Besides, Mark and Sean have everything under control, according to Mark," Bonnie replies.

"Of course they do, sweetie."

"Apparently," Bonnie continues, "things have gotten a little heated between Mark and Hugo recently, which isn't something Mark had wanted to happen. He and Sean are going to try and devise a strategy to repair the damage that has occurred in Mark and Hugo's working relationship due to a recent press release of Mark's."

Jessica is surprised. "I had no idea any of this was going on. Neither Hugo nor Sean gave any indication of friction when I was in Brazil with them."

"That's probably because Ricardo told both of them to behave. Ricardo and Hugo don't really like each other, but Ricardo needs Hugo's political and business connections, and Hugo is just kind of honorable when it comes to family," says Bonnie. "But enough of this depressing stuff. How are the designs going? And do you have any really sexy designs for me in these new collections?"

Jessica smiles and shakes her head. "Everyone seems genuinely pleased with the new lines I've created, and I'm sure you'll find something in there to drive Mark absolutely bonkers once its draped on your perfect body."

"You're too kind," Bonnie scoffs. "It's just because you are such a fabulous designer that I look so good. I can't wait to see them. Will you bring the drawings to the villa, so I can preorder?"

"Of course. I know you just have to have your clothes before the rest of the world."

"That's my girl!" Bonnie says, and Jessica smiles.

CHAPTER 14

DEADLY CALM

Mark kisses Bonnie goodbye and tells her to have a wonderful week with Jessica.

"Thanks, baby. Have a wonderful and productive weekend in McCall with Sean," she replies. Then she double-checks Mark's schedule to make sure she has everything right. "Okay, so you arrive in McCall this afternoon, and Sean will join you tomorrow around eleven o'clock in the morning?"

Mark says, "Yes, that's correct."

Bonnie nods and asks, "Then you and Sean will be home Monday afternoon sometime?"

"Correct again, my love," Mark says, grinning at Bonnie's concern about his schedule. "So, you and Jessica will be returning from Brazil Monday evening?"

"Yes. We hope to get back home no later than nine. Jessica has to get back to work for meetings early Tuesday, and I have the global warming symposium to attend. The one Global Metal Refining is sponsoring." She smiles. "I love you and will see you later Monday evening. You boys behave yourselves in McCall, okay?" She winks at him.

"Yes, dear," Mark replies, smiling, and heads for the door.

Bonnie lingers in the doorway and watches Mark's car disappear from sight, thinking, *this is going to be such an incredible weekend catching up with Jess.* She quickly sends Mark a text that reads, "<3 <3 Text me when you land in McCall. I'll do the same when we get to the villa."

Mark responds with his usual "K" and smiles, knowing that answer irritates Bonnie. He immediately follows the "K" with a second text that reads, "I adore you and have a great time. All my love, darling."

Bonnie smiles and then calls Jessica. She answers, and Bonnie says, "I'm on my way to pick you up, and we can ride to the jet together."

Jessica sounds surprised. "I was just going to meet you there."

"Don't be silly. I can drop you off on the way home, since it's on my way anyway. There's no need to waste any more fossil fuels than necessary."

Jessica, knowing this is just another argument she isn't going to win, just says, "Okay, see you soon then."

⊷⊹ ⊹⊶

Mark arrives in McCall on time, and Bob, Sean's groundskeeper is waiting to drive him to the house on Payette Lake. Mark sends the required text to Bonnie, even though he knows she won't see it until after the girls arrive in Brazil. When Bob drops Mark off, Mark walks into the house, puts his stuff in the guest bedroom, fixes himself a gin and tonic with lime, and then walks out onto the deck, amazed at the beauty of the little mountain town.

Gazing out at the enormous glacier lake, he thinks, *how peaceful.* Even though he's been visiting McCall every year since he and Sean met, he still marvels at the crystal clear water that reflects the brilliant blue sky. As he stands there pondering how good he and Sean have it in life, he notices the lake is calm and smooth, disturbed only by a single kayaker and a stationary pontoon boat about six hundred yards out on the water. Settling into a deck chair, Mark calls Sean in San Francisco, tells him he made it to McCall, and comments on his earlier reflections.

Sean nod. "Why do you think I keep that house? Its beauty always amazes me when I'm there, but what actually amazes me more than the scenery is the silence when you're sitting on the deck."

There's a pause, then Mark replies, "Wow, you're right. No sirens, airplanes, or car horns. How nice."

Sean just chuckles. "I'll see you tomorrow morning at about eleven."

Bonnie and Jessica land in Brazil at midnight, Pacific Standard Time. Bonnie replies to Mark's text with, "We just landed and are heading to the villa now."

Mark responds with, "Glad you made it. I'm heading to bed. Will call you tomorrow evening. I love you."

Bonnie replies, "I love you, too. We are going to sleep a little since we both barely slept on the plane, then we plan on enjoying the pool and as much tequila as we want ;)."

Mark chuckles, then replies, "Good night, my love. Enjoy each other's company."

Bonnie responds, "Don't work too hard this weekend. Kisses, goodnight."

Mark's response is a typical "K." Bonnie just groans and puts her phone in her purse.

Mark awakens at seven o'clock the next morning, fixes himself a cup of French press coffee, and takes a seat on the deck. Once again, he marvels at the serenity and the glass-like appearance of the water. This morning, there are no disturbances to the lake's surface, except for the same unmoving pontoon boat. Mark wonders if the boat was there all night or if one of the locals just enjoys being out on the water enough to get up and get out this early. He smiles a peaceful smile, takes his first sip of coffee, and a moment later he is dead.

There is a slightly muffled sound as the suppressed .308 caliber round exits the barrel, and at almost that precise moment, it strikes Mark Stevens in the forehead, slightly above his right eyebrow. The sniper watches through the scope for the pink mist and listens for the telltale breaking of glass from the window of the living room as the round exits Mark's skull, carrying with it the pieces of his brain. Scanning the deck, the sniper smiles as he surveys his handiwork. Mark slumps in the chair, the same peaceful smile still on his face. His coffee cup is lying sideways on the deck, devoid of its contents, and brain fragments and blood drip from the back of what was once his skull.

The snipers folds the tarp he had laid down prior to the shot in on itself, successfully containing potential gunshot reside, and places it into his small duffel bag. Starting the pontoon boat, he slowly chugs across the water toward North Beach. In the middle of the area of the lake commonly known as the Narrows, he judges from his previous study of the topography that it is the deepest part of the lake. Unnoticeably, he slips the suppressed .308 rifle over the side and into the water. He watches it as it disappears from sight, resting assured that the murder weapon will reach the unfathomable bottom, some three-hundred-plus feet below the surface. He cruises around the islands of the Narrows and moors the boat back in its slip at the marina. He removes his latex gloves, placing them in his duffel bag, then picks the bag up and walks calmly to the vehicle he parked in the upper parking lot on Mill Street. He starts the vehicle and slips away in the early morning mist, completely undetected.

Bonnie sends Mark a text wishing him a good morning while she and Jessica lounge by the pool, sipping mimosas. Bonnie doesn't concern herself when Mark doesn't respond immediately, figuring he might be engaged in work or lounging at the beach. Besides, Bonnie is engrossed in questioning Jessica about her feelings for Sean. Bonnie listens intently as Jessica wrestles with her emotions and words, attempting to describe her feelings.

"A relationship between the two of us would never work," Jessica says, fiddling with the bottom of her champagne glass. "We're business partners for God's sake—"

At this point, Bonnie interrupts, saying, "That is such bullshit, and you know it, girl. I was Mark's executive temp girl when we became romantically involved, *and* he was married at the time."

"I know, but you and I are so different in this area," protests Jessica.

"Look, sometimes in life you can't control everything. Love, or lust, whatever you want to call it, has a way of popping up unexpectedly and changing your circumstances," Bonnie explains.

"But I'm not even sure I like Sean. I've seen what an asshole he can be. Just because he's been charming recently doesn't mean I should seduce him or start a relationship with him," Jessica objects.

"Why not?" Bonnie asks.

"Just because," Jess quips.

"Are you physically attracted to him?" Bonnie asks. Then she adds, "And don't lie to me, girl!"

Jessica rolls her eyes and downs her mimosa. "Of course I am. You'd have to be blind and deaf not to be. But you already knew that, didn't you?"

Bonnie nods smugly. "I just don't see any problem here. Sean is hot, and you are, at least physically, interested, so quit trying to protect your heart and fuck his brains out! If it turns out he is lame in the bedroom, at least you won't have to question your decision any longer, and you won't be disappointed if he doesn't want more."

"But what if he's not lame? What if he is an incredible lover and he still doesn't want more? Then what?" Jessica asks, struggling to express herself.

"Then for God's sake, enjoy the sex. Lord knows you need it. And if it turns out he's an asshole to you, dump his ass, or keep him around, at least for the sex, until something better comes along," insists Bonnie.

Jessica stands up, realizing she and Bonnie aren't going to see eye-to-eye on this issue. "You are a disturbed woman; you know that, don't you?"

Then she turns and dives into the pool, swimming away as Bonnie yells after her, "Yeah, so what's your point?"

Sean's jet lands in McCall just prior to eleven o'clock. He gets into his Jeep Cherokee Limited Edition, which remains parked at the airport when he is away, and drives the ten minutes to his house in the 2400 block of Warren Wagon Road. As he enters the house, he calls out to Mark, but doesn't get a response. Sean throws his bag into the master bedroom and heads upstairs toward the living room, thinking Mark might be out on the deck. Sean can hear the radio playing, and as he reaches the top of the stairs, he sees that

Mark is indeed sitting on the deck. At first, he thinks Mark might be sleeping, because of his slouched position. Then, as Sean takes in the broken window and the appearance of blood, he begins to get tingles of wariness.

As he gets closer, Sean sees a large part of the back of Mark's skull is missing. Gray matter is sprayed on the deck. The French press coffee pot is still on the table next to Mark, and his coffee mug has landed on its side on the deck. Sean gets a whiff of Marks blood and vomits right there on the living room carpet. Grabbing his cell phone, he shakily dials 911.

The dispatch operator answers. "911, please state your emergency."

Sean replies, in a trembling voice, "M-my friend is d-dead."

The dispatcher asks, "What is your address? Is he breathing?"

"No! He is fucking dead. There's blood all over the place, and I can see his fucking brains on the deck!" Sean yells.

"Sir, please stay calm. What is your location? Stay on the line with me while I get help on the way," comes the dispatcher's response.

"2450 Warren Wagon Road, in McCall," Sean responds, feeling the horror leeching out of him as the shock settles in.

"Sir, what is your name?" asks the dispatcher.

"Sean Green."

"What is your friend's name, Sean?"

"Mark Stevens," Sean replies bitterly.

"Do you see any weapons? Are there any weapons in the house?"

"I don't see any weapons, but yes, I have guns in the house," replies Sean.

"Where are they?"

"They are downstairs, locked in the gun safe in the library."

"Okay, thank you, Sean. Can you please go outside and stand in the driveway until officers arrive? They should be there in five minutes or so," the dispatcher pauses, and Sean hears computer keys clicking, "but please remain on the line with me, okay?"

"Yes, I'm going. Please hurry," Sean says, turning his back on the horror before him and walking back downstairs and out the door.

"Can you describe what you're wearing for me, so I can let the officers know who you are when they arrive?"

"Well, I'll be the only fucking one standing outside my house," Sean replies coldly.

The dispatcher almost sighs. "Sean, we assume that, but I need a clothing description for my records," she says patiently.

"Blue jeans, white shirt, and running shoes," Sean says on a sigh.

Just then, two McCall police officers appear walking down the driveway. "Are you Mr. Sean Green?" one of them asks.

"Yes," Sean answers, taking his cell phone away from his ear and hanging up.

The one who spoke nods. "Is there anyone else in the house, Mr. Green?"

Sean shakes his head, unable to do more.

"Okay. Will you please wait here while we clear the residence?" Sean simply nods.

Returning after a few minutes, the officers explain that the agency in charge of the investigation will most likely be the Valley County Sheriff's Office, and deputies should be arriving in about twenty minutes. They ask Sean if there is anything he needs out of the house, because most likely he'll need to stay out of the house for several hours. Sean tells the officers he just arrived and threw his bag in the master bedroom before walking upstairs.

One of them asks, "Was it the red canvas bag?" Sean nods, and the officer goes inside and retrieves it for him.

After quickly searching the bag for weapons, he passes it to Sean. The cop then asks who the deceased person is, and Sean says, "One of my top clients and my personal friend, Mark Stevens. We were supposed to spend the weekend here in McCall working on some business strategies." He pauses, his throat tight, then manages to say, "Mark got here yesterday afternoon."

"From where?"

Sean clears his throat. "San Francisco."

The other officer chimes in. "Did you fly into Boise and drive up?"

Sean shakes his head. "No. I have a jet. Mark used it to fly up yesterday, and then the pilot flew back to bring me up this morning."

There is some nodding. "And who is Mark's next of kin? How can we contact them?"

"Mark's wife, Bonnie, would be the first. But she's in Brazil with a friend at the Stevens' villa for the weekend. That's why my pilot had to make two trips, instead of Mark just taking his own jet... I'll call Bonnie and let her know what's happened as soon as I have a little more information. Please, don't broadcast his name anywhere. He's a very prominent businessman, and the press will be all over this soon enough," Sean replies, regaining a little bit of composure.

A marked Valley County Sheriff's vehicle and another unmarked vehicle approach slowly down the driveway. A tall, blond man slightly overweight in plain clothes introduces himself to Sean as Detective Sergeant Keith Jones.

"Mr. Green, I need to do a walk through and get some photographs, but I'll be right back." Sean nods.

About thirty minutes later, other vehicles arrive on scene, and Sergeant Jones returns from inside the house. He asks Sean many of the same questions the McCall polices officers had already asked.

After answering all of them, Sean asks the sergeant, "Did Mark kill himself in my house?"

Sergeant Jones shakes his head. "I don't believe so. This appears to be a homicide. Did you vomit in the living room when you saw him?" His voice holds tones of sympathy.

Sean swallows as the bile starts to rise again and replies, "Yes I did. I have never seen anything so disturbing in my life."

Jones nods. "It happens to the best of us. Can I speak with you more formally, Mr. Green?"

Sean watches people walking hurriedly around them for a moment, then nods. "Yes, of course. What do you need to know?"

"Well, let me begin by informing you that you are not under arrest, and you are free to leave at any time. Do you understand?"

Sean replies, "Yes."

"Okay," Jones replies, and asks Sean to explain everything from the time he left San Francisco, periodically interjecting a question to clarify his understanding of the sequence of events. "The Sheriff's department called the Idaho State Police for assistance with this investigation, since we don't have the expertise to handle a homicide as serious as this. The house will be off-limits to anyone until the investigation is completed, which I anticipate will be at least a day or more."

Sean doesn't mind. "I'll get a room at the Shore Lodge and fly back to San Francisco tomorrow morning. I don't know if I could stand to go back in there anyway. Can I call Bonnie while I'm speaking with you, so that if she has any questions you can answer them for her?"

Jones replies, "Yes, that would be fine. I will need to speak with her in person, at some point."

Sean says, "We will make that happen somehow. I'll make sure to schedule some time for the two of you to speak. Is it all right if I tell Bonnie that Mark has been murdered?"

Jones considers. "I would rather have you call her and let me speak with her about that. Would you please get her on the phone?"

Sean dials Bonnie's number, then hands his phone to Jones.

Bonnie answers with a jovial, "Sean, dear, how are things? Jessica and I were just talking about you."

Jones says, "I'm sorry, ma'am, this isn't Sean. Are you Bonnie Stevens?"

Bonnie answers cautiously, "Yes, I am. Who is this?"

Jones clears his throat. "Mrs. Stevens, this is Sergeant Keith Jones from the Valley County Sheriff's Office. Unfortunately, I have some bad news about your husband, Mark. It appears he was murdered, either late last night or early this morning. I'm so very sorry for your loss."

Jessica watches from the pool as Bonnie's expression goes from happy, to blank, to shocked, and her phone drops out of her hand as she tips over in a dead faint. Jessica quickly gets out of the pool and yells for the staff to help her. They immediately start attending to Bonnie, fanning her and pressing a cool cloth to her face.

Jess picks up the phone and says, "Hello?"

Jones asks, "Mrs. Stevens?"

"No, this is Jessica Silva. Bonnie fainted. What's going on?"

Jones looks at Sean and asks, "Who is Jessica Silva?"

Sean reaches for his phone, and Jones allows him to take it back. "Jessica, is Bonnie okay?"

Jessica replies anxiously, "Um, no, not really. What the hell is going on?"

Sean is at a loss. "The Valley County Sheriff's Department is with me. It appears Mark was murdered. I had just gotten to the house this morning and I found him on the deck."

Jessica's mouth drops open as she gasps. "Oh my God, Sean. I'll make arrangements for us to head back soon. How did this happen?"

"He was shot in the head," Sean barely gets the words out of his mouth before his voice breaks and he feels the bile start to rise again. Jessica feels the horror seeping into her stomach.

Jones takes the phone back and says, "The investigation has just started. Mr. Green will be staying at the Shore Lodge tonight and heading back to San Francisco tomorrow. I will need to meet with Mrs. Stevens in a few days, and Mr. Green assured me they will be able to fly back to this area soon. Will you be able to join them?"

Jessica replies, "Of course I will. Bonnie is my closest friend."

Jones thanks her and attempts to end the conversation. "We should have some more definitive information for everyone by then."

"Thank you, Sergeant. Oh, Bonnie's waking up I think..."

Sean has regained some of his composure and takes the phone from Jones. He hears Bonnie's hysterics in the background. "Jess, why don't you and Bonnie head back to San Francisco, and I'll meet you at the airport."

Jessica returns to the phone from speaking soothingly to Bonnie. "No, it's okay. Bonnie's car is at the airport. I can drive her home. Why don't you meet us at their house? Can you call the family doctor and ask him to prescribe something for me to pick up for Bonnie? She is a mess, and I suspect it's only going to get worse."

"Yes, of course. Let me know when you'll be getting back as soon as you can," Sean answers. Jess agrees, and they terminate the call.

Next, Sean telephones Evelyn, tells her about Mark, and asks her to have his pilot come get him tomorrow morning at nine. Sean then asks if Evelyn can meet him at the airport and drive him to Bonnie's house, since he plans on being thoroughly drunk by the time he lands in San Francisco.

Evelyn replies, "Of course I can, but don't you think you might need to be functional when you arrive, if for no other reason than Bonnie? You can always get completely drunk later."

Sean agrees, but says, "I'll still need you to drive me tomorrow, probably. I won't get trashed, but I'm also not going to drive if I've been drinking on the plane, which I do still intend to do."

Evelyn replies, "Of course, you got it. What about Mark and Bonnie's cars?"

Sean asks, "Can you arrange with Mark's staff to pick up his car? Jessica said she will drive Bonnie's home from the airport. And can you do me another favor?"

Evelyn's voice is sympathetic. "Anything, Sean."

"Please get the number for the board president of Global Metal Refining. I need to let him know immediately so he can handle the press over the next few days," Sean says tiredly.

Evelyn replies, "I'll have it to you within the hour. I will also notify Jessica's personal assistant, so he can clear her schedule as well. Sean, how are you doing?"

There's a long pause, and Sean finally answers, "I'm distraught, shocked, worried, and pissed all rolled into one big mess. I can't believe any of this is real. Thank you for everything you do for me."

"Of course. Let me get started on getting the numbers for notifications. I'll also have some flowers delivered to Bonnie's before she gets home. I'll notify her staff immediately. Everything is going to be okay, at least as far as I can make it."

Sean thanks Evelyn and hangs up the phone.

⇥⊹ ⊹⇤

Jessica goes into the villa to check on Bonnie and finds her sitting catatonically on the bed, staring out the bedroom window. She pauses; biting her lip, then walks into the room, sits on the bed beside Bonnie, and touches her leg.

"I'm here, sweetheart. What can I do?" she asks quietly.

Bonnie tips into Jess's embrace and says, "Just hold me for now, please."

Jess nods and sits with her arms wrapped around Bonnie, saying nothing for what seems like forever until Bonnie suddenly bursts into uncontrollable sobbing. It's the type of crying that racks the entire body and soul, causing hyperventilation and utter exhaustion. Jessica sits silently weeping with her friend, stroking Bonnie's hair until her sobs subside.

After a while, Bonnie breaks the silence with a question that stabs Jessica's heart. "Jess... what am I going to do?"

Jessica tightens her arms around her friend and replies, "Dear, you are going to grieve and miss him tremendously, and then somehow find the strength to go on living. I don't have any definite answers for you, but I know you will never be alone as long as I live. I love you, hun, more than you will ever know."

Bonnie responds by holding Jess tighter, too, and she says in a broken whisper, "I love you, too."

After a short while, Bonnie falls asleep in Jessica's arms. Jess guides her into a more comfortable position, covering her with a blanket to let her sleep and knowing it will be short-lived. Next, she goes downstairs to speak with the devastated staff, assuring them nothing will change with their employment. They are secure. She asks for their loyalty on behalf of Bonnie. All the staff agrees enthusiastically, and Jessica begins making arrangements to get Bonnie home, and to make dealing with the onslaught of details and complications awaiting them in San Francisco a little bit easier.

Next, Jessica calls Sean back with the tentative plan for their return. Sean informs Jess of all the notifications that Evelyn has already made and asks her to text him when she and Bonnie are about fifteen minutes from the front gate of Bonnie's home.

"I expect a lot of media will be camped outside waiting for a chance to speak with anybody, especially Bonnie. I hired a security team already, to prevent the media from getting close to any of us until we are ready to face the circus. How is she doing?"

Jessica peeks in on her in the bedroom, then murmurs back, "As well as can be expected, but none of this seems real to either of us."

"Yeah, I know. I still can't believe it, and I'm the one that found him. Jessica, it was horrible." His voice catches a bit at the end.

Jess shakes her head sadly. "I can't even imagine what you're going through. Is there anything I can do for you?"

Sean replies, "Yes. Please just take care of Bonnie. Evelyn is helping me arrange everything on this end. And, by the way, I might need someone to confide in after this has blown over a little more. Maybe we can talk then?"

Surprised by the vulnerability in his voice, she replies, "Of course. I'm here for both you and Bonnie. This is just a horrible situation."

"Yes, it is. Thank you," Sean says, and they hang up.

After his second conversation with Jessica, Sean asks if there is anything else Sergeant Jones needs from him at this point and is told to go get some rest. Sean gives Jones Bob's name explaining he is his groundskeeper and asks Jones to call him when the investigation is concluded, so he can secure the house.

"Well," Jones says, "it'll be a few days, I think. And we're going to dust for fingerprints, so you might want to have someone clean after the investigation team is done to make sure all the biohazard materials are disposed of properly."

Sean replies, "I believe Bob will take care of all those details. Thank you, Sergeant."

He heads over to the Shore Lodge. He checks into his room and immediately heads to the bar. Seating himself, he orders Jameson Midleton.

As the bartender moves to pour his drink, Sean says, "Give it to me straight and keep pouring until I leave."

The bartender places the bottle on the bar and says uncomfortably, "Sir, I can only serve—"

Sean waves a hand, interrupting him midsentence, and says, "Never mind. Just put the unopened bottle on my room tab. I'll drink it there."

The bartender eyes him for a moment, then replies, "Very well. As you wish, sir." He pushes the bottle across the bar, and Sean signs for it. Pulling the bottle off the bar, he heads straight to his lake-view suite to drink while staring out at the lake. When the Midleton is nearly gone, he passes out in his chair. Waking at two-thirty in the morning, he gets up, goes to the bathroom, and then climbs into bed. When his alarm goes off at eight, Sean's head is heavy, and his eyes despise the warm sunlight streaming in through the window. He is dehydrated, and he knows he has to get moving to meet his pilot at the airport for his return trip to California and all the chaos awaiting him.

While Sean was abusing his senses and liver, Sergeant Jones and the Idaho State Police forensics team have been scouring his home. From their initial assessment, it is clear this is a homicide, not a suicide. No weapon is located in the home aside from the guns in Sean's safe—no shell casings, not even a sign anyone else had been in the home besides Mark Stevens. Multiple latent fingerprints are located on various surfaces, and while they don't know yet, everyone on the team suspects they will be identified through elimination fingerprinting as belonging to individuals with reason to be in the home, and therefore of no evidentiary value. The team determines the fatal shot had to have come from the surface of the lake, meaning the murderer had to have made the shot from a boat or barge, thus indicating advanced firearms training and skill. They decide the killer is most likely military, former military, or law enforcement. However, this is Idaho, and many hunters also have the ability to make this type of shot. Based on their preliminary trajectory calculations, this was a three hundred to four hundred and fifty yard shot. What unnerves the investigators the most is that a .308 caliber weapon is the weapon of choice for many military or law enforcement trained snipers, not for big-game hunters. To their discomfort, Mark's death appears to be a professional hit.

The initial background investigation information on Mark indicates that he previously held government contracts and has international business contracts, including foreign government contracts. Unfortunately, at this point, there are many more questions then there are answers. The Valley County Sheriff's office

has requested and received assistance from the McCall fire department dive team, who has set up a grid search pattern on Payette
Lake based on the forensic team's trajectory estimates. The search
area involves water in the depth range of fifty feet.

Detectives for the Sheriff's department and the Idaho State police have interviewed neighbors and staff members at the marina.
None of the neighbors heard or remember anything out of the ordi-
nary, and many of them express dismay that such a thing could happen in McCall. The detectives interviewing the marina staff focus on
a barge moored on the east side and two pontoon boats. The staff
advises that the barge had just been brought in last night for the upcoming holiday. It is owned by the McCall Chamber of Commerce
and is used for the town's 4th of July fireworks celebration.

Both pontoon boats are owned by regulars and have not been
out of the marina since last weekend, according to the marina's
records. Nevertheless, after contacting the owners to determine
whether or not either vessel has been tampered with or was of any
further interest, the detectives retrieve the records. Initial reports
from the dive team are disheartening. Nothing has been found,
but the search continues. The forensics team takes photographs
with appropriate measurements of the body's location, then finds
and removes the spent .308 round in the living room wall. It had
struck a thin piece of metal art, penetrating the artwork and lodg-
ing in a stud behind the drywall.

Finally, they have the body removed by the local coroner and
continue to process the crime scene. The brainstorming among
the investigators keeps coming back to the possibility that this was
a professional execution. Yet most of the background they have
received on Mark indicates that he was an upstanding citizen, with
no nefarious business associations whatsoever. Motive at this point
is clearly lacking, and as is always the case, Bonnie Stevens is being
considered as a person of interest, since she presumably has the
most to gain from Mark's death.

The detectives quickly determine they will need additional assistance. The Sheriff's department contacts the Federal Bureau of Investigation's Boise office. They are connected with special agent in charge (SAC), Dominic Hughes. Dominic is a meticulous guy in his early fifties who believes first appearances dictate peoples' initial impression on the type and quality of one's character. His mannerisms are quiet, precise, and calculated. He is the type of gentleman who wouldn't say "shit" if he had a mouth full of it. After a thorough briefing on the events and findings so far, Hughes instructs Jones to secure the scene until the FBI's regional forensic team out of Salt Lake City, Utah, can get to McCall. He assures the investigators already on scene that it won't be more than six hours. Hughes also decides to send four agents up from the Boise office to conduct operations from this point forward. He instructs them to brief him on Monday morning about their findings. The FBI pulls records of known retired and active Special Forces personnel in the area, and Hughes instructs the agents from the Boise field office to begin their interviews with those records.

Hughes then has other agents pull background information on Mark and Global Metal Refining. However, they find no suspicious activity and no connections to questionable organizations or organized crime. Hughes contacts his counterpart in the San Francisco office, who begins looking into Sean Green and SGM, and checks out financial records for the Stevens through Mark's attorney, Todd Stoddard.

Meanwhile, the IRS agents who had been alerted by the San Francisco office have begun tracking Global Metal Refining's international accounts. Agents from the San Francisco office quickly learn that Mark has a personal net worth of slightly more than twenty-two billion dollars, while Global Metal Refining is valued around eighty billion. According to Mark's attorney, there are two primary beneficiaries to Mark's estate. Bonnie, his wife, is the first, along with his only living relative, a sister in San Diego, by the name of Wendy Stevens. Mr. Stoddard politely refuses to give any more specifics about Mark's personal affairs, claiming attorney-client privilege with Mrs. Stevens, without first receiving a subpoena.

The San Francisco FBI agents tell Mr. Stoddard they will have a subpoena duces tecum for him on Monday morning.

Mr. Stoddard is agreeable. "Very well. Why don't you come by my office around eleven that morning, so I can produce all the records you wish at that time?" The agents agree.

⊨⊹ ⊹⊨

The FBI forensics team out of Salt Lake arrives in McCall around eight at night. The entire investigative team—made up of members from the Valley County sheriff's office, Idaho State police, McCall fire department dive team, FBI agents from the Boise office, and the Valley coroner's office—is present for the final briefing prior to officially turning the case over to the FBI. The lead agent from the Boise office, Jay Mather, is a taller man approximately six feet, athletic, with an obsession for marathon running but despite his rugged appearance, he has an endearing quirky smile. He is highly perceptive and his smile often hides his brashness. Jay requests all agency reports be completed and delivered to him via e-mail by Monday at 1300 hours, so he can brief SAC Hughes.

After the briefing concludes, the FBI forensic team begins analyzing and reconstructing the bullet's trajectory from the data provided at the final briefing. Using laser technology, the team determines the previously searched area is too close, and the fatal shot was actually taken from a distance of more than five hundred yards.

Agent Mather calls the McCall fire department team captain and requests assistance for Sunday morning with a new area to grid-pattern search.

"If any potential item is located, please just mark it in place and one of my certified diving agents will accompany anyone you send to retrieve it. We don't want to risk disrupting the chain of evidence, and two pairs of eyes are better than one," he tells the captain. "Thank you in advance for your team's assistance, and I'll see you all tomorrow morning at nine."

Next, Mather requests assistance from the Valley County sheriff, asking her if her marine patrol deputies can block off the portion of the lake that still needs to be searched to keep the area clear of nosy boaters. With everything scheduled and the crime scene secured, the teams all get some much needed rest for the evening.

⇒+ +⇐

Early the next morning, the FBI team arrives to relieve the local deputies and take control of the scene for complete processing. With the bullet trajectory established to their satisfaction, measurements, sketches, and overall photographs, as well as those that require a one-to-one scale, are taken, documenting the blood spatter. Samples of the spatter are collected, and electrostatic technology is employed to lift foot and shoe impressions off the deck, kitchen floor tile, and the entry tiles. Swabs for DNA are taken from the coffee cup on the deck and a glass in the kitchen sink. Latent fingerprints are lifted, and a video documenting the scene as well as the reconstruction is made and entered into evidence. Late Sunday afternoon, the dive team completes its grid search of the new coordinates, unfortunately revealing nothing of evidentiary value to the case. The house is finally secured for the evening and released to Sean's groundskeeper, who decides cleanup will begin the next morning.

Sean has already returned to San Francisco when Bob calls to inform him that the FBI forensics team has released the house back to him. Sean instructs him to have the home thoroughly cleaned, with repairs made as soon as possible, and to have the entire deck replaced immediately, regardless of the cost. The groundskeeper sounds doubtful.

"My best friend and number one client was just killed on that deck. I want it replaced and I don't care what you have to do to make that happen," Sean says firmly.

Finally, Bob agrees, promising it will be done with no hassle for Sean.

Sean thanks him, saying, "If I forget, remind me I told you there is a ten-thousand-dollar bonus coming to you if this is all done before I have to return to Idaho."

"Yes, sir!" comes the excited response from Bob.

CHAPTER 15

FREAK SHOW

Jessica and Bonnie send Sean a text saying, "We are about fifteen minutes from the front gate of the estate." Sean alerts security to anticipate their arrival, reiterating that no press, not even the limited amount currently outside, is to get near either of them.

As the women pull into the estate, there is surprisingly little commotion from the minuscule gathering of reporters. Sean thinks, *the security team has done their job exceedingly well tonight, thank goodness.* Still, he wonders if the same will hold true after the major news stations learn of the tragedy that has befallen the Stevens. He pauses a moment longer, thinking of how McCall will never really be the same for him again.

When Bonnie and Jessica enter the house, they are amazed at the overwhelming smell of fresh cut flowers and visually moved by the prominent array of their beauty. It is all too much for Bonnie, who slumps to the floor and weeps, all the while cursing herself for not being a stronger woman. Both Jessica and Sean sit on the floor in the estate foyer, crying with Bonnie and reassuring her that she is, in fact, an amazingly strong woman to whom the world has delivered an immensely brutal blow.

"You are amongst friends, Bonnie, and we'll be here to help," Sean murmurs reassuringly.

Jessica agrees. "It's safe to let down your guard and grieve. We will support you, no matter what."

Bonnie looks up through tear-filled eyes, mascara running down her cheeks, and asks, "Will you—will you stay with me tonight? I don't believe I can handle being here alone."

Sean and Jessica agree they will both stay at the estate tonight, and maybe even for the next few nights to come. Bonnie rises from the floor, and Sean and Jessica stand with her. She gives them both a hug, then goes to the flowers to read the many cards attached.

After a few moments, she turns and says in a wobbly voice, "You both are good friends. Thank you for the flowers and lovely sentiments." Sean has Bonnie's staff take his things to the guest bedroom, while Bonnie has her and Jessica's things taken to the master bedroom.

She asks, "Jess, would you stay up and talk with me a little longer tonight?"

Jessica just nods. Sean excuses himself, sensing they need some time alone, and retires to the room he is staying in. Upon entering his bedroom, he receives a phone call from Frank Dodge, president of the board of Global Metal Refining.

"I apologize for the late evening call, Mr. Green, but I have to request your presence at the press conference tomorrow morning at eleven. Is that manageable?" Mr. Dodge asks.

Sean agrees, albeit a little reluctantly.

"Thank you. Also, corporate counsel was able to pull enough legal and political strings to get the Security Exchange Commission to freeze Global Metal Refining's stock and suspend trading for Monday. The stock will be able to reopen first thing Tuesday morning, after investors have some time to consider the ramifications and options presented during the morning's press announcement of Mark's murder."

Sean asks, "Who else is going to be at the press conference?"

Frank replies, "The initial lineup consists of SAC Dominic Hughes, who will be flying in from Boise in the morning and will start off the conference with a very brief series of events. Hughes will be followed by SAC of the San Francisco FBI office David Hill. SAC Hill will comment on what steps are being taken nationally and internationally and hopefully dispel concerns about terrorist or criminal associations on the part of Mark or Global Metal Refining. Then I'll give the information the two of us deem is appropriate. If you wish, I'll turn the microphone over to you so you can say something. If not, I'll conclude the press conference."

Sean says, "I don't wish to speak tomorrow. Even if I did, I'm not sure I would be able to at this point."

Frank replies, "I understand. I just wanted you to have the opportunity if you wished."

"Thanks, but not this time,"

The two of them lay out Frank's press statement and then say goodnight. Sean goes to speak with Jessica and Bonnie to let them know when the press conference will be tomorrow. He alerts the security team to be prepared for an onslaught of press shortly after the conference and reminds them of his instructions to keep the media away, primarily from Bonnie and secondarily from Jessica.

"Any reporter crashing the gate or entering the property without permission is to be detained until local authorities can deal with the criminal charges," Sean orders. The security supervisor reassures Sean he understands his instructions completely and there won't be a problem. Feeling slightly better, Sean retires yet again to his bedroom.

He attempts, without success, to get some sleep. His thoughts and emotions haunt him during the night. At three in the morning, he finally gets up, leaves the estate, and drives to his Sacramento Street penthouse. Sean takes a long shower, fixes some really strong coffee, and then heads to his office to gather some things he will need to work on for Global Metal Refining and the Beauty Boutique. Evelyn is surprised to see Sean in his office when she arrives at seven-thirty.

"I couldn't sleep, and I have a press conference with Mr. Dodge in about an hour," Sean explains to Evelyn's curious look.

She nods and says, "I cleared your calendar for two weeks. You need to take some time for yourself, to grieve."

"Thank you for all you have done and for putting up with me for so many years, but I'll be okay."

Evelyn responds with a nod. "I had to, because no one else is as much of a saint as I am. Besides, you would irritate a lesser woman."

Sean chuckles for the first time in two days, then says, "You're right, and I'm lucky to have you." Evelyn smiles and softly closes the door behind her, allowing Sean some time to be alone with his thoughts.

He emerges from his office in time to head to Global Metal Refining's corporate headquarters just a few blocks from his office. He is greeted by Frank Dodge's executive assistant and ushered into a private office.

Sean glances around at the polished wood furniture, then says, "Hello, Frank. How are things around here?"

Frank is visibly antsy and responds with his usual sarcasm, "Couldn't be any better. It's a freak show here today, what did you expect?"

Sean smiles and answers, "Yeah, I guess that was a stupid question, wasn't it?"

"You bet your sweet ass it was," replies Frank.

SACs Dominic Hughes and David Hill arrive a few minutes later. Everyone properly introduces themselves and condolences are offered by the FBI's agents for the loss of Mark. The four men walk into the press conference area, and Sean immediately takes a seat as SAC Hughes takes the podium.

When Hughes looks up, he sees the room is packed with local and national reporters. He takes a quick sip of water, then in his usual soft spoken and articulate manner begins with his opening statement. Hughes introduces himself first, as the special agent in charge from Boise. He then introduces the other speakers for the day, starting with David Hill and then referring to Frank Dodge. No mention is made about Sean, per his prior request. SAC Hughes offers condolences, first to Mark's family, then to all of the employees of Global Metal Refining.

"I'll begin with the facts," Hughes says. "Sometime, either on Friday evening or Saturday morning, Mr. Mark Stevens was fatally shot at a private home in McCall, Idaho. His body was found fairly early Saturday morning by his personal friend, business associate, and owner of the residence, Mr. Sean Green. Local authorities were summoned to the residence and the McCall Police Department secured the scene, followed by deputies of the initial lead agency, the Valley County sheriff's department. The deputies recognized their need for assistance, due to the departments inadequate experience level, and requested assistance from the Idaho State police forensic crime lab. Several hours into their investigation, the teams recognized potential jurisdictional conflicts could possibly involve international issues, and both agencies requested assistance from the FBI. After being briefed of the findings to that point, I felt it was necessary to assign Jay Mather as our lead agent and dispatched the FBI regional forensics team from Salt Lake. The forensics team arrived on scene and was briefed by all local agencies. Then the case was officially handed over to Agent Mather and the Boise field office. I contacted SAC David Hill to request his assistance with interviews and further follow-up investigation needed here in California. That is all I have currently. SAC Hill will advise you of the preliminary concerns addressed by the San Francisco field office. SAC Hill?"

David Hill is a no nonsense hard driving man who is known for his expertise in financial analysis and white collar crimes, blunt speech and profanity. He takes the podium and expresses his condolences to the relevant people. Next, he outlines for the press the fact that initial concerns included any possible links to hostile foreign governments, terrorist organizations, and organized crime on the part of Mark Stevens.

"However," Hill continues, over the mutters of the press, "I am glad to report that no nefarious business associations were discovered involving Mr. Stevens, his family, Global Metal Refining, or subsidiaries. We will be happy to answer your questions at the conclusion of the opening statements, but for now, I will turn the microphone over to Frank Dodge."

Frank nods to Hill as they trade places. "I have no words to express my dismay and deep sorrow on behalf of everyone associated with Global Metal Refining. I extend my utmost condolences to the Stevens family and Mr. Green. The board of directors has appointed Ms. Charlotte Evans as the interim CEO of Global Metal Refining." Dodge continues, describing Evans' twenty-year work history and her education, which also includes her rise through the ranks to chief operating officer and then to president of the international division. "Ms. Evans is currently enroute back to San Francisco from Hong Kong and will be available to the press early next week." Frank concludes his remarks with assurances that while everyone is deeply saddened over Mr. Stevens' tragic and untimely death, he would have wanted and expected Global Metal Refining to go on without him, and that is precisely what everyone within the organization must do, even while grieving his loss tremendously.

Frank then turns the time remaining over to the press. Reporter after reporter peppers the FBI with questions surrounding the investigation.

"Why was Mr. Stevens in McCall?" one calls out.

Frank replies, "I was told he was taking a mini-vacation and working with Mr. Green on business strategies." SAC Hill makes a gesture that he and Hughes will field the questions from here on out, and Frank takes a step back.

"Was Mr. Green in McCall at the time of Mr. Stevens' death?"

SAC Hughes answers, "No, he was not."

"What type of weapon killed Mr. Stevens?"

Hughes answers, "It was a high-powered rifle."

"What type of rifle and caliber?"

Hill chuckles and replies, "Sorry, those types of details will not be disclosed."

"Has the murder weapon been located?"

Hughes replies, "Not at this time."

"Do you have any suspects?"

"We're not going to answer that question,"Hill says, smirking.

"Does the FBI have any ideas about motive?"

"That is currently under investigation," replies Hughes.

"Could this have been a suicide or an accidental shooting?"

"At this point in the investigation, we believe Mr. Stevens was murdered," Hughes says, and points to the next reporter.

"Will Mr. Green answer any questions?"

Hughes shakes his head. "Not at this time. As you can imagine, he is quite distraught over the loss."

SAC Hill steps in again having enough of the media's bullshit and says, "Thank you all for coming. That will be all for today."

With that announcement, all four men leave the room and regroup in the private office. They debrief over the press conference, and all of them are left feeling like it went well. David Hill drives Dominic Hughes to the airport for his return trip to Boise, Sean heads to Bonnie's house, and Frank begins the horrendous task of fielding telephone calls from investors, stockbrokers, clients, vendors, and foreign dignitaries. Frank tells his staff to direct all calls from the press to the public relations department and begins getting ready for the stocks to open tomorrow morning.

Sean arrives back at Bonnie's around one in the afternoon to find Bonnie and her staff answering call after call from friends. Sean notices a mildly attractive petite brunette in her mid-forties sitting with Jessica and Bonnie.

Bonnie glances up, places her hand over the mouthpiece of the phone, and gestures at the brunette. "Oh, Sean, you're back. Thank goodness. This is Mark's little sister, Wendy. She flew up from San Diego early this morning."

Sean extends his hand to shake Wendy's, but Wendy doesn't reciprocate, saying, "I'm sorry, but it's a phobia of mine. Most people don't wash their hands, and many of them recently masturbated. I hope you understand."

Sean makes a face, then raises his eyebrows and chuckles. "Well, given that scenario, I guess I don't have a choice."

Wendy gives Sean a once-over and then says, "Most people don't think of how nasty other people's hygiene habits truly are these days."

Feeling tired and out of patience, Sean sighs at Wendy's apparent drama. "Well, I hadn't until you brought it up."

Wendy sneers and asks, "Are you always this snarky?"

Sean snorts and replies shortly, "Only with drama queens." He turns away, walks farther into the house, and asks the staff for a double scotch on the rocks.

Jess follows him, "Can I join you? She is kind of in your face, isn't she?"

Sean shakes his head and grins. "Of course you can join me. And I'm glad you think so as well. I was beginning to wonder if it was just me being an ass again."

She considers for a moment. "Maybe a little impatient and rude, but not necessarily an ass. Frankly, she had it coming. She's been that way all day."

"Maybe. I'm just tired, emotionally drained, and I also never knew Mark had a sister, let alone one living so close. How the hell can you know someone as long as I've known Mark without knowing he had a sibling?" He accepts his scotch from a staff member with a nod, and Jessica does the same.

"Perhaps he didn't want anyone to know that about him," she replies.

"But why not?" asks Sean. "Why would you hide someone that significant?"

Jessica shakes her head and shrugs. "I have no idea, but I did know him fairly well, and from that I can say I'm sure he had his reasons. Wendy hasn't necessarily been forthcoming about it either."

Just then, Wendy walks in and asks if she can speak with Sean alone. Jessica glances at him for approval and, when he nods, says, "I'll just excuse myself and talk with Bonnie out on the patio. Both of you try to be nice. Nerves are a bit frazzled for all of us right now."

Sean lifts his scotch toward Jessica as if to say, "You got it," while Wendy nods in acknowledgement. Satisfied, Jessica leaves them alone.

Wendy starts the conversation with a quick apology for her reaction to Sean. They chat a while, and Wendy begins to feel comfortable. "I'm not sure if I want to share the information I am about to disclose, and it makes me very nervous, which doesn't come off well. You seem like the best person to tell this secret to. What I'm about to tell you is to remain confidential between the two of us. It is never to be disclosed to Bonnie under any circumstances. Is that clear?" Wendy asks.

Sean ponders for a moment and then says, "I'm not sure if I can agree to something like that without knowing any specifics. Not to mention there's still a criminal investigation being conducted, and I don't want to know anything about Mark that I can't disclose to the investigators."

Wendy replies, "I understand. However, it's nothing like that. You can disclose anything I'm about to tell you to anyone *except* Bonnie. This information would be devastating to her and her image of her late husband, and she doesn't need that right now."

Sean says curiously, "Okay then. You have my confidence."

Wendy takes a deep breath and begins by telling Sean, "Mark was a very secretive man with an extremely dark past—"

Sean interrupts. "Not the Mark I knew."

Wendy sighs and asks Sean to please let her finish before speaking again, because what she is about to relay is very difficult for her to speak about. Sean nods affirmatively, a small pit of dread beginning to build in his stomach.

Wendy continues, "Okay. Mark was extremely brutal in his business practices to start with. Global Metal Refining began simply as Metal Refining. Our father was the original owner, and it was a small regional enterprise until after Mark graduated from college and began working for Dad as an operations manager. Mark was able to cut costs and increase profitability, while also recruiting excellent employees. Dad saw Mark's business skills along with the potential to expand the company from a regional enterprise into a national organization. Mark saw the company as a global organization and began pushing Dad to consider larger things for the company, like going public with placement onto the New York Stock Exchange. Dad told Mark he had no intention of taking the company public as long as he was alive, further explaining that Mark would get his chance to do whatever he wanted with the company after Dad's death. Well, our family has always had longevity on its side, so while Mark was only in his early thirties and Dad was in his mid-fifties, Mark knew his dreams for Metal Refining would not be realized for another forty years or so." Wendy pauses for a shaky breath.

"Anyway, Mark decided the best way to realize his dreams was to take over Metal Refining by ousting his own father. Mark set about silently orchestrating an overthrow, using venture capitalists for the initial purchase of Metal Refining. Through a series of brilliant business moves, Mark was able to oust Dad and get installed as the new president of the company, and then he used the upcoming, yet still fairly prominent, attorney, Todd Stoddard, to take Metal Refining public under the new corporate structure of Global Metal Refining. The two of them were both hungry to make a name for themselves, and from this venture they were able to structure a successful buyout of the venture capitalists. Mark was on his way to achieving his dreams for Global Metal Refining. Because of the hostile takeover, Dad became bitter, at first, then angry and finally despondent. He committed suicide a year later, when Mark was thirty-two and I was nineteen."

She pauses and Sean attempts to wipe the look of dread off his face and understand why she is telling him her life story. He takes a sip of his scotch and motions for her to continue.

"Mom began relying on Mark for support, and Mark took on the tasks that were originally Dad's. Just after I turned twenty, I had a party at the house when both Mom and Mark were out of town. Mark's business meetings ended early, and he came by the house to check on me. When he saw the party in full swing with me both stoned and drunk, he became enraged, kicked everyone out of the house, and shut down the party. After everyone had left, Mark and I started to argue. He called me a drunken whore, and I slapped him across the face. When he spun back around, his fist followed, slamming into my cheekbone. As I lay on the living room carpet crying, Mark grabbed me by the hair and began dragging me to my bedroom. He continued to beat me until he was close enough to throw me on the bed. He pulled the phone cord out of the wall and used it to tie my hands to the headboard, and my feet to the footboard. I continued to yell profanities at him, telling him he was out of control and demanding he untie me. Mark told me that if I wanted to act like a bitch, he would treat me like one. We argued for hours as Mark sat in the chair across from my bed. He drank while we argued, and I continued my verbal assault on his masculinity. Then I made a terrible mistake..." Wendy trails off, sucking in a large breath.

Sean pulls himself out of shock long enough to silently hand her his scotch. She tosses back the rest of the glass's contents and clears her throat.

"I told him he was an overbearing, narcissistic pervert, who killed our father because of his own lust for power and control. When he began beating me again, I said that the only way he could have humiliated me more was to screw me. I watched as this rage filled his eyes, and I was sure he was going to kill me. At that point, Mark walked out of the room, and I heard him make a telephone call. When he came back, he had calmed down. He took another sip of his drink, then said the words that, to this day, still haunt me. 'You have no idea what power and control look like, but you're about to find out.' Then he sat silently, not responding to anything I hurled at him. He simply didn't react. He'd gone stone cold. This went on for what seemed like hours, and then I heard the front door open. Mark called out for the person to come upstairs, then smiled this hate-filled smile that sent chills through my bones. A large male figure arrived wearing a black ski mask, and Mark said, 'Wendy, I'm going to show you what power looks like in the real world, you little snot-nosed slut.' I began crying again when the masked man began cutting off my clothes. Mark told me to plead with him and beg him for mercy or suffer the consequences. My drunken response was a quick 'fuck you.' I would never give him that satisfaction. I thought he was a murdering bastard, but he was even more messed up than I ever knew. The masked man ripped my pants down, revealing everything, because I wasn't wearing underwear. Mark said, 'Beg, you nasty whore.' Again I replied with a 'fuck you.' I watched as the masked man began to remove all of his clothing except the ski mask and put a condom on. He had a tattoo over his heart that I will remember all my life. It was a coiled viper, sinking its fangs into a heart, dripping blood. Mark said, 'This is your last chance. Beg for mercy, or I'll let him do what he wants to you.' As stubborn as I am today, nothing matches the absolute resentment and angst I had in those days."

She begins crying, and then says, "I told Mark to go to hell. His voice was cold and heartless when he said, 'Welcome to my world.' He watched as the masked man raped me repeatedly, all the while insulting me, telling me what a nasty little whore I was. He told his friend to roll me over and humiliate me some more. When his friend said he'd had enough, Mark told him to clean up his condoms and leave. The masked man did as he was told. Mark left me there sobbing for two hours while he told me he had the power to control any fucking slut, whore, or woman he chose to, because he was rich and more powerful than I knew. After he sobered up, he called the police to report I had been raped and he found me tied to the bed. When they arrived, I tried to tell them what Mark had done. Mark told them he was out of town until that morning, when he came home and found me. He gave them names and phone numbers to call for an alibi, and when they checked it out, his story was confirmed. He told the police I was emotionally distraught and disturbed as a result of the attack and had to be placed in a psychiatric facility, where I remained until I stopped blaming him for the vicious assault. No rape kit was done because of Mark's insistence that they not traumatize me any further, and he assured them he would make sure I received proper medical and psychiatric care. He called our mom after the ambulance took me to the facility and explained his version of what had happened. Mom rushed to the hospital. When I insisted on telling her the truth, she got angry and made sure I was medicated. After I got out, I only spoke to Mark once, and he told me I was dead to him. Years later, I found out he had paid all my student loans off. When I confronted him about it, he laughed at me and told me he still had the power to control my life." She sighs and finally concludes, "No one has believed me, so I don't expect you to either, but I swear everything I just told you about my life is true."

Sean sits, stunned, and then says, "Wow. That certainly isn't the Mark I knew." Wendy just drops her head and stares at the carpet. Sean asks hesitantly, "Can I ask you a few questions?"

Her head jerks up and she searches his eyes for what he's thinking. "Sure, why not."

"How is it that Bonnie seems unsurprised that Mark had a sister, but I never knew you existed?"

Wendy explains, "Apparently, a couple of years ago when Mark was drunk, he let it slip about me and Bonnie took it upon herself to find and contact me. We have communicated with each other without Mark's knowledge for years. I have come to love Bonnie, and apparently Mark treated her better than he ever did me, so that's why I don't want her to know any of this. She adored Mark, and she is a good person. She doesn't deserve the pain of knowing what he truly was."

Sean nods and is quiet for a while. "It seemed strange to me that Mark never mentioned you."

Wendy replies matter-of-factly, "It doesn't surprise me. I wanted you to know what I'll tell the FBI if they question me about Mark. Whoever killed my brother is an angel of mercy as far as I'm concerned."

The conversation ends there, and Sean and Wendy head out to rejoin Bonnie and Jessica, who have migrated out to the pool. Bonnie tells them both she has been contacted by Jay Mather, from the FBI, who wants to speak with them as soon as possible.

"I agreed to meet with him early next week, in Boise. He gave me the Valley County coroner's number, and I arranged to have Mark's body shipped to San Francisco for cremation. The memorial service will be scheduled for a week after his body has been returned to me. Nate and Evelyn are coordinating all the details.

They both promised to keep everyone informed as plans are finalized. Also, Mark's attorney, Todd, wants to meet with all of us tomorrow morning for the reading of the will," Bonnie says tiredly.

Sean looks confused, "I don't need to be there for that. None of those details are any of my business."

Bonnie shakes her head and replies, "Todd specifically requested you be there, and I've asked Jessica to come for moral support."

Sean nods, wondering why his presence was requested, and both he and Jess agree to be there at ten o'clock.

The whole entourage arrives at Mr. Stoddard's office just prior to ten in the morning. Mr. Stoddard has everyone sit in the partners' boardroom, overlooking San Francisco Bay. Todd enters the room with a stenographer to record the reading of Mark's last will and testament. After initial introductions, Mr. Stoddard expresses his personal condolences to Bonnie and Wendy. He then thanks Sean for coming and Jessica for supporting Bonnie during this extremely difficult time.

As Todd opens Mark's will, he explains that those who were requested to be present were asked because Mark had named each of them in his will. Todd summarizes for everyone that Mark's personal net worth, as of that day, is twenty-two billion dollars, with Global Metal Refining valued at eighty billion dollars, and he makes sure Bonnie understands that the company value could change dramatically after heavy trading at the closing of the stock market that day.

Todd turns to Bonnie. "You are Mark's primary beneficiary to whom he has left the estate, valued at fifteen billion dollars, and thirty-one percent of his Global Metal Refining stocks."

He glances down at the will and then turns to Wendy. "Mark wanted me to read this short sentence to you. I don't really understand it," he admits, "but it says that you will know what it means. It reads,

'Wendy, with the estate you're about to receive from me, I want you to understand, you are now in total control of your own life.'"

Wendy's cheeks turn bright red, and she shoots a quick glance at Sean. When their eyes meet, she knows that Sean understands Mark is still mocking her, even in death.

Mr. Stoddard continues with, "Mark left you an estate valued at six billion dollars, which includes the beachfront penthouse condominium in San Diego and ten percent of his Global Metal Refining stocks."

A single tear escapes, trailing down Wendy's cheek, and she bows her head, shoulders shaking from silent sobs. Bonnie begins comforting her, thinking, *Poor girl. She must be overwhelmed by Mark's generosity…*

Meanwhile, Sean sits, mortified, realizing that everything Wendy told him about Mark is indeed truthful. The statement Mark left for her proves it. Silently, Sean wishes he had never allowed Wendy to confide in him. After a few moments, Wendy regains her composure, and Mr. Stoddard continues.

"Finally, Sean, Mark left you one billion dollars in assets along with ten percent of the Global Metal Refining stocks. He specifically wanted to tell you this: 'I believe you have reached every goal you set for yourself and us, and my last concern is for you to embrace our success, stop pushing so hard, and enjoy the fruits of your labor.' He also wanted me to mention that he thought you should invest yourself in a mentoring relationship, like the one he had with you. That's all. Do any of you have any questions?"

All of them shake their heads, mutely.

Todd nods and says, "I would like to meet with each of the beneficiaries privately to finalize all the transfer paperwork and, hopefully, be able to establish an ongoing working relationship with all of you as well. Thank you for coming."

As everyone is leaving the partners' boardroom, Wendy grabs Sean's arm and asks, "Can I have a few minutes? In private?"

Sean looks to Mr. Stoddard, who nods that they can use the. "Take all the time you need."

After the door has closed behind him and the others, Wendy looks at Sean and whispers frantically, "That evil motherfucker. What a fucking narcissistic pervert to think I'd accept anything from him!" She turns on her heel and stares out the window. Sean waits for the next wave of anger to come out of her mouth, but she doesn't say anything else.

Finally, Sean speaks. "Wendy, I can't even imagine the horror Mark put you through. But I think the best thing you can do is take his money and do something good with it, for others as well as yourself." Wendy turns and looks at Sean, listening. He sighs. "I knew a different Mark than you did, but after today I have no doubt that everything you told me you went through that horrible night is true."

Wendy takes a shuddering breath. "Thank you. You have no idea what that means to me."

Sean touches her shoulder and continues, "Take the money, condo, and stocks, and help other victims, like yourself. Besides, the best revenge you can get is to live a happy, healthy life, having overcome Mark's sadistic tyranny."

It is the first time in Wendy's life since the night of the party she feels well enough to embrace another person, so she hugs Sean and cries for what seems like an eternity to him, but he silently holds her until she lets go of his neck. After extricating himself from her embrace, he hands her a handkerchief and waits for her to clean up a bit. Then, they go to meet the others and return to Bonnie's house.

CHAPTER 16

A GREAT AND DECENT MAN

S ean calls Bob to see how close the renovations are to being
completed and is informed they will all be done by the end of
the week.

Sean says, "As soon as everything is completed, have a realtor
call me so I can list the house for sale."

Bob clears his throat and says, "Sir, it's not really my place, but that
might not be a good idea so close to the homicide, because everyone
in town is still talking about it. I already took the liberty of speaking
to a friend of mine about it. The property value at this point is significantly reduced, and you'll lose market value to sell it now."

Sean swears. "How much would I be losing?"

"Prior to the murder, the property was worth around one point
three million. Today it would sell for, maybe, three hundred and
ninety thousand. A year from now, it should be back up to around
seven hundred and fifty thousand, with the value returning to
normal in probably two years, after everything calms down and
people forget about the murder."

"Would you be interested in buying the house today for three
hundred and ninety thousand?" Sean asks suddenly.

Stunned Bob says, "Well yes, but I would need some time to find a partner to invest with me."

"How much time?" Sean presses.

"A month or so. Are you serious, Mr. Green?"

"I'm as serious as a heart attack. If you're interested in buying the place, I'll sell it to you and carry the paper. I just can't go back after Mark was killed there. If you hold the property for two years then sell it, you'll have funded your own retirement."

"Consider it sold then."

, "Great, but let me throw in another twist for you."

Bob, somewhat dejected, asks, "And what is that?"

"I'll sell it to you on these terms only: I don't want you to bring on a partner. Tell me what you can afford on a monthly basis. Then we'll structure something fair for both of us. I want you to get the benefit from this relationship, nobody else. Oh, and the ten-thousand-dollar bonus you're going to receive from me should be set aside to help make the first year's payments."

"This is incredible," Bob replies, still stunned. "I can't thank you enough."

Sean asks, "It won't bother you to live there after the murder?"

"No, sir, it won't."

"Very well then. Get back to me on the monthly payment you're comfortable with. Try to make it a bit of a stretch for yourself, and we will structure a fair deal for us both," Sean says and terminates the call.

As soon as he hangs up the phone, Evelyn calls and tells him she just received another call from Agent Mather at the Boise FBI field office.

"He wants to know when you, Bonnie, and Jessica are planning to be in Boise, so he can schedule a meeting."

"Okay, would you set up the interviews in Boise for Friday morning starting at ten, if he's available then?"

"Of course. I'll call you back later with confirmation," Evelyn replies.

"Thank you."

Sean then calls Jessica and Bonnie to inform them about the interviews in Boise. Meanwhile, SAC David Hill contacts Wendy to inform her that since she won't be joining Bonnie, Sean, and Jessica on their trip to Idaho, he would like to schedule a meeting with her in San Francisco.

"Of course, Agent Hill. How about Friday afternoon at three?"

"That would be fine, Ms. Stevens. Thank you. I'll see you at my office."

Friday morning, FBI Agent Jay Mather introduces himself and two other agents to Sean, Bonnie, and Jessica.

"Thank you all for making the trip to Boise to speak with me. I would like to interview Bonnie, and my colleagues will speak with you two," he nods toward Sean and Jessica. "Does that work for everyone?" Everyone agrees. "Wonderful. I believe if we get started right away, we can finish the interviews up today, so let's get this over with, shall we?" Everyone disperses to separate interview rooms.

Mather begins his interview with Bonnie by expressing his condolences for her loss, and then he informs her, "If at any time during this interview it becomes too much for you, we will stop and finish it after the funeral. Okay?"

"I understand, Agent Mather. I would prefer to get this all behind me as soon as possible, as I would like to allow myself some personal time for the grieving process."

Mather nods. "I expect that would be best. Let's begin. Please describe your marriage with Mark."

Bonnie takes a deep breath. "I began working for Mark as a temporary executive assistant while he was still married to his second wife. After we realized our attraction for each other, he confided in me about the fact that his marriage was dissolving and he was getting divorced. We became intimately involved. After a couple of weeks, Mark had finalized his divorce paperwork, and he proposed to me. It was a great marriage, mutually supportive, sexually dynamic, and very satisfying for both of us I think—"

Jay interjects. "So, no problems in the marriage then?"

Bonnie shakes her head. "Not as far as I am concerned. We were both very happy."

"Thank you. Do you have any idea why someone would want to kill your husband?"

Bonnie replies, "I have no idea. He was such a good man, fair to others, and environmentally sensitive in a business where most companies don't care about the planet. They just want its riches, no matter how badly they destroy the earth in the process—"

Once again, Jay interrupts to clarify, "So Global Metal Refining was an eco-friendly organization?"

Bonnie nods, "Absolutely. That's one of the traits I admired most in Mark."

"Do you know anything about Global Metal Refining's problems in Brazil, with Diablo Mining, Inc.?"

Bonnie explains, "I know Diablo Mining was coming under pressure for their mining practices, and when Mark found out what they had been doing, he told them he wouldn't do business with them until they followed proper environmental practices."

Jay raises his eyebrows and asks, "Did Mark tell you that himself?"

Bonnie says, "Yes. Why?"

Jay shakes his head. "No reason. I was just clarifying. Can you explain how Hugo Montes and Ricardo Montes are related?"

Bonnie looks suspicious, then answers. "They are cousins. Hugo has the political power and connections. Ricardo is a player and needs Hugo to help him build his real estate development and management company, so they work closely together."

Jay considers for a moment and then decides he will test the waters. "Would you be shocked if I told you Mark backed the environmental practices Hugo employed in Brazil, in order to maximize the gold delivered to Global Metal Refining?"

Bonnie's eyes widen and she says angrily, "Yes, I would! How dare you try to disparage the good names of my husband and Global Metal Refining!"

Jay holds up his hands in surrender and says, "I apologize. Do you know of any business associate who had any reason to want Mark dead?"

A single tear leaks from Bonnie's eye, but her voice remains strong when she says, "No. He was a great and decent man, who was loved by many, disliked by few, and respected by all."

Mather pauses, taking in the emotion on her face and regrets the next question he has to ask. "I see. So the person who would benefit the most from Mark's death would be you, then?"

Bonnie gasps, sitting upright with her hand on her chest, and looks Agent Mather in the eyes. "I don't like what you are insinuating. If you have grounds to arrest me, then do so now. Otherwise, you can go fuck yourself, because this interview is over!"

Agent Mather sits back, barely refraining from sighing. "You are free to leave at any time," he replies evenly, watching her closely.

Bonnie stands up, walks out the door of the interview room and up to the front desk, and demands to speak with Dominic Hughes immediately.

The receptionist says, "I will see if he's in. Who can I tell him requires his assistance?"

Bonnie replies, "You can tell him that Mrs. Stevens would like to speak with him. If he doesn't have the time, I'll have my pilot fly me to Washington D.C. to speak with the director, instead. Is that clear?"

The receptionist represses a sigh and says, "Yes, ma'am. Quite clear."

Dominic Hughes comes out into the waiting area and escorts the still distressed Bonnie back to his office. When Bonnie begins ranting about her interview, Dominic stops her.

"Mrs. Stevens, Agent Mather has also filled me in on what happened. If you will wait just a minute, I'll have him present in this meeting as well." He steps out of the room for a moment and returns with Agent Mather, who walks up to Bonnie.

"I apologize for the way our conversation ended, but please allow me a few minutes to explain—" he begins.

Bonnie interrupts, "There is no explanation for your accusatory, rude, and disgusting interrogation!"

Hughes says, "Excuse me, ma'am, but yes, there is an explanation. Please, allow Agent Mather the opportunity to explain, and if you are still not satisfied, I'll handle your complaint personally." Bonnie considers for a moment and then nods grudgingly.

Agent Mather takes a breath. "My last question was designed to elicit a reaction from you, Mrs. Stevens. The reaction you displayed is that of an innocent person being wrongfully accused of a very serious crime. Had you not been offended by my insinuation, it would have caused me to look further into you as a person of interest. However, based upon what others have told me about your marriage and your reaction to the 'accusatory, rude, and disgusting' question, it is apparent you loved Mark very much. As such, I have eliminated you as a possible suspect in Mark's murder."

Bonnie glares at him, but her expression slowly clears and she sighs. "Well, I suppose a thank you is in order, but that's a pretty crappy thing to do to someone."

Hughes says, "Yes, unfortunately it is, but it is still one of the most effective in our experience."

Agent Mather smiles ruefully. "The others will be finishing up their interviews shortly. Can I buy you a cup of coffee to apologize?"

Bonnie replies, "A shot of tequila would be much better, but since you're still on duty, a cup of coffee will do. I'd love one."

⊶ ⊷

Jessica's interview is rather uneventful. She is questioned about Mark and Bonnie's marriage, her friendship with Bonnie, and her working relationship with Sean. Jessica explains that Bonnie and Mark referred her to Mr. Green for marketing services for her company. She talks about how she disliked Sean when she met him and how it came about that his firm is now representing her.

"Without Mark and Bonnie, I seriously doubt SGM would have ever taken my company on as a business client, simply because we're small potatoes compared to SGM's other clients," she says. "I have a lot to thank them for, and they have always been wonderful people."

The agent asks, "And how do you know Hugo and Ricardo Montes? What is their connection to Juan Zamora?"

Jessica looks puzzled at how the FBI would know about her connection to Mr. Zamora, but figures they probably know a lot of strange stuff. "Well, I met each of them through Mr. Green. He located a factory that he thought my company might look at as a possible expansion site. I was performing due diligence for Beauty Boutique Clothing, and each of the individuals mentioned was involved, to some degree, in that due diligence," she replies.

The agent asks for examples of their involvement.

Jessica explains, "Ricardo owns and manages the factory. Hugo, in an effort to help Ricardo land a long-term tenant, opened the communication channels into the government, through Juan. As a favor to Juan, I suggested that while I was in Brazil, I could have one of my designs custom-made for his wife. She loves the fact that she owns the first Beauty Boutique design manufactured in Brazil. It was just good marketing. I believe it will shorten and minimize the cost of expedited approvals, thus allowing me to open the factory for production in three or four months."

The agent raises his eyebrow at the questionable business practice of bribing the Brazilian government, but is convinced that Jessica has no knowledge surrounding Mark's murder and concludes his interview with her.

Jessica meets up with Agent Mather and Bonnie at the Starbucks coffee shop in the lobby of the federal building.

Agent Mather welcomes her, then explains, "Sean's interview was expected to be the longest of the three, due to the close working relationship he and Mark shared over the years. They should be done soon though."

The three of them decide to continue in conversation until Sean's interview concludes.

———

Most of Sean's interview is benign, until he is questioned about the struggles Global Metal Refining was experiencing with Diablo Mining, Inc. Sean immediately realizes this could get very difficult because of his smuggling U.S. currency past Brazilian customs in order to buy Hugo Montes' cooperation. He tries to explain.

"Well, I devised a strategy to shift the environmental blame off of Global Metal Refining and onto Diablo Mining as it pertained to Mother Earth Cooperative. Diablo Mining had technically not violated any Brazilian laws, even though all parties knew international best practices were ignored in order to maximize the gold yield for both Diablo Mining and Global Metal Refining," he says, hedging around how he managed a compromise.

The agent presses. "Why would Mr. Montes agree to such a one-sided arrangement?"

Sean's response is plausible. "Because Diablo Mining is a small company in comparison to Global Metal Refining, and if they wanted further contracts with Mark, they had to agree to this arrangement or find themselves losing future contract bids and therefore business."

The agent raises his eyebrows and says, "So, just to confirm, you blackmailed them into acquiescing?"

Sean gives the agent a wry smile and replies, "That's a bit harsh. We simply persuaded them to accept our terms. It's called business."

The agent snorts. "Spin it however you want to, Mr. Green. Mr. Montes didn't really have a choice, did he?"

Sean almost chuckles. "Of course he did, agent. One always has a choice. Fortunately for me, in this case, most people are greedy. When you control the dollars, you control the terms. Mark Stevens taught me that simple fact and I'll never forget it."

The agent scoffs. "Bullshit. The two of you extorted your terms out of Diablo Mining."

Sean presses his fingertips together, feeling a bit frustrated. "It's all a matter of perspective, isn't it? What is your name again, by the way?"

"Bill Parks," the agent replies. He ponders his next question before asking, "So, Sean, who would want Mark dead? Consider your answer carefully, because this same person may want to kill you next."

Sean tries not to act disturbed, but he is actually shocked about the idea. It isn't anything he ever considered, and frankly, he is unsettled by the possible ramifications of the question. The agent notes his distress, but is quiet.

Sean thinks for a moment with several names rattling around in his head, then responds, "I have absolutely no idea who would ever want Mark dead."

Bill sits quietly for what seems like an hour, his piercing eyes locked onto Sean's. When he breaks the silence he says, "Really? Let me see if I can think of a few possibilities for you to consider then. How about Bonnie or Wendy Stevens? Hugo or Ricardo Montes? What about Juan Zamora? Or any one of the members of the Mother Earth Cooperative? Hell, it could even be you."

Sean meets Parks' gaze and says coldly, "You don't think much of me, do you? What the hell is your problem? Besides, what would be my reason, or Bonnie's, or Wendy's, to kill Mark?"

Agent Parks says, "I could think of a billion reasons."

"Well then, maybe you killed him. See how ridiculous that sounds?" Sean counters, annoyed. "What about the others who didn't inherit any money from Mark's estate?"

"Oh, you mean those other individuals whom you and Stevens have controlled and extorted from to make more money?"

Sean, actually angry now because of Agent Parks' juvenile antics, decides to play along just a bit more. "Agent Parks, do you know what I think? I think the FBI hasn't a fucking clue who shot Mark, and every one of you are grasping at straws, hoping to find the proverbial needle in the haystack." Parks laughs out loud but there's an edge to it, and Sean decides to piss him off some more. "Oh and, Bill, I forgot to explain that 'proverbial' means customary, or well-known. Am I free to leave, or do you have more sophomoric theories you would like to espouse?"

Agent Parks sits back in his chair yet again. "You are free to leave at this time, but we very well may wish to discuss matters further with you later."

Sean pats his heart and says, "I cherish the thought." He stands up and walks out of the room. "Where are the others?" he asks the receptionist, and is directed downstairs to meet them in the coffee shop.

The minute Bonnie sees Sean coming; she knows things didn't go well. Sean walks up to her, Jess, and Agent Mather at their table and says, "I don't know about you, but I'm getting on the jet and getting the fuck out of this podunk, redneck town. You two can join me or you can stay, but the jet leaves as soon as I get to the airport." With that, he turns on his heel and heads for the door. Bonnie and Jessica share a moment of confusion, then grab their purses, leave money and a tip at the table with Agent Mather, and hurry after Sean.

When they get into the car, Jessica asks, "What the hell was that all about?"

Sean replies, "I'm just tired of all the bullshit today."

For the rest of the trip, he doesn't say a word. He drinks scotch after scotch until they land in San Francisco. Jessica makes Sean give her his car keys and drives them all back to Bonnie's house. When they arrive, Wendy is waiting for them, reading a book. Sean walks unsteadily past her without acknowledgement, heading straight to his bedroom.

Wendy is about to say something to his back when Jessica touches her arm and murmurs, "Let him go. We'll talk about everything in the morning. Apparently his interview wasn't very cordial." Jessica goes to Sean's room, knocks on the door, and peeks inside. Sean is sitting at his computer, shirtless.

She clears her throat. "Hey, are you okay? Do you want to talk about it?"

Sean looks at her over the top of his computer screen, sigh, then says, "Not tonight. I'm just pissed, and now pretty drunk. We can all talk in the morning, okay?"

Jessica nods and closes the door gently. She stands there for a moment, her hand still on the doorknob, thinking, *oh my God, that man is fine, even when he's pissed.* In that moment, she realizes just how much trouble she is in as far as Sean Green is concerned.

━━◈ ◈━━

The next morning, the four of them sit down to compare observations of their interviews. Bonnie, Jessica, and Wendy want to know what happened in Sean's interview, since his reaction was extreme compared to the others.

Sean explains, "Agent Bill Parks made several accusations about Mark's and my business relationship, suggested that I could potentially have killed Mark for money, and then proceeded to tell me that if I didn't do it, whoever killed Mark may want to come after me next."

All the women are shocked. Recognizing his comments are disturbing to the others, he adds, "It just shows that they have no idea who killed Mark." Attempting to change the subject, he asks Wendy, "How was your interview here?"

Wendy shrugs. "I met with David Hill, who was absolutely charming. He asked about Mark growing up, our relationship as kids, and then about our adult relationship. When I told him Mark and I really didn't have much of a relationship as adults, he asked me to explain why." She glances over at Sean momentarily, and he knows Wendy disclosed everything that caused the rift between the two of them.

Bonnie fingers her coffee mug. "You know, you never have discussed the reasons you two never spoke as adults. What did happen?"

Wendy touches Bonnie's hand gently and says, "It's a long story, dear. But the short version is that Mark was into making money and I just wanted to help people. Perhaps that's why he took over Dad's company and I became a counselor specializing in treatment for domestic abuse victims. We simply saw the world too differently. Did I ever tell you, I found out years after Mark and I stopped talking that he was the person who anonymously paid off all my student loans, all the way through my PhD?"

Bonnie smiles as a tear rolls down her cheek. "No, you didn't. That was just like Mark."

Wendy swallows and replies, "Yes, it was, dear."

Sean sits there, unable to fathom Wendy's strength. *What a kind gesture that was, for Wendy to turn a horrible circumstance into a loving memory for Bonnie,* he thinks. He wonders if he would have been able to be so kind had he gone through all that Wendy had endured.

The conversation is abruptly interrupted by a telephone call from Nate and Evelyn. Jessica puts them on speakerphone so they don't have to repeat everything separately. They explain that all the plans for Mark's memorial have been made. They reserved Grace Cathedral for the service and emailed the program to Jessica for Bonnie's approval.

"Sean," Evelyn asks, "will you be up to delivering the eulogy?"

Sean nods. "It would be my honor." He looks to Bonnie. "Unless you have someone else in mind?"

Bonnie shakes her head. "I would love it if you delivered the eulogy."

Nate chimes in, "Our intent was to keep the service under two hours, but several people have contacted us wanting to speak on Mark's behalf. A senator, some business associates, and a few friends have come forward so far."

Bonnie asks, "Can we please keep it under two hours? I don't think I can endure much more while still maintaining my composure."

Nate and Evelyn agree that they will make sure that change occurs, then request approval on the program as soon as possible.

Bonnie says, "Hold on, I'll have Jessica pull it up right now."

After reviewing the program, Bonnie approves it and thanks them for all their hard work in preparing everything.

Sean asks, "Did you allow time for the press to ask questions?"

Evelyn replies, "After the service, we have reserved time for a brief press conference with questions and answers for them. We were hoping you would handle that immediately after Bonnie leaves the church."

Sean sighs and says, "I knew it was coming. It might as well be then, so I can just be done with it."

Nate says, "There is one other thing everyone should be aware of. The FBI will be at the service, but they have promised to keep an extremely low profile, so if you recognize one of the agents, just ignore them and they will do the same for you. From our best estimate, we are expecting around twenty-five hundred people to be in attendance. We've already informed everyone there will be no reception following the service, because the next of kin has requested privacy. Bonnie, we've also set up a charity foundation in Mark's name for any donations, specifically to help with environmental problems, and you are the chairperson of the foundation. We named it the Stevens Environmental Relief Fund."

Bonnie starts to cry and says through her sniffles, "Thank you. I'll make sure Mark is honored through this foundation."

With all the plans for Mark's memorial in place, Wendy, Bonnie, and Sean schedule appointments with Todd Stoddard to complete all the necessary transfer documents. Wendy informs Mr. Stoddard that she will find other legal representation in San Diego and will not be in need of any further services from him or his office.

"Pardon me, Ms. Stevens, but why?" Todd inquires.

Wendy is very blunt as she states, "Because, Mr. Stoddard, I hold both you and Mark responsible for my father's death." Todd is surprised and says so, so Wendy explains, "You're the asshole who assisted Mark in the hostile takeover of Metal Refining, which caused my father to lose his company, become despondent, and commit suicide."

When Todd attempts to protest, Wendy interrupts, saying, "I don't want to hear your excuses. I'll simply take my six billion dollars and find other counsel. Have a nice life." With that, Wendy terminates the conversation. Both Bonnie and Sean, however, decide to remain clients of Mr. Stoddard.

CHAPTER 17
A DAY AT A TIME

Grace Memorial is a beautiful, iconic chapel in San Francisco. Today, it is filled with flowers and wonderful, happy images of Mark Stevens' life. When Bonnie, Jessica, Wendy, and Sean arrive, they are not surprised to see the place is packed. The pastor begins the service by reminding everyone present that God is still in control of all that happens.

"While we don't understand why such tragedy could befall anyone in this life," he says, "there is always a higher purpose being achieved. There is shelter and hope to be found in the Lord during trials and difficulties. Let us pray."

There's a rustle while everyone bows their heads. Then the pastor prays for the peace found only in God to transcend their hearts, minds, and emotions in Christ Jesus. After the prayer, the service is turned over to Sean, who delivers a brief but powerful eulogy, in which he outlines Mark's many accomplishments, successes, goals, and dreams.

Sean concludes with touching words to Bonnie. "I was a close friend and confident for Mark through both of his failed marriages. While I am sure Mark loved his previous wives, I had never seen Mark as happy as he was with you, Bonnie. Mark cherished you and would have done anything to make you as happy and fulfilled as you made him. One day, while trying to explain your relationship to me, and also convince me why I should find someone and settle down, Mark told me you completed him and his life, and there would never be another woman for him. It was that simple! I remember thinking, at the time, that Mark was becoming a sentimental old fool," Sean pauses, a sad smile on his face. "But now, looking back, I recognize what the two of you had. I pray someday I'll find someone to complete my life like you did for Mark."

After finishing this statement, Sean turns the service back over to the pastor, who allows many other friends to share special moments and memories. Other than the grateful tears shed during Sean's eulogy, Bonnie sits stoically throughout the service, although she is extremely gracious to well-wishers at its conclusion. She maintains her poise as she, Wendy, and Jessica exit the church and drive away. It is only in the car that Bonnie allows herself to feel the totality and searing pain surrounding Mark's murder. In that moment, she feels completely lost, alone, abandoned, crushed, and broken. She weeps uncontrollably, surrounded by the arms of the two people who love her most in the world.

While Jessica and Wendy are comforting Bonnie, Sean is heading to the press conference. He grabs SAC David Hill and asks the agent to accompany him, to prevent him from saying more than is permissible at this point in the investigation.

Hill agrees and says, "Of course I'll help monitor you. Thank you for asking." They walk into the press room together.

Sean takes the podium with his opening statement. "Thank you all for honoring the family's request for privacy during these difficult days. In the next few weeks, I am sure Mrs. Stevens will feel up to handling requests for interview, but again, I ask for your patience. In the event you wish to request an interview with Mrs.

Stevens, please contact Nate Styles, at Beauty Boutique Clothing, or my executive secretary, Evelyn Brooks at Sean Green Marketing. These two extremely competent individuals will coordinate with each other, so please don't try and play them against each other to get your request expedited. We will know, and we will not be amused." He pauses, considering what to say next.

A camera flashes in the background as he continues. "As you can all imagine, this has been a difficult time for everyone involved, from Mark's loved ones, to his employees, to friends and acquaintances. It has, personally, been the most difficult time in my life. Mark was my mentor, friend, and first big client at SGM. Without him, I sincerely doubt I would have realized the success I have with SGM. A week ago, Mark and I scheduled a mini-vacation and strategy session regarding many of the difficulties surrounding Global Metal Refining's association with Diablo Mining, in Brazil. As many of you already know, Global Metal Refining was evaluating its relationship with Diablo Mining. We were in the process of ensuring Global Metal Refining's desires to comply with best practices, environmentally, and taking Diablo Mining along with us. Mr. Hugo Montes, the CEO of Diablo Mining, explained to us he hadn't violated any laws in his mining practices, which Mark acknowledged, but Mark wanted Mr. Montes to adhere to stricter industry practices. The two were in the process of reevaluating their positions and desire to work together when Mark was killed. This mini-vacation and strategy session was going to take place at my vacation home in McCall, Idaho. Mark arrived Friday night. I had prior business commitments, so I was scheduled to arrive around eleven the morning after Mark arrived. When I got to my home, I found Mark's body on the deck." Sean proceeds to explain the way the scene was handled. "At this point," he continues, "I'll open this conference to any questions you may have, with the understanding that elements of the FBI investigation will not be discussed."

Next come the barrage of reporters' questions. "Mr. Green! Can you describe what you saw when you discovered Mr. Stevens' body?"

Sean represses a shudder. "It was the most horrendous thing I have ever seen in my life. It made me sick."

"But can you describe Mr. Stevens' body position and surroundings?"

At this point, SAC Hill steps up to the podium and introduces himself, saying, "I apologize. Sean will not be able to answer these types of questions, as they may compromise our investigation."

A collective sigh moves through the media, and the next reporter asks, "What happens to Global Metal Refining and Diablo Mining now?"

Sean suggests, "That question could be better addressed by Ms. Charlotte Evans, the interim CEO of Global Metal Refining."

"How will the death of Mr. Stevens affect your company?" comes the next question from the crowd.

"Mark's death will have an immense impact on SGM in several ways. First, I have lost a mentor and close personal friend—in fact, I would say my best friend. Second, I would hope the services SGM performed to date have been profitable to Global Metal Refining, and that long-term business can continue. However, I'm fully aware each CEO has their own relationships that they like to maintain. Should Global Metal Refining choose to go a different direction that doesn't include SGM, while I would certainly be disappointed, SGM is still and would remain a leading marketing firm internationally, thanks to Mark's mentorship. We will continue to move forward and grow with all of our clients."

The next reporter asks, "Can you tell us who has been interview by the FBI so far?"

Sean looks to Agent Hill for approval and when he nods, Sean says, "As far as I know, the immediate family, myself, and Ms. Jessica Silva."

"Do they have any suspects? Are *you* a suspect?" comes the follow-up question.

Once again, Agent Hill steps up to the podium and says, "At this point in the investigation, no suspects have been identified. The interviews conducted to date are routine and should not cast suspicion on any of those spoken to. Interviewing family and close friends of the family is standard protocol."

Sean nods to Agent Hill as he steps away from the podium. "Last question, please," he announces.

"How is Mrs. Stevens really doing?"

Sean looks surprised at the question. "She is a strong woman, but she is devastated by losing the love of her life. Now that the memorial service is over, I suspect she will be able to truly let go and grieve. Bonnie has good friends and family surrounding her, so for now, we'll all take it one day at a time. Thank you all again for coming."

Sean then steps down off the podium, even as a barrage of questions explodes from the press. He exits the press area with David Hill and thanks him for his time. Then each of them goes their separate ways.

After a moment of appreciating the quiet in his car, Sean returns to Bonnie's house. Jessica immediately asks how it went with the press. Sean says he felt it went well. He suggests everyone should relax by the pool and share in some downtime for the rest of the day. Bonnie has the staff prepare a light snack of fresh fruit and various cheeses, and they all share wine and good memories of Mark. It is a silent struggle for Wendy that only she and Sean understand what Mark truly was, so she concentrates on the things Mark did as a big brother before he went to college. It is good for everyone to see that, at least for a couple of hours, Bonnie's emotions are focused on good things, and she appreciates it very much.

Suddenly, she turns to Wendy and asks, "When are you leaving?"

Surprised by the sudden turn of conversation, Wendy blinks, then answers, "I'll stay tomorrow, but I'd like to fly back to San Diego the next day, if I can book a flight. I need to meet with my attorney and accountant regarding the new assets I own."

Sean snorts. "Don't be ridiculous. I'll have my pilot fly you home."

Wendy glances at him. "Really? Thank you. I appreciate it."

For some reason, Sean's generous gesture toward Wendy really bothers Jessica, so much so that she has to force certain unpleasant thoughts out of her mind. She struggles to maintain her indifference to her business partner.

"What about you, Sean?" Bonnie asks. "What are your plans?"

Sean considers. "Well, I need to spend some time in the office tomorrow, but I'll go in early. I promise I won't spend the entire day there, though."

Jess reaches over and pats Bonnie's hand. "Don't worry, honey. Nate can handle things for one more day, so I'll be here to spend the day with you. Maybe the three of us can lounge by the pool and have girl talk?"

Bonnie glances in Jessica's direction with her all-knowing 'what's up?' lift of her eyebrow, then says, "I would love to catch up with both of you tomorrow." Wendy agrees as well, and they return to conversation.

Sean decides to head to his room early, hoping to actually get some sleep. He excuses himself under the guise that the three of them need to spend some time alone, without him around.

Bonnie, into her second bottle of wine, giggles. "You're not fooling me. You just feel like there is too much estrogen in your life right now."

Sean smiles. "You got me there. Besides, the game is on tonight, so that's the real reason. I need my sports fix."

Bonnie smiles groggily and says, "Enjoy your fix then." On a more serious note she continues, "Thank you for everything, Sean."

After Sean leaves, Wendy asks Bonnie, "What's the real story on Sean?"

Bonnie begins explaining by saying, "Well, he's a really terrific guy. He's just the consummate bachelor, interested only in work, who doesn't know how to enjoy downtime."

Wendy asks, "Has Sean ever been married?" After a moment's thought she adds, "And what was his business relationship with Mark like?"

Jessica shifts in her chair. As Bonnie begins to answer Wendy's question, Jessica's movement catches her attention and she sees the little look of jealousy on her face. Bonnie thinks, *huh, this could get interesting and ugly at the same time.*

She returns her attention to Wendy. "Sean was the first marketing guy to get Mark's attention. First, they developed a business relationship, and their deep friendship followed. Sean is a brilliant, self-made millionaire, with enough of his simple arrogance to make him edgy for most women. You know, the kind of guy you would want to take to bed, but not home to meet your parents." She chuckles.

Wendy smiles and says, "Oh, my. Well, I don't have any parents for him to meet—"

Jessica clears her throat and jumps in. "You know, Sean can be a real asshole. The first time I met him, he was condescending, rude, arrogant, and sarcastic all wrapped up in a confident swagger."

Wendy replies, with a raised eyebrow. "Interesting. Have either of you slept with him?"

Jess makes an indignant noise and Bonnie chuckles, then says, "No. I haven't because he was Mark's best friend. And Jessica hasn't because she's been too busy pursuing business excellence to enjoy carnal pleasures."

With that, Jessica rolls her eyes and decides to call it a night and head to bed. Bonnie now knows she's correct that Jessica was seriously thinking about her feelings for Sean, and this conversation has made her jealous.

After Jessica excuses herself, Bonnie tells Wendy she believes Jess is romantically interested in Sean.

Wendy laughs and says, "Oh, heavens. He is definitely not my type. I just wanted to know if you guys thought he could be trusted. Is that why she left so abruptly?"

Bonnie replies, "I think so. Jess hasn't been involved with anyone for over a year. Not even just flings. I think it's cute that your questions about Sean bothered her. It's a good sign."

Wendy, still chuckling, says, "I'll let her know tomorrow that coast is clear for her. I just wanted to know if you both felt like you could confide in him and if he was stable."

Bonnie nods her understanding and they chat for a while longer before heading to bed themselves.

⊷ ⊶

The next morning, Bonnie, Wendy, and Jessica enjoy a leisurely breakfast and head out to the pool.

The conversation is light, and Wendy says to Jessica, "I hope I didn't offend you last night with my comments about Sean?"

Jessica looks surprised and responds, "Of course not. Why would you think such a thing?"

Wendy smiles. "Oh, I don't know. I just got the vibe you are interested in him in more than a business sense."

Jessica chuckles and tries to brush it off. "We are business associates, and as such, nothing can ever happen between the two of us." Thinking she has ended the conversation, she turns to rub some suntan oil on her legs.

Then Wendy and Bonnie simultaneously ask, "Why not?"

Jess flinches, then turns back to them and answers, "Because it just wouldn't be right. It could seriously complicate the working relationship we currently have."

Wendy nods and says, "Okay, as a psychologist, I will concede to that point. However, as a woman, if you're interested in Sean, you're stupid not to see how dating him would turn out. Times have changed, honey. It is perfectly acceptable for business associates to pursue romantic inclinations. Sean isn't your boss, so that's not an issue. He also isn't one of your employees, so that excuse is off the table. I just have to ask… Why wouldn't you take things a day at a time and see what happens? He is obviously attracted to you."

Jessica starts at those words. "Really? Why would you say that?"

"Well, for one," Wendy says, laughing, "I'm not *blind*. I see how he looks at you, and also how you look at him. Let's be honest here. You're attracted to him, aren't you?"

Jessica opens her mouth, then glances at Bonnie, who is glaring at her in a way that tells her she better not lie. She shuts her mouth, sighs, then turns back to Wendy. "Yes. I'm attracted to him."

Bonnie chimes in then. "So, go after it, woman! What have you got to lose?"

Wendy chuckles and agrees, then says, "Look, he is a very attractive, successful man who has one kick-ass set of abs, arms, and a nice chest. Quite frankly, I've never even looked at his ass, because I've been too distracted by his upper half."

Jessica laughs and admits, "His ass isn't bad either."

The three of them dissolve into giggles, then Wendy asks, "Why are you afraid to get involved or even explore the option of dating him then?"

Jessica hesitates, then attempts to explain. "The last guy I dated was a serious douche bag. He treated me like someone who was totally insignificant in his life. My opinion never mattered, and he used to ignore me for weeks at a time as punishment when I did something he didn't like, even if that something wasn't wronging him in any way. I'm not sure I'm emotionally ready to get into another relationship… especially if it turns out that way again."

Wendy nods sympathetically. "Okay, that's an excellent reason to be hesitant. Has anything about Sean led you to believe he would be the same way?"

Jessica bites her lip. "Maybe…"

Wendy says, "Go on."

"Well, I told you last night that when I first met him it didn't go well. I wasn't lying about any of the things I mentioned. I guess the way he acted did kind of reflect my ex for me."

"Understandable. But didn't he later apologize for his behavior, and didn't you two correct the issue enough to travel to Brazil together?" Wendy asks.

"Yes. Yes, we did exactly that," Jessica replies, a little suspicious that Wendy seems to know so much. She gives Bonnie a look, and Bonnie simply shrugs with a slight smile on her face.

"Has he ever treated you, or anyone else that you've noticed, like that, since?" asks Wendy.

Jessica shakes her head slowly. "No. He has actually been an amazing supporter, mentor, and gentleman."

Wendy smiles. "Let me tell you right now, from much psychoanalyzing experience, I believe Sean Green is an amazing man, and I can see he is attracted to you, but if you aren't going to pursue any possibilities with him, you need to make that very clear. I would also like to know your intentions, because if you're going to pass on that hunk of prime meat, I'm going to try and get a huge mouthful for myself—" She is interrupted by Bonnie, who chokes on laughter and spits out the sip of water she had just taken to continue laughing. Wendy grins, then looks back at Jessica. "What's it going to be?"

Both of them stare intently at her, waiting for the answers, and Jess says, "All right, fine! I'll pursue my feelings for Sean!"

Just then, Sean steps out of the house onto the patio and asks, "Um, what are you going to pursue with me?"

All three women jump and all the blood drains from Jessica's face. Bonnie quickly jumps in. "Oh, you're back. Um, how long have you been eavesdropping?"

Sean shakes his head with a confused look. "I just got here and heard Jessica say she would pursue something with me. What?" When his question meets an awkward silence, he glances at Bonnie and asks, "Did you tell her what we discussed yesterday?"

Bonnie clears her throat. "No, I didn't, but now that the cat is out of the bag, let's do it together." Jessica shoots a piercing glare at Bonnie, who catches the look and continues, "Oh, jeez, relax. We talked about a business proposal I have for you." Bonnie watches Jess relax, then says, "I have been discussing your expansion plans with Sean. He went to the office this morning to put some numbers together for me."

Jessica looks surprised, then asks, "What have you two been dreaming up then? And what about my expansion?"

Bonnie smiles at her. "Well, I'm glad you asked. I figure your expansion into the international fashion scene will cost you around two million dollars, is that correct?"

"Initially, yes, that's the number I came up with," Jessica agrees.

Bonnie nods and, jerking her thumb at Sean, says, "And then you have to pay this marketing leech five hundred thousand for his services, is that right?"

Sean smiles and shakes his head, and Jessica raises her eyebrows. "For the first year, yeah, about that much. What is this all about?"

"Be patient, I'm about to tell you!" Bonnie exclaims, then pauses, all dramatics. She takes a breath and announces, "Jess, love, I have already paid for all your expansion fees. I've paid SGM's first-year service contract, and I've set up an expansion fund of five hundred thousand dollars for incidentals in the Beauty Boutique's name."

Jessica's mouth drops open, and then she exclaims, "Absolutely not! I can't accept all of that."

Bonnie scoffs. "I knew you would react that way, so all the funds were entrusted to Sean. You see, you can't say no." She giggles a little diabolically. "It's already done. However, I would accept a hug and a thank you. Besides, it's not like I can't afford to. I just received a fifteen-billion-dollar estate. There is one condition you must meet though. You must keep me in the latest designs from the Beauty Boutique."

Jessica, speechless, gives Bonnie a huge hug. Finally, through tears of gratitude, she manages, "I'll never forget this amazing gift. Thank you."

Bonnie gives her a squeeze and then whispers, "When I let go of you, I'm going to give Sean all the credit, so you better give him a hug as amazing as this one. Please just go for this opportunity, girl."

Jessica is crying and laughing when she and Bonnie pull away from each other. Lifting Jessica's face in her hands, Bonnie says, "This was all Sean's brainchild."

Jess nods once, decisively, then stands up, walks over to Sean, and throws her arms around his neck. "Thank you so much. You are a truly amazing man."

Sean is startled at first, then goes with it. He hugs Jessica amazingly close and holds her tightly in his arms. Wendy and Bonnie wink at each other as they watch the almost physical vibrations of emotion begin to solidify between Jess and Sean.

When they release each other, they make eye contact for a moment, and then Sean clears his throat and sits down on a lounge chair. "Okay, on to the next item. We all need to talk a bit."

Through a huge amount of willpower, Bonnie represses a sigh. "Alright. Spit it out."

Sean begins explaining to Wendy and Jessica that Bonnie has also decided she wants to purchase the old Nike factory from Ricardo.

"Jessica, this means that Bonnie will be your landlord. I have done some calculations, and if you sign the lease on the factory with Ricardo, Bonnie will most likely have to pay double what she would to purchase it without a tenant. What I'm proposing is that you should immediately tell Ricardo you have found a more promising property and, while you appreciate his help, you have decided not to lease his property. All of us can take a trip to the villa two weeks after this announcement, and I'll take Bonnie to meet Ricardo as an apology for the misunderstanding about your deal with him. This way, Bonnie can strike a new deal with Ricardo for half the price in cash. Mr. Stoddard will have the purchase agreement all drawn up, as well as your lease agreement with Bonnie. When the purchase agreement is signed, we'll contact Lidia and get the production schedule fired up. Are you willing to play along?"

Jess looks extremely uncomfortable, but after a moment of considering and remembering the way Ricardo had talked to Lidia, she says, "Of course I am. Bonnie just gave me three million dollars. Why wouldn't I do that for her?"

Bonnie smiles. "What a payback that will be. If you do this for me, I'm going to make over a ten-million-dollar profit on my three-million-dollar investment in you."

Jessica laughs and says, "Then I guess it's a win-win for everyone here."

Sean nods. "Great. We should all plan on being in Brazil in two weeks. Perhaps this time we can take a week to relax and recover from everything that has happened, then be ready to hit work hard again."

Bonnie nods, then suggests, "Wendy, why don't you join us at the villa?"

Wendy politely declines. "I have clients to take care of, and I have to move into a beachfront penthouse. By the way, Bonnie, how do you want me to handle things, like furniture and stuff, at the penthouse? I think I'd like to keep my own furniture."

"I'll come by and get my clothing, if you will donate Mark's things before I get there? I don't think I could bear to do that myself, and I'm not one to keep everything of his..." Bonnie replies quietly.

Wendy says, "Absolutely, I can do that."

"Thank you. Everything else in the condo is yours, with the exception of a few photos I might want. I spent very little time there, as it was really for Mark when he had business in San Diego. If the furnishings aren't what you want, do what you will with them. I'm not interested in any of them."

Wendy considers. "Perhaps some of it will be better than what I have, and I can donate anything I don't want I'm sure."

Bonnie reminds her, "You no longer have to worry about budgeting so tightly. You are now a very rich woman, and I ask that you please learn to enjoy it with grace and humility."

Wendy shakes her head in disbelief and replies, "You're right. I keep forgetting my net worth basically went from nothing to six billion overnight. It's going to take some time to sink it before it becomes real for me." She gives Bonnie a wry smile.

"It will happen faster than you think," Bonnie tells her. "Just don't forget the less fortunate individuals and remember to help others often."

Wendy smiles, a real smile this time, and says, "I have several causes I'll be helping very soon. I'm glad to know you feel the same way about money that I do."

The two women clasp hands, and Sean goes to put on his swimming suit. They enjoy the rest of the day in leisure, preparing for the weeks to come.

⇒⊰ ⊱⇐

Wendy leaves the next morning after thanking Sean again for the use of his corporate jet.

She hugs Bonnie, telling her, "If you need anything, please call me anytime and I'll be here for you."

Bonnie barely holds back the tears as she replies, "I know you will, and I promise to call if I need anything, but only if you do the same."

Wendy says, "Okay, I promise too, and you better."

Releasing Bonnie, she turns and gives Jessica a huge hug as well and whispers in her ear, "By the way, I was never interested in Sean, but I knew if you felt there might be some competition, you would go for it. Just take it one day at a time and enjoy the ride for all it's worth."

Jessica laughs a little tearfully and hugs Wendy back tightly, surprised at how fond she has gotten of the seemingly annoying woman. "Thank you for forcing me to make a decision, and by the way, if the ride is anything like my imagination, it will be awesome."

Wendy giggles and says, "Then for your sake, I hope it surpasses your imagination."

"Me too!"

Wendy then hugs Sean, whispering in his ear, "You should really ask Jessica out. I can see you're attracted to her, and I'm pretty sure she would say yes. Your choice though."

Sean replies awkwardly, "Um, thanks for everything, Wendy. Enjoy your first flight in a private jet."

Jessica makes a sound of delight. "You'll be amazed. I certainly was when we flew to Brazil."

Sean smiles at her, then turns to Wendy, "Do you have a car at the airport, or should I have transportation arranged for that as well?"

Wendy smiles, overcome by the amount of concern she's getting from her new friends. "Thanks everyone, but I left my car at the airport, and I'll be just fine. I love you all."

They watch as she walks down the steps to the waiting car and waves as she rides away. Her return to San Diego marks the change back to real life and the daily responsibilities that everyone has to return to. Sean needs to get back to his clients, Jessica needs to prepare her staff for the fully funded expansion, and Bonnie needs to get the purchase agreement and lease prepared for their trip to Brazil in two weeks.

As Sean and Jessica are leaving the estate, Bonnie recognizes her need to deal with the emotions and pain of being without Mark at their home for the first time. She realizes he will never be returning home. The thought comes to her that she may never get closure on Mark's murder. As all these realizations come flooding in for her, she sits by the pool, remembering fondly the last time she and Mark enjoyed the pool together, and how she teased him. Silent and alone, even while surrounded by staff, Bonnie allows herself to accept the reality that Mark is dead, truly grieving for her loss for the first time since that shocking phone call.

After what seems like hours to her, she is approached by one of the women on the staff, who apologizes for disturbing her.

"Mrs. Stevens, I just received a call from a reporter who would like to interview you. What should I tell him?"

Bonnie looks up at her blankly, then comes back to herself and asks, "Could you please take a message and promise him I'll get back to him in the morning with my schedule? Also, if you would be so kind as to bring me the best bottle of chardonnay we have, I would appreciate it. I don't want to be disturbed for the rest of the day."

The woman replies, "Yes, of course, Mrs. Stevens. If you need anything, I'm right here."

Bonnie nods. "Thank you." Then she returns to her thoughts and memories of Mark. She spends the rest of the day in deep thought and contemplation. She cries and laughs on and off throughout the day. She sips wine and eats the snacks that magically appear as the day progresses, but most of all, she truly misses Mark and wonders what is in store for her life now.

⇥⊹ ⊹⇤

Jessica enters her office at nine in the morning, much to Nate's surprise.

"Girl, what are you doing here? Shouldn't you be with Bonnie right now? Everything here is under control. You didn't have to come in today."

Jessica replies, "I know, I know, but Bonnie needs some time to be alone right now. I checked on her last night, and she was exhausted, but doing really well considering everything. She is a really strong woman. But anyway, we need to call an emergency staff meeting. It is mandatory that all staff be present, so if anyone is off duty, call them in. Let's move." She bustles into her private office with Nate on her heels.

He looks quizzically at her and she settles back into her desk, cocks his hips, places his hands on them, and says, "Well? Do you want to tell me what this is all about, before I stir everything in the place up?"

Jessica laughs and answers, "Why, yes, of course. Beauty Boutique Clothing is expanding into the international market through Brazil immediately."

Nate gasps and says, "Oh my God, Jess! We have so much to do!" He throws up his hands and turns to leave her office, but immediately reappears. "Wait, how are we funding this?"

She stands and walks over to Nate, taking his hand. "The expansion and SGM's first year's fee are prepaid, and a five-hundred-thousand-dollar expansion fund has already been established, courtesy of Mrs. Bonnie Stevens."

Nate's jaw drops and, without thinking, he squeaks, "Holy shit!" Catching himself, he clears his throat and apologizes for the impropriety.

Jess just smiles and says, "It's okay. I can't believe it either. I need you to do two things immediately. First, I need you to reject Ricardo's lease agreement, and second, call the staff meeting."

Nate's excitement turns to complete confusion. "Wait, what do you mean, reject Ricardo's lease? It's everything you wanted!"

Jessica waves a hand and says, "Yes, I know it is, but tell him we have located a more promising site we are pursuing at the moment."

Nate raises an eyebrow and asks, "And where exactly is this site?"

Jess then goes on to explain to Nate the plans Bonnie and Sean came up with for the purchase of the factory.

"Bonnie will profit enormously from the gift she gave me in funding the expansion," she says in conclusion. "It works better for everyone, especially since Ricardo seems like such an asshole."

Nate nods, understanding. "Wow, I never realized Bonnie was that smart, business savvy, or shrewd. But what do you suppose Ricardo is going to do when he finds out? He will find out, Jess, and he is going to be pissed. Can't he interfere with any governmental approvals you need through Hugo?"

Jess shrugs. "I don't think so. We already have the approvals from Juan Zamora in hand, and I don't believe Ricardo has the political clout on his own. Hugo is worried about losing his contracts with Global Metal Refining, so it's not anticipated that he will help Ricardo in any way when Bonnie and I have so much influence with Global Metal Refining now."

Nate seems concerned. "It still seems like a pretty risky plan. No one knows how Ricardo is going to react."

Jessica replies, "I guess we will find out soon enough. Bonnie, Sean, and I are all heading to Brazil in two weeks to finalize everything and hire the laid-off factory workers and Lidia. After this is finished, I'll need several production supervisors to head to Brazil for a couple of weeks. Please develop a strategy for implementation by the end of next week. And hold onto your hat. We have just entered the realm of international fashion design and marketing."

After the entire staff of the Beauty Boutique is assembled, Jessica makes the announcement, explaining the company's expansion into Brazil.

"Funds are already in place to fully pay for this expansion, from hiring the necessary staff for the factory there, to paying for the company's first year of marketing through SGM. We've got nothing to lose, people," she tells them all excitedly.

Everyone is happy to hear the news, but they also recognize that each of them will now be required to step up their game, because the rules have changed dramatically. There will be an increased operational tempo required for organizational survival in the much more competitive realm of international fashion.

Jessica further explains, "Nate is devising a strategy for immediate implementation whereby several of the production supervisors will be heading to Brazil for three week stints on a rotating basis until each is convinced, as a team, that the factory workers in Brazil are performing up to our standards. Furthermore, the team of supervisors will also need to identify and properly train production supervisors for the Brazil operations, with whom they will coordinate shipping and receiving logistics both within the United States and abroad. So keep your eye out for anyone promising during each of your shifts in Brazil," she says, making eye contact with each of her supervisors, then continues. "In two weeks, I will be in Brazil with Mrs. Stevens and Mr. Green getting all the contracts signed, along with hiring the initial factory staff for the production supervisors to evaluate and train. If there are any workers hired that you feel are under, or not at all, qualified to perform the functions of the job descriptions, you are to document them and notify me so I can make the necessary changes. Any questions?" She pauses, giving everyone time to consider, and when there are no further questions she finishes, "Thank you all. Without your hard work and dedication to the continued success of Beauty Boutique Clothing, none of this would have been possible. As this organization prospers so will each of you."

There is a resounding round of applause, and everyone returns to their daily functions with a renewed sense of purpose and resolve. Time passes quickly with all the preparations necessary for the upcoming trip back to Brazil. Wendy checks in with Jessica to see how things are going, especially between her and Sean.

Jess is forced to admit that it isn't going very well. "Unfortunately, I haven't seen or spoken to Sean in person since the day you left for San Diego."

Wendy asks playfully, "Do I need to come back up north to get your competitive juices flowing again?"

Jessica snorts, "That won't be necessary. My juices are flowing quite well anticipating our trip and the constant interaction we should have in Brazil. But thanks for the offer."

Wendy reminds her, "If you don't make your move on Sean, someone else probably will, and there is nothing more demeaning than to regret letting a chance slip by you because you were too indecisive to pursue your own heart's desires."

Jessica assures her, "Wendy, I won't let any more time pass without letting Sean know how I am feeling about him. I swear."

Wendy doesn't sound convinced. "Okay, well, I'm going to update Bonnie on this conversation so that she can hold you accountable for the promise you just made."

Jessica grins. "As you wish, but for the record, I'm going to call Sean after we hang up and remind him he owes me dinner. I have decided on sushi and whether he likes it or not, that is where he will be taking me."

Wendy chuckles. "Great idea! Just remember, I'll be checking on you."

Rolling her eyes, Jess changes the subject and asks, "How is the penthouse? What do you think of it? And how are your clients adjusting to you being a billionaire?"

Wendy laughs. "The penthouse is fabulous, with views that amaze me during every sunrise and sunset. I really haven't adjusted to being a billionaire, but the clients who have heard are all very pleased for me and seem to be easier about it than I am. I set up a foundation in the name of one of my deceased clients. She was murdered during a domestic violence incident. The organization will help assist domestic violence organizations nationally in cooperation with several other large foundations."

Jessica replies, "Wow! I'm so pleased to see you expand your influence in the domestic violence arena from counseling victims to helping them on so many other levels. From my perspective, you are a guardian angel for all the victims of domestic abuse."

"Thank you," Wendy says, her voice tight, "but it is just my passion to help others in such unfathomable circumstances. Nothing more."

Jessica shakes her head. "That may be so, but it takes a truly special person to do what you do day in and day out."

As soon as they hang up the phone, Jessica calls Sean's office. When Evelyn answers, Jess identifies herself and asks if Sean is available.

Evelyn snickers a little, "Hold on, Ms. Silva, I'll check and see if he can find a moment to take your call."

Pushing the hold button, she gets up from her desk, knocks on Sean's door, and then walks in without waiting for an answer.

Sean looks up at her and says on a sigh, "If you're not going to wait for a reply, why do you even bother knocking?"

Evelyn shrugs. "I guess I'm just being polite."

Sean grins and retorts, "Actually, being polite requires you to abide by the etiquette that *follows* a knock, which is waiting for an answer from your boss."

Evelyn rolls her eyes and says, "Stop being an ass. Ms. Silva is on line one. Shall I tell her you're busy?"

Without even responding to Evelyn, Sean hastily grabs the phone, presses line one, and says, "Jessica, good to hear from you. How are things going?"

Evelyn stands in Sean's office doorway with one eyebrow raised and an incredulous smile on her face until he waves his hand, shooing her out the door.

As she turns to go, she says, "Give Ms. Silva my best, would you, Sean?"

Sean cups his hand over the phone, glares at her, and whisper-shouts, "Out! And close the door behind you!"

Evelyn blows him a kiss and quickly closes the door behind her.

Getting back to his phone call, Sean listens as Jessica says, "Things are progressing well with my preparations for Brazil. Need I remind you of our bet regarding Ricardo taking my deal?"

Sean laughs and says, "No, but you didn't accept the deal, so how did I lose the bet?"

Jessica retorts playfully, "A bet is still a bet, so I believe you owe me dinner soon, and I have decided I would like to get sushi. I hope you like it, but even if you don't, that's where we're going."

Sean replies, "Are you kidding? I love sushi. I would be honored to pay my bet to you. How about tonight, do you have time?"

She giggles, "If you can wait until about seven, I can make it. I need to get some things finished up here first."

"Actually, that's perfect. I'll pick you up at your office at six forty-five. I know a great place not far from there."

Jess shrugs. "Okay, that will be great."

Nate watches from the door of Jessica's office, initially stopping because she is on the phone, but once he recognizes whom Jessica is speaking to, he can't help but eavesdrop on the conversation.

When she hangs up the phone, she gives an audible cheer of 'Yes!' accompanied by a fist pump. As she turns in her chair, still doing a mini happy dance, she sees Nate standing in the doorway. She tugs down her suit jacket, clears her throat, and asks in her most dignified voice, "How long have you been standing there?"

Nate puts his hands on his hips, grinning, and replies, "Long enough to know your panties are wet with anticipation over your date with Mr. Green, the pompous ass. Girl, you are in so deep. Didn't I tell you he was exactly the type of guy you swoon over?"

Jessica closes her eyes and says a mini prayer for her salvation. "Oh, must you be so crude? I'm not swooning over Mr. Green."

Nate laughs. "Oh please, this is me you're talking to, and I haven't seen you this excited about any man as long as I've known you. You are simply smitten with him, but good for you. You go, girl!"

Jessica smiles sheepishly. "Yeah, well, maybe a little."

Nate asks, "So when are you going out and where?"

"Tonight and sushi. Sean said he knows a place near here that's good."

Nate nods. "I bet he does, and just think of all the possibilities with a guy who likes sushi." He gives her a slight smile and a wink.

Jessica rolls her eyes. "Ugh! Must you be so crude?" Then she smiles back at him and says, "Yes, it makes a woman's head spin with possible scenarios."

Nate giggles as he starts to walk out of Jessica's office, then stops in midstride and turns back toward her, saying, "Oh, I came in here to tell you my preliminary thoughts on who should go to Brazil to train the new workers. Do you want me to just brief you on these selections and their schedules, or do you want to review them first?"

She motions for Nate to sit down and says, "Let's just discuss it now, so you can move forward on the strategy. I don't want to hold you up."

Nate nods, sits, and explains why he selected each supervisor and the strength each brings to the table. Jessica is pleased with the mix of skills Nate has put together and tells him she agrees with both his reasoning and selections. She makes a few alterations to his rotation schedule, explaining the strengths and weaknesses with the current factory setup, along with how the timing of the scheduled improvements will impact the training flow.

Nate asks about hotels in the area, but Jessica interrupts him, saying, "Oh, I'm so sorry, I forgot to tell you. Bonnie has graciously confirmed with her staff for each of our supervisors to stay at her villa and be spoiled while they are there."

"Ha!" Nate says, shaking his head and smiling, "Well then, I'll have to schedule some time for me to be necessary there, and perhaps Phillip will be able to join me."

Jess replies, indignant, "Absolutely not! I need you on the ground here, running things while I'm out of the country." She watches Nate's face fall and then bursts into laughter. "Don't worry. I already booked a two-week vacation stint just for you and Phillip at the villa when the transition is completed. All expenses are on me, and you'll also have one thousand dollars of spending money to enjoy Brazil."

Nate's mouth falls open and he says, "Girl, this is why I absolutely adore you and will never work for anyone but you."

"You're welcome," she replies with a wink. "Now get back to work!"

He looks at his watch and then gives her a once-over. "Are you wearing that out to dinner tonight?"

Jessica looks down at herself and says, "Yes. What's wrong with what I'm wearing?"

Nate replies, "Well nothing, darling, if you were going to a business dinner. But you aren't. You're going on a date. So come with me right now. I have an idea."

She glances up at him, almost pouting, then sighs and gets up from her desk to follow Nate into the showroom. He pulls a green silk dress off the rack, then asks her, "What type of underwear are you wearing?"

She takes the dress and, without thinking, replies, "A thong." Then realization dawns on her, and she glares at him, "*Not* that it's any of your business."

Nate just keeps going with the conversation. "Oh, thank God, you didn't do granny panties. Go try that on."

She sticks her tongue out at him as she disappears into the dressing room. When she steps out, Nate gives her his evaluation by saying, "That is absolutely gorgeous on you, and Sean's going to have a bitch of a time hiding the boner he pops when he sees you in it."

Jess steps around Nate to look in the full-length mirror. "Really this is a bit much for sushi, don't you think?"

"Nope, I don't," Nate responds bluntly.

She looks at the dress, sizing it up. It's slit up the middle to mid-thigh level. Remembering what Sean told her about his preferences about women's clothing in Brazil, she simply smiles to herself. The dress also has a V-cut front that exposes just the right amount of cleavage to be suggestive, but not slutty, and again she smiles.

Nate, watching her expression, says quietly, "That's just perfect for tonight. You're going to knock his socks off. You look fabulous." She beams at him in the mirror, and he smiles and says, "There, I've done my job. The rest of the evening is totally up to you."

"You always think of everything for me," she says, smoothing the front of the dress. "Thank you."

Nate smiles and replies, "Enjoy your date, and I'll see you tomorrow morning." He turns and starts to exit the showroom, but then turns and adds, "And *try* to enjoy tonight as a date, not a business meeting. Flirt, tease, and above all make sure you kiss him goodnight. You need to know from the get-go if there is a spark between you two." With that bit of advice, Nate leaves for the day.

Jessica is in her office working when Sean is escorted to her by one of her production supervisors. She immediately rises from her desk and watches as Sean's eyes survey her body. She walks around her desk toward him, and he manages to get out, "Wow, you look terrific. Is that one of your new designs?"

Jessica thinks, *Damn, Nate was right again! Thank God for that man.* Then she smiles and replies, "Yes, it is. I'm glad you like it."

Sean looks incredulous. "Like it? I think it is phenomenal."

She smiles again, a little more shyly this time. "Thank you, Sean. Shall we?"

As he holds the car door open for her, she slides into the car and allows the slit of her dress to fall off the side of her crossed legs, revealing her athletic frame to mid-thigh. Sean tries to be discreet as he closes her door, but after he is seated in the driver's seat, Jessica catches him sneaking a peek at her leg while putting the key into the ignition. During his brief lapse in concentration, Sean misses the ignition and drops the keys onto the floor board. Jessica quickly looks out her window to hide her grin at the idea that what she is wearing is unnerving this particular man.

Sean regains his composure by starting the car and saying, "We will be there in ten minutes or so."

"Great! I'm starving. What about you?"

Sean says, in a husky voice, "You have no idea."

When they arrive, the valet takes Sean's keys and says, "Good evening, Mr. Green. Table for two?"

, "Yes, thank you. And can we make it a special table tonight?"

The valet nods with a grin, and as Sean walks over to help Jessica out of the car, the valet relays the message to the hostess. Jess swivels in the seat and takes Sean's hand as she gets out of the car. Once again, Sean is extremely pleased with the dress, admiring the V-cut that leaves just enough up to his imagination.

The hostess takes them to a secluded table overlooking the San Francisco Bay, then asks, "Is this sufficient, Mr. Green?"

Sean looks at Jessica for approval, and she says a little breathlessly, "This is wonderful."

Sean nods to the hostess, who then asks Jessica, "What would you like to drink, ma'am?"

"Hot sake, please." Sean orders his usual scotch on the rocks.

Jessica can't help herself and asks, "How much do you pay by the drink for your scotch, if you don't mind me asking? I'm not trying to be rude, I'm just curious."

Sean shrugs. "Oh, don't worry about it. It's one hundred dollars a drink."

Jessica's mouth drops open, and she exclaims, "Holy crap! I would never pay that."

Sean chuckles at her reaction and replies, "Then you obviously don't appreciate fine scotch."

"Not at a hundred bucks a drink I don't," she says with a grin.

When their drinks arrive, Sean hands Jessica his scotch. "Here, you must experience what truly fine scotch tastes like, before you ruin your palate with the sake."

She looks doubtful, but takes a tentative sip of the scotch. She swallows, looks at Sean, and after a moment says, "Okay, that is amazing, but I still wouldn't drink it on a regular basis."

Sean laughs, saying, "Well, it's one of the few luxuries I allow myself."

Jessica snorts, "Now that's bullshit. I've flown in your jet, and you said the same thing about that."

Sean raises an eyebrow and challenges, "Well then, let's compare. How much do your dress, jewelry, shoes, and purse cost?"

Jessica does a quick calculation, wincing at the comparison. This particular dress is eight hundred dollars, her matching gold and emerald necklace and earring set ran about two thousand dollars, and her shoes came to three hundred.

She smiles apologetically at Sean and says, "Right around three thousand dollars."

Sean smiles and replies, "Well, there you have it. I would have to have thirty-one drinks to match what you are wearing."

Jessica smirks and attempts to turn the tables. "But that's not really a fair comparison. I *have* to wear clothes. You don't *have* to drink eight-hundred-dollar scotch."

Sean retorts, "Point well made, but you don't *have* to wear three thousand dollars' worth of clothing either."

Jessica nods and laughs. "Okay, point taken."

Their conversation is light over dinner and dessert. Each of them asks the other why they aren't involved with someone. Jessica explains about the last guy she dated again, while Sean replies that he experienced a possessive and jealous woman once. Both of them relate similar difficulties with the time they give to their work as an issue in their previous relationships.

After dinner, Sean drives Jessica back to her office and walks her to the door.

She clears her throat. "I had a delightful evening," she says, and Sean agrees.

He extends his hand to shake hers, but she ignores it and steps in to hug him. Sean leans in to kiss her, and when he does, he unconsciously laces his fingers through her hair. Jessica gives a pleasure filled moan as they kiss. Sean releases her hair and pulls back. Both are surprised by their reactions, and Jessica regains her voice first.

"I just want you to know, you can definitely kiss me like that again, sometime soon."

Sean smiles, his hands still on her waist, "You should count on it." He gives her another hug, says goodnight, and watches her walk back into her office.

On the drive home, Sean can't stop thinking about kissing Jessica, and how the feel of her in his arms really turned him on. He decides it was a great evening and he truly enjoyed her company and conversation. He arrives home without a clue in the world how he navigated the streets of San Francisco.

Jessica walks into her office and sits down at her desk, unable to remain on her feet. Without thinking about it, she calls Bonnie. Bonnie answers, sounds like her normal chipper self, and asks how Jessica is doing. Jessica tells Bonnie she isn't really sure.

Bonnie's voice fills with concern. "Oh no, honey, what's wrong?"

Jessica replies, a little confused, "Nothing bad. I just had an absolutely wonderful first date with Sean, and I'm not sure how I feel now."

, "Oh, girlfriend, you must give me all the details, *now!*"

Jessica relays the evening in chronological order, including the kiss. After she finishes describing everything and how she felt, Bonnie says, "So when are you two going out again?"

, "I don't know. The next date will be up to Sean, I guess, since I forced this one, on Wendy's insistence."

Bonnie laughs. "Isn't she terrific? I know she can seem a bit annoying at first, but she really grows on you. I just wish she and Mark could have worked out their differences while he was alive."

Jessica smacks a hand to her forehead and says, "Oh man, I'm so sorry! I didn't mean to be indelicate talking about Sean…"

Bonnie scoffs. "Don't be worried about every little thing. I miss Mark terribly, and I have good days and bad days, but he's gone and I have to go on living. That's what Mark told me he always wanted for me, should something ever happen to him. I don't think I'll ever marry again, and I'm certainly not interested in dating anyone right now, but I'm so happy for you. I've always thought you and Sean would be a good fit for each other."

Jessica says admiringly, "You are an amazing woman."

Bonnie chides, "Yes, I know, and don't you ever forget it, because I know I'll need your strength sooner or later."

"Well, you know I'm always here for you."

"I'm so thankful for that."

⊨⊧

When Jessica walks into work the next morning, Nate wants all the details of her date. Jess admits that Nate helped her out quite a bit with the choice of clothing, describes the delightful conversations they had, and then explains about their kiss. She also explains she was stunned by her reaction to Sean grabbing her hair during their kiss and how much it turned her on.

She says, "No one has ever done that to me before, but I really enjoyed it."

Nate listens very patiently to Jessica with a growing grin on his face, and when she finishes he asks, "So when are you two getting back together again, because it sounds to me like you both are very passionate individuals. When, or if, you have sex, I bet it will be mind-blowing for both of you."

"How can you possibly know that?" Jessica asks.

Nate just laughs, "Based upon what you told me about your and Sean's reactions, that's how. Both of you have been free of any relationship entanglements, and both of you sound like the pent-up sexual emotion inside you guys is going to erupt like an old, dormant volcano. When it happens it's going to be hot, hot, hot! Just mark my words, Jess." He winks and leaves her considering sex as hot as lava.

CHAPTER 18
PLAYED

Later in the day, Jessica receives a desperate phone call from Ricardo wanting to know why Beauty Boutique Clothing has suddenly changed its mind on executing the lease agreement, especially since he agreed to all the conditions she laid out during their conversation in Brazil.

Jessica tells him, "You didn't sound too enthusiastic about our offer, so I browsed elsewhere."

Ricardo protests, "That may be true, but you also understood everything I told Lidia, Juan, and Hugo when we thought you couldn't understand us, didn't you?"

"Yes, I did, but any type of lease arrangement of this proportion needs to begin as a win-win agreement. If the Beauty Boutique begins its relationship with you on a bad note, for example if you feel like you were forced into the deal, then when issues do arise, you'll be less likely to work with us. I'm simply looking at other options that have a better chance of a mutually supportive relationship."

Ricardo asks, "Is there any possibility of changing your mind?"

Jessica replies with an emphatic, "No. I am sorry."

Ricardo says in a cold voice, "I'm sorry to hear this decision is final. Maybe when this new location doesn't work out for you, we will renegotiate terms more favorable to *me*."

The line goes dead, and Jessica pulls the phone away from her ear to stare at it. *How rude,* placing the phone back in the cradle.

⊷ ⊶

Ricardo calls Sean next. "What the hell happened, Green? I thought we had a deal!"

Sean grimaces. "Slow down, Ricardo. What happened?"

"Ms. Silva," Ricardo replies, disdain dripping from his voice, "has just refused to sign our lease agreement after I met every term she asked me to meet. This is unacceptable. Now I must scramble to see if I can come up with another alternative to alleviate some of the stress that comes with owning a building without any tenants lined up—"

Sean interrupts to ask Ricardo if he had ever considered selling the building.

Ricardo snorts. "Not without a tenant in the place. To do so with an empty building would reduce the price of the property substantially."

"Well, it's a good thing you can hold the empty building for the long term then."

Ricardo admits, "I thought I could, but after Mr. Stevens death, Hugo is very concerned Global Metal Refining will cancel his contract and not look favorably on any future bids. It puts extra pressure on me to find a tenant, because I may need to seek additional funding soon."

, "I understand. Global Metal Refining was my largest client, and I, too, fear the same response from the interim CEO. You know, I will be at the Stevens' villa with Mrs. Stevens and Ms.

Silva in a week. Perhaps we can meet, put our heads together, and come up with a new solution that would work to take some pressure off you?"

Ricardo agrees and asks Sean if he thinks Ms. Silva might change her position.

, "I seriously doubt it. I'll level with you… the three of us are coming to Brazil to view land close to the new Nike factory for Mrs. Stevens to buy and, eventually, build another factory to perfectly suit Beauty Boutique Clothing. Ms. Silva would be able to lease long term on very favorable conditions, since Mrs. Stevens has substantial cash to invest. I must remind you, Ricardo, that Mrs. Stevens and Ms. Silva have been lifelong friends, so Jessica pretty much has backing to do whatever she wishes. Including not hiring SGM for the marketing or anything else drastic."

Ricardo responds grudgingly, "I will make all the time you want available in order to solve what might rapidly become a difficult predicament for me."

Sean tells Ricardo he looks forward to working with him in a week.

After they hang up, Sean calls Bonnie. He tells her that the plan is right on track and relays the facts of the conversation he just had with Ricardo.

Bonnie tells Sean, "Excellent. Jessica telephoned about an hour ago informing me of the conversation she had with him, also. From what you both have told me, all I have to do is remind Hugo and Ricardo that between you, me, and Wendy, we still have controlling majority in Global Metal Refining and the three of us are in agreement on basically everything. What I need you to do next is get in touch with Hugo and set up an appointment between you, me, and him. Tell him of my environmental preferences, and mention I would like to discuss his future with Global Metal Refining. This should be enough to pucker his sphincter and gain us the leverage we need with Ricardo."

Sean says incredulously, "Bonnie, you are evil, but I really like what you seem to have learned from Mark. This is a brilliant plan."

Bonnie chuckles, "That is a true compliment coming from you."

Sean grins, "Well, I'm glad, because it's also a sincere one."

━┿ ┿━

Bonnie, Jessica, and Sean arrive at the villa mid afternoon on Monday. The staff is prepared for their arrival and has lunch ready on the veranda, complete with mango margaritas. The food, as usual, is fantastic. Everyone decides to relax by the pool and once again share wonderful memories of Mark. It is decided that Bonnie and Jess will spend the next day shopping while Sean meets with Ricardo. On Wednesday, Hugo is scheduled to come to the villa to meet with Bonnie and Sean.

The next morning, Jess and Bonnie are up early and out the door for their shopping excursion while Sean prepares for his meeting with Ricardo. When Ricardo arrives, Sean once again has the meeting on the veranda. They enjoy a leisurely breakfast and, over coffee, Sean explains the circumstances of Mark's estate and the need for Ricardo to tread very lightly around Bonnie, not only for himself, but also for Sean and Hugo.

Having concluded his spiel, Sean says, "On a lighter note, Mrs. Stevens has authorized me to offer fifteen million U.S. dollars, in cash, to purchase the old Nike factory. She feels bad for pulling your only tenant prospect away from you, and she wants to make up for it. She has decided, if you agree, to make it a center for environmental studies surrounding issues specific to the Brazilian rain forest."

Ricardo objects, saying, "The value of the property exceeds thirty million dollars. Fifteen is a toddler's offer."

Sean gently reminds Ricardo, "Yes, that's true, but only if it were a fully leased complex with a financially stable long term tenant, which you don't have at this time and probably won't get in the near future."

Ricardo glares at Sean. "I appreciate the offer," he says through gritted teeth, "but I am inclined to reject outright. However, because I know you well, I will consider it."

Sean shakes his head sadly. "Unfortunately, this offer is only good until Thursday evening. If the deal isn't done, Bonnie will take her chances on the property deteriorating futher and purchase it at fire-sale prices."

"Understood," Ricardo replies, and he rises to leave.

When Sean rises and offers his hand to shake Ricardo's, Ricardo simply looks at it and walks away with a gruesome sneer. Sean watches as his tense shoulders disappear with a staff member. Then he sits down and calls Bonnie with an update.

"We need to implement plan B with Hugo. Ricardo doesn't seem inclined to work with us." Sean figures the increased pressure on Hugo will force Ricardo's hand, knowing he still stands to make several million dollars for himself and his investors or risk the possibility of losing both the money and his investors for good.

Bonnie tells Sean, "I know the drill. I'll implement the plan as scheduled. Can I go back to shopping now?"

Sean chuckles and replies, "Yes, see you later."

When Wednesday rolls around, Hugo is on time for his meeting with Sean and Bonnie. Jessica goes for a run, then lays out by the pool while the meeting is in session. Bonnie begins the conversation by chastising Hugo for his mining practices, indicating that Mark was far more forgiving than she will ever be.

Hugo defends himself politely. "Mrs. Stevens, you do understand that Diablo Mining hasn't violated any laws in Brazil."

Bonnie clucks her tongue and says, "I don't much care, Mr. Montes. Brazilian laws are far inferior to international best practices, which, as a prominent shareholder in Global Metal Refining,

I will expect any of the vendors we work with to adhere to, unless you simply do not wish to do business with us anymore."

Hugo, sensing he has seriously irritated Bonnie, backtracks hastily and asks, "What could I do, as a genuine faith gesture, to demonstrate my sincerity in Diablo Mining's ability to comply with your wishes?"

Bonnie considers for a moment, then replies, "You know, I'm actually very interested in purchasing the old Nike factory to develop an environmental study's center. I'm prepared to pay Ricardo fifteen million dollars for the property, but he doesn't seem inclined to accept my offer. If I must, I'll wait him out and purchase the site when the price has come down even further... Or, on second thought, perhaps I'll just buy out his investors one at a time, until I control the majority interest, and fire him as the managing partner." She pauses, allowing the implications to sink in, then continues, "However, I would prefer not to go that route. If I have to, I may not look kindly on your promise of sincerity or Diablo Mining's supposed intentions to follow the mining industry's best practices. Mr. Montes, have I made my intentions clear to you?"

Hugo, looking slightly pale, replies, "You are quite clear. I understand completely, and I'll have a very serious discussion with Ricardo today. He will either contact you directly by tomorrow morning, or I will reach out to you personally very soon. Thank you for this opportunity to show Global Metal Refining my loyalty."

Bonnie smiles sweetly and says, "Wonderful. I'll be waiting to hear from you soon. Have a good day, Mr. Montes."

⋙ ⋘

Hugo drives straight to Ricardo's office, walks in, and tells him to cancel all of his meetings and plans until they have decided what to do with Mrs. Stevens' offer to purchase the factory.

Ricardo, annoyed at the interruption, growls, "There is nothing to decide. I'm not selling the factory at that price, period."

Hugo tells Ricardo to listen to him before making that type of decision, because it also has ramifications for Hugo's business.

Ricardo gives Hugo a dubious look. "How does this affect Diablo Mining?"

After Hugo explains his conversation with Bonnie, Ricardo looks pissed and says flatly, "They are pressuring you to get to me."

Hugo agrees. "You know, without my political connections, that factory would have never been built," he tells Ricardo forcefully.

"Well, that's true, but that is all in the past now!" Ricardo insists.

Hugo is angry at Ricardo's blatant disregard of his help. "You still need my connections, and one of the main reasons I have those connections is because of Global Metal Refining. If Diablo Mining loses that contract, my political connections, and subsequently yours, disappear. This isn't a fucking joke."

Ricardo asks, "Jesus Christ, what do you want me to do?"

"Contact your investors, explain the problem with losing the potential long-term tenant, show them that accepting this offer produces a thirty percent per annum gain on their investment, and ask for their support in the proposed deal. If the investors reject the offer, explain the possible ramifications of losing some, if not all, of their investment capital. If they still reject the sale, then we will all have to live with the consequences, but at least that way I may be able to salvage Diablo Mining's relationship with Global Metal Refining."

Ricardo swears openly as Hugo struts nervously around the office. He makes the calls to each of his investors, who all agree, given the circumstances, they should take their profit and get out of the property as soon as they can. Ricardo calls Sean and puts him on speakerphone for Hugo's benefit.

"I have decided to agree to sell the factory to Bonnie, at her stated price. We will sign the contract as soon as it is delivered to us."

Sean requests that Ricardo come by the villa. "The contract is already drawn up and awaiting your signature," Sean says, and then asks Hugo to come with him so Bonnie can see he fulfilled his promise of loyalty.

Hugo answers, "Yes, alright. We'll be there within the hour."

"Perfect. I'll let Bonnie know the good news." He hangs up the phone.

"Get ready," he announces to Bonnie and Jessica. "Hugo and Ricardo are on their way so Ricardo can sign the contract. I'll let the staff know to have champagne ready for the celebration when they arrive." Upon the Montes' arrival, everyone meets on the veranda. They toast to each other and profitable relationships for years to come.

When Hugo and Ricardo have left, Jessica immediately signs the long-term lease with Bonnie. They then share a private toast to a well-planned and executed strategy.

Jessica calls Lidia and asks, "Can you meet with me tomorrow at the villa? We have some things to discuss."

Lidia replies, "Yes, of course."

Lidia arrives on time and is surprised to find lunch prepared. She is also surprised to learn that she will be meeting not only with Jessica, but also with Sean and Bonnie.

Jessica explains everything to her. "I would like to offer you the position of production supervisor for the new Beauty Boutique Clothing factory. You would be given authority to hire the people as you please, subject to my review of course. Within one week, my management team would be here to get the factory up and running and we'd be going at full throttle in three months."

Lidia looks slightly confused. "I am very surprised, because the last everyone had heard was that the Beauty Boutique had refused the lease, and we thought that meant that you wouldn't be doing business in Brazil."

Bonnie chimes in, "Ah, yes. We apologize, but that was a negotiation ploy in order to buy Ricardo out of the property at a very favorable price. We can assure you that this is a very serious offer." Bonnie shows Lidia the lease agreement and the government approvals, and thanks her for all her help so far and continued support in the future.

Lidia excitedly accepts Jessica's offer, and then she says, "You won't regret this. All the workers hated Ricardo. He's a sexist pig. I'll get the workers I initially planned to hire scheduled to meet the management staff coming from the U.S. next week. Thank you so much for this opportunity, Ms. Silva." Jessica thanks Lidia in return and welcomes her to Beauty Boutique Clothing: Brazil.

When Lidia leaves the villa, she is torn between joy for her new job and the ability to support her family and the realization that Ricardo has been played by individuals much better at the game than he could ever dream of being. Lidia is delighted that, for once, it is Ricardo getting screwed.

After careful consideration, she decides she must go to Ricardo's office and give him the news, so that she can watch his reaction herself. She arrives and tells him about everything, explaining, "The Beauty Boutique is still opening in that old factory. I have seen the lease agreement, and they hired me. I am sorry I have to give you this news."

Through clenched teeth, Ricardo replies, "How could you work for someone as dishonest as Ms. Silva? I can't blame you for accepting, I suppose, given it's your only opportunity to provide for your pathetic family. But by agreeing to work for that bitch, you and all the other worthless women from the factory have screwed me out of ten million dollars. What did I do to deserve this type of disrespect from you uneducated bitches?"

Lidia, finally able to stand up to Ricardo without fear of retaliation, tells him, "You have always treated us as second-class people and now—"

He interrupts, saying, "You are second-class people! All of you! You are just women and factory workers. You mean nothing."

"I don't have to care what you think anymore, you asshole," Lidia retorts, then adds insult to injury by saying, "And if that's your point of view, then you should be thrilled to know that all of us are going to make very good money on this transaction, except you."

Ricardo spits, "Get the fuck out of my office, you ungrateful bitch."

As soon as Lidia leaves, Ricardo jerks the phone off the hook and calls Hugo, yelling at him furiously for pressuring him. He explains what he just learned from Lidia.

Hugo simply laughs, "Well, both of us were played very well, cousin."

Ricardo retorts, "Yes, but I am the one that ultimately gets screwed! Fuck you, Hugo."

Hugo says, "Calm down. All we can do is count this as a lesson learned and not make the same mistake twice—"

Ricardo hangs up before Hugo can finish his statement and drives over to the villa to confront Sean, Jessica, and Bonnie.

As he speeds up the driveway, Sean warns the staff to get ready for a hostile meeting. "Jess, hurry and go get Bonnie before she gets into the shower. Someone is speeding up the driveway, and I'd bet my ass it's Ricardo."

Jessica nods and runs upstairs into Bonnie's bedroom. Bonnie is slightly surprised when Jessica catches her completely naked, about to step into the shower, but Jess explains that someone is racing up the driveway, and Sean is expecting to need some backup.

"It's probably Ricardo, and he probably knows about our scheme," she says with a grim set to her mouth.

Bonnie sighs, throws on a sundress, then quickly follows Jess downstairs.

CHAPTER 19

A WOMAN SCORNED

Ricardo gets out of his vehicle and storms up the outside stairs, and then onto the veranda, where he is intercepted by Sean and Eduardo.

Jessica and Bonnie arrive moments later.

Ricardo looks right at Jessica and shouts between the two men, "You bitch! Why would you lie to me this way? You forced me into taking a deal at half price so you could turn around and make the same deal with someone else and immediately realize a tremendous gain! Then, to add insult to injury, you contract with the woman I introduced you to? Fuck you! What pisses me off the most is that you waited until you had all the governmental approvals before any of this was put into action. You used me and my cousin's political connections to get what you wanted, then tossed us aside like garbage and cut us out of the actual profits."

Before Jessica or Sean can respond, Bonnie steps in. "Now, Mr. Montes, it was my idea to structure the deal this way. I gave the Beauty Boutique a very large gift, so Jessica would be forced to cooperate in this negotiation, and I formed the plan. If I had not, you would still have an empty factory, no potential tenants, a large debt, and nervous investors. How long did you think you could hold on paying for an empty building? If you will calm down, we can have a civil conversation by the pool, but if you continue to yell and be extremely rude, you can leave my estate. What's your preference?"

Ricardo replies snottily, "Oh, I'd like to have a discussion."

Bonnie nods. "Very well then," she says and instructs the butler, Eduardo, to prepare a quick brunch for everyone, to be served by the pool. Then, with a sweep of her arm, she motions toward the tables that are poolside.

After everyone is seated and some mimosas are served, Bonnie opens the conversation with Ricardo by pointing out that Hugo's political connections only came after Diablo Mining contracted with Global Metal Refining.

When that comment meets a brooding silence, she continues, "Ricardo, much of your ability to produce the vast amount of wealth that you have in the last four years has been due to the doors Hugo was able to open for you. Again, this was as a result of the political connections he gained by associating with my husband's company." She pauses, and Ricardo opens his mouth to respond when Bonnie raises a hand, stopping him, and says, "Please, allow me to finish. Then I'll give you as much time as you need to respond to what I have said."

Ricardo nods, sullenly, his cheeks flushed with anger.

Bonnie considers for a moment, and then concludes, "You, of all people, should understand my desire to help Jessica like Hugo has helped you, and I apologize if the way we went about things seems unfair to you, but understand that Jessica has been my best friend my entire life, and if either you or Hugo do anything to interfere with the Beauty Boutique's success here, I'll cut off both of your balls. Do you understand me?"

Ricardo, not being used to this type of challenge from a woman, pushes his chair back from the table and stands up, red-faced.

Jessica jumps in, holding her hands up to Ricardo. "Please, calm down and listen before you overreact."

Ricardo throws his napkin on the table, saying, "I can't believe you just said that to me after all you have done, you lying bitch!" Bonnie immediately shoves her own chair away and places herself between Ricardo and Jessica. Ricardo turns his attention to her. "Just who in the hell do you people think you are? You, especially, are nothing but a little rich bitch who came into wealth by using her body to get her boss wrapped around her finger. You were just a temporary office skank!"

Bonnie gasps and slaps Ricardo across the face, causing him to spin slightly to his right. When Ricardo spins back, he follows up with his fist, striking Bonnie hard on her cheek and knocking her to the ground. The fall causes her sundress to rise up, revealing she is naked underneath, and adding embarrassment to the pain in her cheek.

Sean jumps up and gets between Ricardo and the women, while Jessica leaps to Bonnie's aid.

Ricardo jerks a switchblade out of his back pocket, snarling at Sean, "If you come any closer, I'll kill you."

Sean stops advancing, never taking his eyes off Ricardo's face, he says, "Everyone, calm down. This is out of control."

Ricardo taunts him. "What's the matter? Can't you figure out how to spin this to your client's advantage?" Glancing down at Bonnie, he continues with a sneer, "Why do all you American bitches think it's sexy not to wear underwear? You are all filthy, nasty little whores."

Eduardo, having come to see what the commotion is all about, is appalled to see Ricardo holding Sean at bay with a knife and reaches behind the door to grab the shotgun.

Stepping out onto the veranda, he racks a round into the chamber. Ricardo turns to look for the sound, and Eduardo points the gun at him, descending the stairs slowly.

"Mr. Montes," Eduardo says, his voice unwavering and cordial, "you have ten seconds to put that knife away and leave this estate, or the authorities will be fishing your bloody, lifeless body out of the pool."

Ricardo snarls at him and then slowly returns his knife to his pocket. He begins walking to his vehicle with Eduardo following him, still aiming the shotgun at his back. Only after Ricardo starts his vehicle and drives off the estate does Eduardo return to the veranda. Bonnie is now being attended by the staff, and Jessica is kneeling next to her, concern written on her face. Bonnie's left cheek is swollen and a massive blood-filled sack has formed under her left eye.

Sean shakes his head in disbelief at what has just happened. "Bonnie, you need to go to the hospital," he says quietly.

Bonnie replies stiffly, "Since we are heading home in the morning, I'd prefer to go to the doctor in San Diego that Mark really liked. I'll call Wendy and ask if she can get an appointment scheduled, if you guys could drop me off there on your way back to San Francisco?"

Sean says, "Of course we will, but if you can't confirm everything with Wendy, I'm taking you to the hospital here." Jessica calls Wendy for Bonnie and briefly explains what happened, then expresses Bonnie's request for Wendy to make the doctor's appointment.

Wendy tells Jessica, "I know that doctor fairly well. I'll pull every string I have with him. She'll get an appointment. And please, let her know that I expect her to stay with me over the weekend, so I can be sure she's okay before she heads home."

Jessica asks, "Could you meet us at the airport?"

"Of course. I'll be there. I'll call you back as soon as I get a hold of the doctor."

Jess hangs up and fills Bonnie in. Eduardo brings both of them dirty martinis, made to Bonnie's liking, and an ice pack. Bonnie tells him, "Just keep these coming until I say stop, please. And thank you for your quick response to Ricardo's violence. You are irreplaceable."

He replies. "Not a problem, just say when." He gives her a short, formal bow, and she almost smile, then winces at the pain in her cheek.

Wendy calls back fairly soon and tells Bonnie, "I got a hold of the doctor, and he said I should call him when you get here. He said he will meet us at his office to x-ray your cheek and decide on the best course of action from there."

"Thank you," Bonnie mumbles, the swelling making it a little bit difficult to talk.

"What the hell happened?" Wendy asks, wanting to hear the story from Bonnie's perspective.

Bonnie says, "I'll bring you up to speed tomorrow. Right now, my head is pounding and I'm going to get very drunk."

Wendy sighs. "Okay, but I want every detail, do you understand?"

Bonnie replies, "Yes, I know. I promise, but right now, I feel like shit and don't want to talk, okay?"

"Okay. I'll see you tomorrow afternoon. Take lots of ibuprofen and get some ice on it in the meantime. Love you," Wendy says, and they hang up the phone.

CHAPTER 20

BROKEN

Sean, Jessica, and Bonnie arrived at the San Diego airport on time. Wendy is waiting at the gate, worried, but completely unprepared for what she sees. She is stunned and very angry. The entire left side of Bonnie's face is swollen, she has two black eyes, and her speech sounds like she has just undergone major dental surgery. Wendy tells Sean and Jessica she is taking Bonnie to the doctor immediately and will call them when she has some results. She hugs them both and leaves with Bonnie in tow.

The doctor's office is prepared, anticipating Bonnie's arrival, and moves her into the examination room without delay.

Dr. Peckman examines her and asks, "How did this happen?"

Bonnie explains, "I was in Brazil and an angry business associate punched me after I slapped him for being rude."

Dr. Peckman gapes at her for a moment, then regains his composure and orders immediate x-rays. He tells Bonnie he will see her again before she leaves to discuss the results and form a treatment plan, because he is pretty sure at least something is broken.

After about an hour, Dr. Peckman returns with the results. Bonnie has a broken orbital socket, but it won't require surgery. He prescribes Vicodin as needed for pain, telling Bonnie to keep ice on her cheek for the swelling. Wendy and Bonnie thank the doctor for seeing her on such short notice.

Dr. Peckman nods and rubs Bonnie's arm gently. "I'm so sorry about your husband, Bonnie. If there is anything else I can do, please let me know."

Bonnie thanks him as she and Wendy leave the office.

Wendy tells Bonnie on the ride to her house, "I have fresh lobster, a salad, and a wonderful bottle of wine waiting for us."

Bonnie replies, "You didn't need to go to all that trouble."

Wendy says, "Oh yes, I did, beautiful. Besides, you need to tell me everything that happened yesterday, without skipping anything. I need to know if you'll need counseling." The two laugh, but Wendy knows she is only partly kidding.

When they arrive at the penthouse, Wendy immediately pours a glass of wine and gives Bonnie the wine and Vicodin. They sit on the deck overlooking the ocean. There is a slight breeze and the temperature is warm and comfortable right around eighty-five degrees.

As Bonnie begins relating the events leading up to the incident, the wine and Vicodin begin relaxing her, making it easier, as Wendy had planned, for her to speak in detail. As she's explaining, Wendy notices tears forming in her eyes. A drop falls when Bonnie murmurs, "Ricardo called me Mark's temporary office skank… that's why I slapped him. Then, to make matters worse, when I fell my skirt came up and I wasn't wearing any underwear. It was so embarrassing, and he said I was a filthy, nasty little whore. How could any man be so cruel to any woman?"

At that statement and question, Wendy feels something snap in her brain, followed immediately by a wave of recognition and then rage that she hadn't experienced since her traumatic experience fighting with Mark.

"He said that specifically? Nasty little whore?" Wendy asks, trying to keep the anger and realization out of her voice.

Bonnie just nods miserably, and Wendy is glad she's under the influence of wine and Vicodin, because it gives Wendy time to regain her composure. She hugs Bonnie and says, "Not all men are pigs. I'm so sorry you had to endure such a thing." Then she stands and walks into the house, furious at Ricardo for opening old wounds in her and bringing out the rage she thought she had resolved.

"Bonnie, just relax," she calls from the kitchen. "I'm going to make dinner. It should only take about fifteen minutes." Bonnie leans back in her chair and lets her eyes drift shut.

While waiting for the lobster to boil, Wendy melts the butter and completes the salad, then sets the dinner table. She pours Bonnie another glass of wine and considers how she can restore strength and confidence back to the somewhat broken woman on her terrace.

Wendy walks back outside, hands Bonnie the glass of wine, and assures her that dinner will be ready momentarily. After slipping back inside, Wendy calls Jessica and informs her of what the doctor had discovered. "Physically, Bonnie will heal just fine," Wendy says, "but I'm worried about her emotional state. How much trauma do you think she can handle in such a short time frame?"

Jessica responds with concern in her voice. "I don't know, but she has always been such a strong, resilient woman. I'm sure if we just support her, she'll be okay."

Wendy sighs and replies, "Okay, well dinner is ready here. I want an update on Sean, but I will call later, after Bonnie has fallen asleep, if that's okay? I really need more detailed information about what happened with Ricardo as well."

Jessica says, "Absolutely, call anytime. I'll fill you in on any details from the incident that we may have missed so far."

Wendy hangs up and has Bonnie come in from the deck for a beautifully prepared dinner and more wine.

Bonnie says, slurring slightly because of the medication, "I had no idea you had such extraordinary culinary skills. This is prepared to perfection and tastes absolutely fabulous."

Wendy replies bashfully, "I wanted you to have something homemade and comforting, and really worthy of your sisterhood."

Bonnie looks at Wendy with nothing but kindness in her eyes and says quietly, "You are the only family I have left, and you will always be my family, dear."

Wendy is deeply moved by Bonnie's kindness. As tears start to fall from her eyes, Bonnie says, "Oh, no. That is enough of that. Tonight is a celebration of love and family." She holds her glass up for a toast, and then the two enjoy the lobster in all of its deliciousness.

After Wendy gets Bonnie into bed, she calls Jessica back and explains Bonnie's apparent emotional state. "That asshole has pissed me off more than any of you will ever know," she says ferociously, "Please, fill in every detail so I can develop a strategy on how to help Bonnie recover from this mess."

Jessica nods, "Well, I wasn't in the initial meeting. That was between Sean and Ricardo, so Sean will have to fill things in there." She goes on to explain every detail leading up to Ricardo's violence and the terrible things he said. "It was something like, 'Why do you American women think it's sexy not to wear underwear. You are all nasty little whores.' It was absolutely horrible of him."

Her throat tight with confirmation, having gotten the same sentence from two sources, Wendy asks again, "He said that? I mean, those *exact* words?"

"Yes. I'm certain, because they seemed so unbelievable to me. Why? Does the wording matter?" Jessica asks.

Wendy says, "Yes, because of how to counsel them. And also because there was only one other time in my life where I heard a comment like that. It was from a man I once respected, and since then, I've loathed him, even to this day."

Jessica is shocked. "I'm so sorry. Who was it?"

Wendy replies, "It doesn't matter. That man is dead and can't affect my life any longer. But those words cut to the core of my being and destroyed my sense of self-worth back then, and today I find they still enrage me. I want to make sure Bonnie doesn't end up in the same position."

Jessica agrees. "They are just words from an angry, ignorant asshole. Not you, nor any other woman, have to accept them as a reality in her life."

Wendy nods and says, "Intellectually, of course I know you're right, but emotionally they still make me want to cause the same amount of emotional pain to the guy who says such things to anyone."

Jessica chuckles, "I understand. It would be nice, wouldn't it?"

⇒+⋅+⇐

The next morning, Bonnie awakens to the smell of fresh coffee brewing, coupled with another pleasing aroma she can't quite distinguish. When she walks into the kitchen, she finds Wendy putting an egg concoction onto fresh baked croissants.

Bonnie watches her working feverishly for a few moments before she says, "I'll hire you as my personal chef any day."

Wendy turns around quickly, surprised because Bonnie jolted her back to reality. Then she smiles and says with a wink, "You could never afford me."

Bonnie chuckles. "That's probably true, but I'd be happy going broke and getting fat on your cooking."

Wendy beams at the compliment, "Well, breakfast will be ready in about fifteen minutes, so enjoy your cup of coffee in the living room and I'll finish things up here."

As she's cooking, Wendy hears Bonnie's cell phone ring, and from parts of her conversation she assumes Bonnie is speaking with Sean. Wendy comes into the living room with breakfast, then notices the unsettled look on Bonnie's face.

"What is it?" she asks, as she and Bonnie enjoy a wonderfully prepared French breakfast.

Bonnie raves about her first bite, and then explains, "Sean called because he received a call from Ricardo, apologizing for his behavior. He requested that Sean schedule a meeting between us, so Ricardo can personally apologize to me. Sean wanted to know if I would consider such a meeting, and I'm not sure."

Wendy nods. "Well, I don't know if meeting him in person so soon is a good idea, but I'll tell you what. Give me Ricardo's number and let me call him as your counselor. I'll ask him a few questions, and if I feel comfortable in the fact that it is safe for you to meet with him, I'll let you know. Would that be okay?"

Bonnie nods gratefully. "If you're willing to do that for me, I certainly would appreciate it."

Wendy replies, "Of course I will. You're my sister-in-law and I love you." Bonnie gives Wendy Ricardo's number. Then the two of them finish up their breakfast and enjoy lighter conversation. Bonnie thanks Wendy for everything she has done for her, then mentions she would like to head back to San Francisco that afternoon, if Wendy will take her to the airport.

Wendy complains, "But you've only been here one night!"

Bonnie acknowledges. "I know, and it was far too short, but I really have to get back. I have things I have to work on with Mr. Stoddard and others. But I promise my next stay will be much longer."

Wendy says, "I guess I understand, but I will definitely hold you to your promise, both for another visit and a longer one."

After Bonnie leaves for San Francisco, Wendy telephones Ricardo. She introduces herself as Bonnie's counselor and tells him, "Before I advise Bonnie on whether or not to meet with you, I would like to have dinner with you to discuss the event, in order to determine if it would be safe for her, given the physical abuse during your last meeting. Perhaps, more importantly, I will be better able to determine if it is emotionally safe for her to see you in person."

Ricardo sighs, resigned. "Fine. When and where?"

"Not so fast," Wendy admonishes. "I have one condition. This meeting must be confidential, due to my client's delicate feelings on the issue. No one, especially not Bonnie, is to know that you and I are meeting. If anyone finds out about it, I'll make sure Bonnie never speaks with either you or your cousin ever again. Understood?"

Ricardo agrees to Wendy's condition, and they both agree to meet in three weeks in San Francisco. Wendy thanks Ricardo for his willingness to work with her and tells him she looks forward to helping him and Bonnie restore their business relationship.

Ricardo replies, "Thank you, as well, Ms. Stevens. Our meeting will certainly remain confidential. Goodbye."

Next, Wendy calls Bonnie to tell her she would like to stop by for a visit to discuss her phone call with Ricardo.

"Really? You spoke with him already? Wonderful!" Bonnie exclaims. "When would you like my pilot to pick you up?"

"In three weeks? It gives me some time to schedule time off," Wendy replies.

"Perfect! I can't wait."

Wendy replies, smiling, "I can't either, sister dear."

After the conversation ends, Wendy goes to the market, buys some fresh pork chops, and leaves them in the see through packaging on the kitchen counter in the sun. They develop mold rapidly. She also bakes a potato in aluminum foil and places it on the counter next to the pork chop. As the days progress, she checks on the mold's development continuously. When either of the items is covered in the mold, she scrapes it off and places it in a jar containing a small amount of pork broth. Wendy continues this procedure over the next three weeks, then she transfers the moldy broth into three small nasal spray containers and places them in her purse.

Wendy meets Bonnie's pilot at the airport, boards the jet, and flies to San Francisco to meet with Ricardo, then visit Bonnie. Ricardo has agreed to meet her at a small restaurant, the Bistro on Union Street, for dinner. When she arrives, she is greeted by the hostess and seated with Ricardo, as he arrived first. Wendy is struck by his good looks and charming personality, and she thinks of what a shame it is that he is such an evil bastard.

Their conversation is cordial as Wendy questions him about the incident, but she is completely unimpressed with the way he displays his so-called remorse for his actions and demeaning behavior. The server comes to take their orders and Ricardo orders pork chops in a port sauce and a good glass of cabernet sauvignon. Wendy enjoys a private smile at how fortunate his dinner selection will prove to her, and then orders fresh grilled salmon with a salad bar combination and a glass of chardonnay.

"Excuse me, Ricardo. I need to get my salad," she says.

She surveys the bistro, and seeing to it that no one is watching, she removes the first nasal sprayer from her jacket pocket, squirting a small amount onto the salad bar after retrieving her salad. She places the sprayer back into her pocket, then returns to the table to have a pleasant conversation with Ricardo. Fairly soon, the server brings their dinners, but just as he arrives Ricardo excuses himself to go to the restroom. Wendy is extremely pleased with the timing and retrieves the two remaining sprayers from her purse, again surveying the bistro for observers. She mixes the entirety of one sprayer into Ricardo's port sauce and the other she pours into his glass of cabernet.

When Ricardo returns to the table, the two return to polite conversation. Wendy watches him take a bite of his pork chop and drink some of his cabernet before she settles in to enjoy her own meal. She keeps a watchful eye on him as he finishes his dinner and wine, leaving nothing for leftovers. The two of them also enjoy a wonderful dessert of blueberry crepes and coffee.

At the end of their meal, Wendy says, "I am surprised to say, I have had a delightful time with you. I'll make sure Bonnie contacts you at your hotel in two days. If you haven't heard from her by then, call me, and I'll find out what is going on and possibly bring her to meet with you."

Ricardo thanks Wendy for a wonderful dinner and her willingness to help him restore an important business relationship, then excuses himself under the guise of much needed rest.

Ricardo returns to his hotel, places the 'do not disturb' placard on his door, and calls the front desk to request no room service tomorrow. He informs the clerk that he intends to sleep in late after his long trip.

The front desk clerk assures him he will not be disturbed in the morning and says, "Sleep well, Mr. Montes."

"Thank you," Ricardo replies, then watches television, makes a few short phone calls, and goes to sleep.

The next morning, the hotel staff doesn't disturb him, as requested. He wakes up around noon, fatigued, and goes to the bathroom. He crawls back into bed, thinking he must be getting old because he has never experienced such extreme jet lag before. He awakens again around six in the evening with a dry mouth and stomach cramps, then rushes into the bathroom to vomit. Realizing he probably has the flu, he grabs some water and phones the front desk again to explain about the flu and asks not to be disturbed again.

"Of course, Mr. Montes. Is there anything you need?"

"No," Ricardo replies rudely, "I just don't want to be disturbed."

Once again, she assures him he won't be and Ricardo hangs up.

He awakens in the middle of the night having a little difficulty breathing. Taking some aspirin, he decides to go back to sleep. When he awakens yet again in the morning, he can't even get out of bed to reach the telephone. Knowing he is in trouble, he hopes the cleaning lady will check on his room, but he forgets he requested to not be disturbed.

Ricardo falls back to sleep, simply unable to keep his eyes open. Having not heard from him well into the afternoon, the staff knocks on the door. When they don't receive an answer, they go inside and find him having extreme difficulty breathing. They attempt to help and also discover he is almost completely unable to move. The staff immediately calls for medical attention, and one of the maids stays with him, waiting for the paramedics to arrive.

Ricardo grabs her arm and pulls her closer to him. Struggling immensely to find the breath, Ricardo whispers hoarsely, "I think I'm dying, and I need to tell someone. I hired... the killer." He wheezes. "And I'm the one who—" His revelation is interrupted as the paramedics enter, and he is intubated and rushed to San Francisco General Hospital.

He arrives in severe respiratory distress with overwhelming sepsis. The staff immediately rushes to place him on a respirator, and then get him into intensive care. Blood cultures are taken, but Ricardo is now completely unresponsive. His liver and kidney functions begin failing and, within six hours, he dies from multi organ failure.

The hospital laboratory, concerned about some type of outbreak, continues testing the cultures and finally determines that Ricardo died from botulism. The hospital notifies public health officials, who focus on recent reports of food poisoning in San Francisco restaurants and, through the process of elimination, determine Ricardo contracted the botulism after eating at the Bistro on Union Street. Local news reporters broadcast the death, which prompts an onslaught of individuals reporting to local hospitals, claiming symptoms of botulism. Most of the reports are false, but a few disturbing cases test positive and confirm the place of origin.

—+—+—

That evening, Bonnie turns on the news and immediately calls Wendy, who had returned to San Diego after their brief visit.

"I just saw on the Channel 7 News that Ricardo just died at San Francisco General of botulism. I didn't even know he was in San Francisco, did you?"

Wendy allows surprise to tinge her voice when she replies, "He what? Yes, I knew he was in San Francisco. I had dinner with him at his request. After some conversation, I told him I wasn't in favor of you seeing him, and since he never tried to arrange a meeting himself, I didn't mention it. Did you just say he's *dead*?"

"Yes! Did you feel sick after eating with him?"

"No, I feel fine. I had a wonderful dinner."

Bonnie sighs. "Well, it's a good thing because several people have come forward with food poisoning. It's all over the news."

Wendy smiles to herself, feeling a perverse sort of pride that her plan has worked. As Bonnie continues to speak and explain everything she is seeing on the news, Wendy recognizes just how easy it is to commit a well-planned murder. Almost subconsciously, with a small, satisfied smile on her face, she begins to consider the possibilities.

A GLIMPSE OF: UNMERITED FAVOR: BOOK 2

Oh, the possibilities... Wendy thinks and wonders, throughout the new investigation and the horror the owner of the Bistro on Union Street in dealing with, if anyone will discover the restaurant owner is the former abusive husband of one of her clients.

Throughout the second book, the author has Wendy contemplating the 'spin' that has occurred because of her brother's unconscionable abuse, and new events continue to feed her enthusiasm for the kill.

Meanwhile, Beauty Boutique Clothing opens in Brazil, with more success than Sean and Jessica could have ever dreamed. As their sexual attraction grows, so does the profitability of their relationship. With encouragement from Bonnie and Wendy, Jessica explores more than just Brazil with Sean.

Jerry Summers takes us deeper into romance and investigations, while Wendy contemplates her next merciful act. It was Sean who told her to "Take the money, condo, and stocks, and help other victims, like yourself," but he has no idea the help Wendy intends to give. After all, isn't 'mercy' the definition of Unmerited Favor?

Available at Amazon.com and on kindle.